CHARITY'S BURDEN

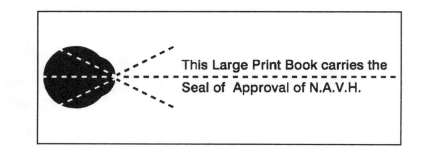

This Large Print Book carries the
Seal of Approval of N.A.V.H.

A QUAKER MIDWIFE MYSTERY

CHARITY'S BURDEN

EDITH MAXWELL

THORNDIKE PRESS
A part of Gale, a Cengage Company

Farmington Hills, Mich • San Francisco • New York • Waterville, Maine
Meriden, Conn • Mason, Ohio • Chicago

Copyright © 2019 by Edith Maxwell.
Thorndike Press, a part of Gale, a Cengage Company.

ALL RIGHTS RESERVED
This is a work of fiction. Names, characters, places, and incidents are either the product of the author's imagination or are used fictitiously, and any resemblance to actual persons, living or dead, business establishments, events, or locales is entirely coincidental.
Thorndike Press® Large Print Mystery.
The text of this Large Print edition is unabridged.
Other aspects of the book may vary from the original edition.
Set in 16 pt. Plantin.

LIBRARY OF CONGRESS CIP DATA ON FILE.
CATALOGUING IN PUBLICATION FOR THIS BOOK
IS AVAILABLE FROM THE LIBRARY OF CONGRESS

ISBN-13: 978-1-4328-6272-5 (hardcover alk. paper)

Published in 2019 by arrangement with Midnight Ink, an imprint of Llewellyn Publications, Woodbury, MN 55125-2989 USA

Printed in the United States of America
1 2 3 4 5 6 7 23 22 21 20 19

For Amesbury's historical museums: the John Greenleaf Whittier Home Museum, Amesbury Carriage Museum, and Bartlett Museum. Thank you for keeping local history alive, and for helping me with nineteenth-century details large and small.

For Amesbury's historical museums: the John Greenleaf Whittier Home Museum, Amesbury Carriage Museum, and Bartlett Museum. Thank you for keeping local history alive, and for helping me with nineteenth-century details large and small.

AUTHOR'S NOTE

I came across an article about the infamous Madame Restell before I wrote this manuscript. She was Ann Trow Lohman, a self-trained midwife who also performed surgical abortions and sold abortifacients to women in New York City in the mid-nineteenth century. She opened a boarding house where women could give birth safely, but was much maligned. She was called the Wickedest Woman in New York and the Abortionist of Fifth Avenue. Kate Manning wrote a novel, *My Notorious Life,* based on Lohman's life and named the Lohman character Madame DeBeausacq. I then read *Contraception and Abortion in Nineteenth Century America* by Janet Farrell Brodie and decided I had my theme for the fourth Quaker Midwife Mystery, modeling my own Madame Restante on the infamous Restell.

In this book I mention John Greenleaf Whitter's "The Golden Wedding of Longwood," although the poet himself does not make an appearance this time.

Many thanks to Patty Hoyt, Education Coordinator at the Lowell's Boat Shop in Amesbury, who gave me a personalized tour of the working museum. Lowell's is the oldest continually operating boat shop in the country, and has been making sturdy and graceful wooden boats since 1793. I set several scenes in this book in the shop.

John Douglass was a real physician in Amesbury, but I'm sure he was a much more congenial man than I portrayed him in this book. My apologies to his descendants. Amesbury reference librarian Margie Walker continues to be helpful with whatever I ask her about local history and I thank her.

Nancy A. Pope, Curator/Historian at the Smithsonian's National Postal Museum, kindly shared information about post office boxes in the late nineteenth century. I attended an invaluable kitchen-centered presentation in a nineteenth-century mansion in Wiscasset, Maine, presented by Historic New England, and several historic lectures and walking tours sponsored by the Amesbury Carriage Museum. I continue to refer constantly to the Online Etymology Dictionary to make sure the words my characters utter are authentic. Obviously, any remaining errors in historical detail are of my own doing.

The ubiquitous research tool YouTube enabled me to watch videos of equine births. Thanks to fellow authors (and people with horse experience) Annette Riggle Dashofy and Martha Reed for checking my foaling scene.

ONE

The crimson on the rag Charity Skells removed from between her legs was too bright. Blood soaked the long strip of muslin. The painfully thin woman bent into herself, her arms crossed over her emptying womb.

"Am I dying, Rose?"

I silently prayed she wasn't. I stroked her hair back off her damp brow. "Of course not. But I need to have a doctor see thee." I am a skilled and experienced midwife, but this was too much bleeding for an early-term miscarriage. I opened a drawer, looking for more cloths. A pamphlet printed on red paper lay half buried in a stack of neatly folded linens.

I glanced around the threadbare bedroom where a note from my client had summoned me this frigid Second Month morning. "Does thee have a telephone?" I was certain she didn't. My modest home a mile away

11

had acquired one of the new devices only a month ago.

She shook her head without looking up. "But I'm going to put one in. When I get the money."

The money? What money? Maybe she meant her husband's next pay from the boat shop, but surely that would go first to food, clothing for the children, and paying off debts. He had been working for Lowell's a scant few months.

"I won't let Ransom say no." She smiled sadly. "When we first married, he said yes so very often. He was always sweet with me, Rose."

"I am sure he loves thee very much." I hadn't seen him be publicly sweet with her, but one never knew what went on behind closed doors in the life of a married couple.

A moan escaped Charity's lips.

"I'll take thee in my buggy. We must move along quickly, though." I grabbed the last of the rags on the dresser and handed them to her. The small Methodist hospital was only a short distance up Market Street, and my beau, David Dodge, had insisted I accept the loan of a dun-colored gelding named Peaches and a doctor's buggy for the winter months. I was grateful today I didn't have to waste time trying to hail a hansom cab.

After I helped her into her coat, wincing at the frayed cuffs and thin fabric, I wrapped a woolen shawl closely over her head and around her neck.

As we made our way down the front steps, I asked, "Where are the younger children today?" Charity was a Quaker like myself, and despite being a scant five years older than my twenty-seven, was the mother of six. The oldest, a friend of my niece Betsy Bailey, was only nine. She and the next three siblings would be at the Whittier Grammar School today.

"Mother took them." Her voice was barely a whisper.

"Good." Transporting a toddler and a four-year old to the hospital along with their very ill mother would have been an added burden. In the buggy, I tucked the traveling blanket securely around Charity and clucked to the ever-patient Peaches. The ten o'clock sun struggled to light the day, but an icy cloud cover barely allowed it. I sniffed the damp metallic scent of snow in the air.

It took less than fifteen minutes to arrive at the hospital; much faster than if we'd attempted the trip over the Merrimack River to the larger Anna Jaques Hospital in Newburyport. Charity didn't have that kind of time. This hospital building looked no different on the outside than any other home built by a wealthy merchant or mill owner. A mansard roof covered the square house, with open shutters framing large graceful windows. I handed Peaches off to a waiting stable boy and helped Charity up the wide steps to the front door.

The building's inside made it clear this was not a private residence. The air smelled of disinfectant and to either side of the foyer I glimpsed wards full of beds. A nurse wearing a starched full-length pinafore glanced up from a desk, where a small metal nameplate identified her as Nurse Jeanne Peele. I kept my arm firmly around Charity's bony shoulders, afraid she'd fall if I didn't.

"I am Rose Carroll, midwife, and this is my client Charity Skells, who summoned me an hour ago. I believe she is having a miscarriage, but the bleeding is excessive."

"I'm Nurse Peele. Welcome." She blinked and her eyebrows went up when she gazed at Charity's face, now the color of bleached linen. The nurse stood and hurried to a corner under the stairs, wheeling a wicker chair to Charity.

Charity slumped into the seat, closing her eyes with a faint moan. Her coat fell apart, revealing a dark blossom on the skirt of her light gray dress. I pressed my lips together.

14

The bleeding had worsened during our short ride. I followed the nurse as she pushed the chair through the women's ward at our left to the only empty bed at the end of the room. A young nurse without stripes on her starched cap hurried over and helped Charity onto the bed.

"I'll get Doctor," the nurse said. "Miss Gifford, see that Mrs. Skells is warm. She'll need fresh rags for the bleeding."

"Yes, Nurse Peele." The student curtsied.

"Come with me, Miss Carroll, and give me a history as we go."

"She's an impoverished mother of six, Jeanne." I kept up with her brisk stride through the halls of an addition to the back of the house. "She birthed a premature baby at the end of Eleventh Month — November — that was too small to survive. Her husband had been out of work and I believe Charity was going hungry so her children would not. I was discouraged to learn she thought she was with child again. I've been encouraging her to space her pregnancies, but whatever measures she's been taking clearly aren't working."

The nurse sniffed. "And Mr. Skells likely refuses to use a safe, am I correct?"

A safe, one of the many euphemisms for a male prophylactic sheath. "That is what

Charity says, yes."

Jeanne Peele shook her head. "A man who disregards his wife's health isn't worth her affections."

Two

I sat at Charity's side an hour later, stroking her hand, her cool skin as pale as the pillow slip beneath her head. She lay resting with blankets up to her chin. The doctor had prescribed extract of ergot to contract the uterus, which should stanch the bleeding — a remedy I could have given — but otherwise had no real help for her. The student nurse had cleaned Charity and dressed her in a cotton gown, with plentiful cloths wedged between her legs to absorb the blood. The flow at least now ebbed, but she had lost so much of life's precious fluid. I closed my eyes and held her in the Light of God that she might survive this onslaught to her health.

Could her bleeding truly be a miscarriage? I thought back to the date she'd birthed her premature baby at the end of Eleventh Month. Surely she couldn't have ovulated before First Month, in which case this pregnancy would be in its initial phase. On the other hand, she clearly had a healthy fertility or she wouldn't have had seven pregnancies — maybe eight — in ten years. And if Ransom, her husband, had forced himself on her while she was still recovering from the lost child, it was certainly possible that she was miscarrying today. Still, I was surprised at the extreme way her body was expelling the tiny, tiny fetus. Often women merely thought it was a late and heavy monthly when they lost a pregnancy at this stage.

The life of a hospital ward bustled around us. A woman cried out in pain from the other end of the large room. An older lady with lips pressed together shuffled past gripping a cane, as if each step hurt but she was determined to be active and recover from what ailed her. A nurse brought a syringe to a young woman sitting up two beds away, and a man mopped the hall beyond the open door, bringing a fresh wave of acrid disinfectant. Still, it was better than the scent of disease.

Charity's eyes fluttered and opened. She turned her head slowly toward me. I leaned in.

"Rose, don't let Ransom get the money."

The money again. "What money, Charity?" I asked gently.

She gave a creaking moan. "I am sorry. May God forgive me." She closed her eyes again, lashes dark against the bruised-looking skin under them.

"For what, Charity? A miscarriage is not thy fault."

"No. Ask Orpha," she whispered. "She warned me not to go to . . ." Her voice trailed off into a murmur I couldn't understand.

Orpha? Ask my elderly teacher and mentor what? Where had she warned Charity not to go? Of course Charity knew Orpha Perkins, because she had delivered Charity's first babies, the fifth with me as apprentice. I'd caught babies six and seven after Orpha retired and I took over her business.

As I watched, Charity's mouth fell open. Her breathing became labored, raspy. My heart filled with the sad certainty that these were her last moments on this earth. I beckoned to Jeanne Peele, who hurried over, but I did not release Charity's cool hand. The nurse sat on the other side of the bed and we held the death vigil together.

I kept my finger on my client's barely detectable pulse as I tried to pray for her, but instead my thoughts turned to imaginary remedies. Would that we had a medi-

19

cine to more effectively stop bleeding, or the means to replace all the blood she had lost. I had read about experiments in England to transfuse blood from a healthy donor to a patient suffering with extreme loss from hemorrhage. So far there were as many deaths from the procedure as lives saved. Perhaps blood from one person was incompatible with blood from another. Regardless, it was too late to take such a risky step with Charity. Had I done all I could to save her? I believed I had, and only wished there was more in my power to do.

She didn't breathe for a long minute, then gasped in another breath. But this one was her last. Under my fingers her pulse ceased and she became still. The nurse glanced at me and I nodded my head once. I reached over and gentled Charity's eyes closed as I held her released soul in the Light.

Three

Outside some minutes later, I considered my next step. My first obligation was to convey the sad news to Lowell's Boat Shop, where Ransom Skells was employed. This was the worst part of my job — the rest of which I loved — telling a husband his wife's life had been extinguished. I always questioned my care — could I have done something differently to save the woman's life? Certainly not in Charity's case. Knowing that fact didn't make it any easier to tell a man his cherished spouse was gone. I also yearned to talk with Orpha and learn about her conversation with Charity, but that would have to wait.

After Peaches was underway reversing our route on Market Street back toward town, I reflected that I hadn't seen Ransom act as if he particularly cherished Charity. At the time I'd attributed his surly moods to his lack of gainful employment. What was a chandler to do when the world had turned to gas lighting instead of candles? These days electricity seemed poised to take over even for gas. Ransom had finally secured a position as a carpenter at Lowell's Boat shop. At least now he had work, the money from which he was going to need to feed and care for their children. Charity had said he'd been sweet with her at the beginning of their life as a couple. That implied he might not be so sweet now. Maybe he'd been surly because the marriage had turned sour for him. I might never know.

After I slowly made my way through busy Market Square, I pointed the horse up Main Street and continued where the road turned the corner and headed toward the wide Merrimack River some two miles away. As I passed frozen Pattens Pond in the hollow, I heard a fast clopping approach from behind. My dear friend Bertie Winslow pulled next to me astride her handsome steed, Grover, and kept even with Peaches's slow, steady pace.

"What news, Rosetta?" she asked with her trademark grin and stylish hat pinned at a rakish angle.

Only Bertie, our town's unconventional postmistress, used that nickname for me, and I loved it. "Sad tidings, I'm afraid. I lost a client to bleeding from the womb this morning. I'm off to inform her husband he's now a widower."

The grin slid off her face. "I'm sorry to hear that."

"With six children at home, too." I shook my head. "It was strange, Bertie. Charity couldn't have been more than two months along but the blood was copious. She also mentioned something curious about money, and apologized for not doing what Orpha had advised her to do, or not do. I confess to being puzzled."

"Puzzled? You, the master mystery solver?"

It was true. I had assisted the police in the investigations of several murders in the past year. I seemed to have a facility for noticing odd behavior, asking the right questions, and pursuing bits of conversation I heard, often from my pregnant clients. I also had an advantage — I could speak with women about subjects they would be reluctant to discuss with the police, and I heard secrets during the throes of labor. I wouldn't call myself a master, though.

"You'll figure it out." Bertie guided Grover around a dip in the paving stones. "But hold on there. Did you say Charity? Charity Skells?"

"Yes. Does thee know her?"

"I had a disagreement with her oddly named husband. Not a pleasant sort, that one."

Bertie was unfailingly good-natured with me, but she was also a strong-willed public figure who didn't tolerate nonsense or bad behavior, no matter the source. I had seen her refuse the mayor of the town in an unreasonable request once.

"What did thee quarrel with Ransom about?" I asked. "By the way, Ransom is his middle name. His given name is Howard, but Charity told me there are other Howards in the family, so he prefers Ransom."

"Whatever his appellation, he was being rude in the post office. Trying to push his way to the front of the line." A loud bell clanged several times behind us. "It's the trolley needing to pass, and I'm off to make a delivery at the high school. Let's have a real visit soon," Bertie said before she urged Grover into a trot and turned right up the hill toward the large four-square secondary school building.

"Yes, let's do," I called after her, pulling as far to the right as I could. I kept a tight rein on Peaches as the horse-drawn trolley clattered by my buggy, but I didn't really need to. A calmer horse I'd never met. I wasn't so calm myself at this moment. Charity's death disturbed me. Something didn't feel right about it. I would like to discuss it with David, my betrothed and a physician, but he was away for a few days at a medical conference in Portsmouth, New Hampshire. That busy port city was only twenty miles to the north, but he was staying in a hotel there to avoid having to travel back and forth. I thought he said he'd be back on Fifth Day. I could send him a note when I got home asking him to come and see me when he returned. Of course I missed his loving care, his handsome smile, his devotion to me, which I gladly returned. But it was his quiet wisdom and professional expertise that could serve useful at a time like this.

FOUR

I entered Lowell's Boat Shop under a sign reading OFFICE. A neatly put-together young woman regarded me over a wide desk. A carved wooden name plate on her desk read *Miss Delia Davies.* The hammering and sawing sounds of boat construction drifted through a closed interior door, but not a trace of sawdust marred her neatly arranged piles of paper and account books.

"May I help you?" The woman's starched shirtwaist was of a pinstriped fabric and she'd done up her flaxen hair in a chignon with the new fringed bangs that were becoming increasingly popular.

I removed my glasses and wiped off the fog clouding them from coming in out of the cold. "Good morning. My name is Rose Carroll. I am here on a matter of some urgency and must speak with Ransom Skells."

She blinked several times. "What is the

business you need to conduct with Mr. Skells?"

"I prefer to speak with him directly about it."

"This is most irregular." She stood. "What is your occupation and place of residence?"

I cocked my head. "Why does thee need to know that?"

"The owners have to be cautious about our competitors disguising themselves and learning our proprietary methods."

"Very well. I am most certainly not thy competitor. My name is Rose Carroll and I am a midwife caring for Ransom's wife."

Her nostrils flared as she pressed her lips into a thin line.

"I reside on Center Street," I finished. "Now, may I speak with Ransom, please? As I mentioned, it is an urgent matter." Sadly, it wasn't really urgent. Charity was dead, and nothing could change that tragic and final fact. Still, I needed to inform Ransom as soon as possible.

Delia's expression returned to that of an officious gatekeeper. "Follow me." She ushered me through the door and pointed to Ransom, who was perched on an overturned wooden crate eating his dinner.

"I thank thee." I covered the few yards in a moment, still feeling Delia's eyes on my back. No matter. It was too noisy in here for her to eavesdrop on my sad tidings.

A stocky man, Ransom held half a meat turnover as he gazed out at the white expanse of the frozen river. Behind him saws and planes, chisels and hammers, awls and gimlets were hard at work in the hands of craftsmen, creating the dories and whalers the shop was known for. Motes of sawdust floated in the light that was reflected off the Merrimack and the air smelled deliciously of fresh wood. My mission here was not so delicious.

Ransom glanced up at me with a start. "Miss Carroll?" He stood, swiping crumbs off his mouth with the back of his hand. "What are you doing here?" he asked in his reedy voice, then smiled, the gap between his front teeth giving him a boyish look even though I thought he was at least thirty. He had remarkable light blue eyes framed by smile lines, and curly carrot-colored hair. Although Charity was a regular at Friends Meeting and her husband had converted to our faith, Ransom rarely accompanied her, and clearly hadn't embraced the Quakerly manner of speech.

I took in a deep breath, then began. "Ransom, I am very sorry to tell thee that Charity was taken quite ill this morning."

"Taken ill?" He shook his head. "There's always something with that woman. I keep telling her —"

I held up my hand. "Please let me finish. She sent for me. She was bleeding heavily, so I took her to the hospital on Market Street. But we were not able to save her."

"Save her what?"

Was he willfully trying to shut out bad news, or was he simply not understanding me? "Her life, Ransom. Charity's soul was released to God a little over an hour ago. I am so sorry."

He stared at me. "Do you mean to say she's dead?" His pie hit the floor with a splash of sawdust, and his whisper was as harsh as rough sandpaper.

I nodded once.

"What will I do?" he murmured, more to himself than to me. He turned away, his face to the tall window. A hammer nearby fell silent, and the man holding it watched Ransom as he faced me again.

"Bleeding, you say." Ransom's ruddy face had gone ashen. "Did she cut herself making dinner?"

"No." I spoke softly. "She bled from inside."

Ransom's nostrils went wide. He opened his mouth and shut it again. He rubbed his

29

thumb with his fingers on both hands. "It's my fault, isn't it?"

I touched his arm. "Please don't blame thyself. We don't know the cause." In fact, I didn't. A hemorrhage from such an early-term pregnancy was unlikely. Perhaps Charity had another malady I wasn't aware of. I hoped she hadn't sought out an abortionist, but it was a possibility. She might have visited one of the many unscrupulous and shadowy ones, most of whom were also dangerously unskilled, eager to make money off women desperate not to bear the child they carried. That could have been what Orpha had warned Charity against doing. But wouldn't Charity have told me the reason for her bleeding?

It was curious, what Ransom said. Why would he think his wife's death was his fault? Because he'd forced himself on her and knew she was with child again so soon? If she'd sought out an abortion because of her pregnancy, in a circuitous way her death would make him guilty.

"Where is Charity now? Her, her body, I mean." He winced at the term.

"They are holding her at the hospital until thee comes for her." As Quakers we didn't believe in embalming, but it wouldn't be possible to bury Charity promptly because of the frozen ground. She would need to go into Union Cemetery's receiving vault until spring brought a thawing of the soil. That service came at a cost, however, and I wasn't sure Ransom could afford it. Perhaps our Meeting could take up a collection to help defray the expense, or Charity's parents would assume the cost.

The man holding the hammer, a fellow with graying hair and spectacles perched on his nose, stepped forward. "Mr. Skells, I heard what the lady said. May Mrs. Skells rest in peace." He crossed himself, then pushed up the spectacles perched on his nose.

"I thank you, Mr. Sherwood." Ransom straightened his shoulders. "This is Midwife Carroll. She was looking after my wife. Miss Carroll, Mr. Sherwood is my supervisor here, teaching me to make boats and all."

"Pleased to meet you, miss."

"And I, thee." I extended my hand and shook his, feeling his calloused carpenter's skin next to mine.

"Now Mr. Skells, you go on home." The supervisor's quiet voice held authority. "You'll be having arrangements to make, a wife to grieve, children to comfort."

"Oh, but I can't leave, sir. I need to finish my day. I need the pay, you understand."

Ransom darted a glance at me. "The little ones, where are they, Miss Carroll?"

"Charity told me thy mother-in-law has them," I said. "Thee will need to break the bad news to her, I'm afraid."

"It's all right, Mr. Skells," the supervisor said. "Don't come back until Monday. I'll inform Miss Davies that you're to be paid for a full week's work."

This was an exceptionally generous manager.

"Very well, I'll go, then. Thank you, sir." Ransom tugged at his nonexistent hat.

"I'll take thee, Ransom," I said. "I have a horse and buggy." Transportation I hadn't expected I would use for a sad purpose such as this.

FIVE

Ransom remained quiet as we drove toward Charity's mother's abode. I glanced at him.

"Who was that nice young secretary at the shop, Ransom?" I ventured.

He snapped his face toward me. "Secretary?"

"The one thy supervisor referred to as Miss Davies. She showed me in." I didn't add that she'd been reluctant to do so. I pulled Peaches to a halt to let a wagon heaped high with coal turn in front of me.

"Oh, her. Delia Davies. She's nice enough." His fingers set to rubbing his thumbs again, even through his worn leather gloves.

"Has she been there long?"

He shrugged. "Was there when I started, but that was only two months ago."

"Does she live here in Amesbury?" Peaches clopped along again.

"Why do you care?" His tone was brusque.

"Here my wife has gone and died, we're on our way to tell her mother the terrible news, and you're asking about some girl, some chippy?" He stared away from me at Pattens Pond as we passed by.

He was right to admonish me. He had just lost his wife, after all.

"She's just a girl," Ransom continued. "I don't understand why you need to know about her. She's nothing." His clenched jaw worked almost as hard as his fingers.

What was that line from William Shakespeare? *I think thou doth protest too much,* or something similar. I let my questions lapse and soon pulled up in front of Virtue and Elias Swift's home on Lincoln Court.

"Would thee like me to accompany thee to convey the sad tidings?" I very much wanted to visit Orpha and learn what Charity had meant in her dying words. If Ransom wanted me to come in with him, though, I would.

He blew out a ragged breath, once again looking the grieving husband. "If you will. I would appreciate the help, and I expect Mother will want to know the details of Charity's death. She's never taken to me much. I'm glad it's daylight hours. Mr. Swift will be away at his office. He don't like me at all."

"I will come in with thee." Another curiosity, that he called his mother-in-law Mother rather than Virtue but referred to Charity's father as Mr. Swift. The use of "thee" and "thy" wasn't the only Friends way of speaking that Ransom ignored. Or maybe he addressed Virtue as "Mother" because it irked her, but he didn't dare attempt the same with his father-in-law.

The thought brought my own difficult situation to mind. My dear David had asked for my hand in marriage last summer, and I had gladly agreed. We'd received my parents' blessings as well as David's father's. But his mother was firmly against our union. Amesbury Meeting didn't approve, either. David was not a Friend, attending the Unitarian church in Newburyport. I would be marrying out, as Friends referred to it, and would be read out of Meeting, at least for a time. My mother had let me know the Lawrence Meeting, where she and my father worshipped — and where I had grown up — was more lenient and would welcome us to be married there. But the obstacle of Clarinda, David's mother, was another matter. We had yet to schedule our wedding.

"Does Virtue employ a stable hand?" I asked, wrenching myself back to the present. The Swift home was a large one and I glimpsed a matching carriage house set back on the right. If Charity's parents were so well off, why hadn't they helped her and Ransom financially? Because they didn't like their son-in-law? At least they hadn't shunned Charity. Virtue would not have taken the children for the morning if they had. I knew her only slightly from seeing her at Friends worship. She wasn't regular in her attendance, and of course I had not grown up in Amesbury but rather on our farm in distant Lawrence.

"Yes." His mouth twisted. "They have a goodly number of servants, but wouldn't give their daughter a red cent."

As I suspected.

"Go along back there." Ransom pointed to the carriage house.

But before we traveled the several yards, a man with disheveled dark hair under a battered fedora stomped out of the structure leading a rather sorry-looking gray horse. Ransom jerked in the buggy next to me and swiveled in his seat as if to hide his face from the man, who mounted his steed before he spied us. He clopped up next to my buggy and grinned down at Ransom.

"Ransom Skells, my man. I've been looking for you." He tipped his hat at me. "Miss."

I detected the smell of alcohol on the man's breath. The day had barely passed its midpoint.

Ransom met his gaze. "Hello, Joey." He lifted his chin. "Joe Swift, this is Miss Rose Carroll, my late wife's midwife."

The man's expression turned serious. "Your late wife, is it? Do you mean my cousin Charity has crossed the dark river?"

His cousin. Interesting that Ransom had seemed to want to avoid speaking with him. "Yes," I said. "She died this morning of complications from a miscarriage."

The man nodded slowly. "Well, I'm sorry to hear that. Be seeing you, Skells." He clucked to the horse and trotted away.

Ransom muttered to himself, but I couldn't make out the words.

"Shall we proceed?" I asked.

"I would rather not, but we must."

I drove up to the open door of the carriage house. Inside were a drop-front phaeton and a lovely Bailey carriage. I thought I spied a wagon in the back, too. I handed off Peaches to the stable boy, barely older than my nephew Luke's fourteen years, and followed Ransom to the house.

Virtue opened the door. "Why, Ransom,

what is thee doing here?" She was tall and angular, like Charity had been, but elegant where her daughter had been careworn. Virtue's silvering hair was done in a neat knot, and her maroon day gown was of a fine wool. "Good afternoon, Rose. I am surprised to see thee, as well." She stood back. "Come in, come in. Don't just stand there in the cold."

"I thank thee, Virtue." I preceded Ransom into a tastefully furnished front hall.

Charity's husband lingered on the stoop, twisting his tweed cap in his hands. "Mother, we . . ." His voice trailed off.

"Ransom Skells, I will never for the life of me understand why thee can't just call me Virtue like the rest of the world does. Now come in and close the door. Thee is letting all the heat out." She tapped her foot, shod in a cream-colored kid shoe.

He finally obeyed. I felt badly for him, but it was his news to bear. And who knew, perhaps he had lost his own mother at a young age and was happy to be able to use that word again to address his mother-in-law.

"Now, what's this all about?" Virtue asked. "And how's my daughter? She said she was ill this morning, that's why I fetched the little ones."

"Papa!" Little Howie, the couple's only son, ran into the hall and hurled himself at his father. A white-clad woman in her mid-twenties followed, holding the Skells' eighteen-month-old girl. Ransom lifted his son to his chest and buried his face in the boy's curly red hair that was a brighter shade of his own.

"I'm sorry, ma'am," the maid said. "Master Howie heard his father's voice and insisted on seeing him."

"As of course he should," Virtue said. "Let's go through and sit." She led the way into a comfortable sitting room decorated in shades of rose and green. A wooden rocking horse occupied a corner and was surrounded by books and blocks scattered on the floor, clearly the children's play area when they came to visit.

The maid headed in a different direction as Ransom touched my elbow.

"I can't. I can't tell her, Miss Carroll, not with —" He pointed to his son's back. Ransom's expression was slack, his eyes puffy, his shoulders slumped.

I nodded, sighing. "I will, then."

"Thank you." He nuzzled Howie's neck. "Let's see if Cook will give us a treat, shall we, my boy?"

Howie perked up. "Treat!"

39

Ransom carried the boy toward the back of the house, while I carried my burden of sad tidings to Virtue.

Six

Charity's mother stared at me, her hand to her mouth. "How can she be gone? She merely said she wasn't feeling well." Her eyes filled but she kept her back erect, perched on an upholstered chair. "Is thee sure?" Her lips wobbled.

I sat at the end of a settee next to her. "I stayed by her side until the end. I'm so sorry, Virtue. She was bleeding excessively. I believe it was from a miscarriage." I laid a hand on her knee. "She lost too much blood, and there was nothing we could do."

"That man," she muttered, anger apparently vying with her grief. "She had no business carrying another child so soon after losing the last one." She bowed her head, sorrow winning as her shoulders shook.

That man. Ransom himself. I pulled out a clean folded handkerchief I always kept in reserve for exactly these cases and handed it to her, then waited without speaking. It was not the right order of things, for a mother to lose an adult daughter. Sadly, such was life in our times.

At last Virtue straightened. She dabbed at her now-reddened eyes. "I should have helped her more. I tried every way I could imagine to slip money to her now and then without my husband's knowledge. Elias insisted she'd made her bed with Ransom and we had to leave her in it. I think he thought she would finally leave the man and bring her babies home to us. And she never did. Now it's too late." She sniffed. "I encouraged her to space those babies farther apart, too, and I provided her with money to obtain the necessary herbs. To no avail."

Was that the money Charity had referred to?

"Now we have two deaths in the family," Virtue added.

"Thee lost someone else recently?" *The poor woman.*

"My husband's brother, Joseph." She tilted her head toward a framed portrait on the far wall, a picture now draped in black crepe. "He lived in Newburyport and was much older than my husband. Had made a fortune in rum." She wrinkled her nose. "He'd fallen away from being a Friend, as thee can imagine, may he rest in peace."

"I'm sorry to hear of his demise." I pictured the man on the horse Ransom had addressed as Joey. "Does he have a son by the same name?"

"Yes. He was here just before thee arrived." Her mouth pulled. "Joey doesn't follow Quaker values, either. He's my husband's nephew, but he's a drunken gambler."

"I see. I met him briefly as I arrived with Ransom." Every family had its black sheep, it seemed.

We sat in silence for several moments. I closed my eyes and held Charity's released soul in the Light, as well as that of her mother, still very much of this world. I opened my eyes to see Virtue rubbing the back of one hand with the other.

She lifted her chin. "I must see my girl. Where did thee say she is?"

"At the Methodist hospital on Market Street."

"Would thee accompany me, Rose?" Her eyes pleaded her case.

One more delay to my visiting Orpha. But I had to say yes. "Is thee sure thee doesn't want to remember Charity as she lived, rather than with her soul already released to God?"

"I have many happy memories of my

daughter. Nothing will erase them. But I must say my farewell in the flesh."

"Of course I will come. But Ransom —"

"He can stay here or he can go home. He's not coming with us." She stood with her chin lifted.

"I'm not coming where?" Ransom appeared in the doorway, now without Howie. His shoulders drooped and his face still had that stricken appearance.

"I'm going with Virtue to view Charity." I caught myself before I uttered the word *body.*

"I have every right to see my wife." Ransom glared at Virtue.

"Then thee can exercise that right later today," Virtue said in a low, steely tone that brooked no argument. "I don't wish thy company on my sad mission. Now if thee will excuse us."

"I don't mean to intrude, but what about the older children?" I asked Ransom. "Will thee be home for them after school today, Ransom, or will they come here, Virtue?" Someone had to look out for them now.

Ransom looked from me to Virtue and back. "Charity always took care of the little ones. I'm not sure I know what to do."

Virtue's nostrils flared but she kept her composure. "I will fetch them and bring them here. They are always welcome at my house."

"Thank you, Mother. My wife would have appreciated that."

Virtue gave a soft snort. "We'll be going now. Rose?"

SEVEN

On the way to the hospital, Virtue said, "We need to fetch my husband. Elias will want to see our girl, too."

"We can stop to tell him, but we can't accommodate a third person in this buggy."

She brushed away my comment. "He has his own carriage, of course."

I steered Peaches to the haberdashery that Elias had started years ago as a small enterprise making hats for Quaker men. It had blossomed into one of the most highly regarded hat shops in the area, making all manner of toppers for men as well as fanciful head creations for women. It was an ironic business for a Friend to own, since his own wife and daughters wore only plain bonnets.

"I'll return in a moment," Virtue said as she climbed down.

As I waited, I mulled over Ransom's reactions to the news of Charity's death. He'd first asked himself what he would do, and then said her death was his fault. This grieving father was reeling from the news, and must have realized that her pregnancy was due to his insistence on resuming relations too early. I had only lost two clients to childbirth, and both had succumbed by natural causes, but their distressed husbands had not claimed responsibility.

Virtue reappeared and climbed into the buggy. "He'll be right along." She clasped her gloved hands tightly, her gaze downcast.

A mass of vehicles clogged Market Square ahead and I was forced to pull Peaches to a halt. Men yelled, horses whinnied and huffed, and a church bell tolled twice. A stiff cold breeze chilled me and I pulled my woolen shawl closer around my neck.

"Rose, if I'd only known," Virtue said as we waited.

Her voice was so low I had to strain to hear over the clamor. "Known what?"

"Charity and I, we'd had a falling out. She was upset I couldn't help her more. I wanted her to come around. Leave that worthless husband and bring the children home to live with us." A tear splashed on her glove, and then another. "We'd been estranged for months. I didn't know how bad it was for my girl. I didn't know she would die before I could say I loved her and missed her." She drew out an embroidered handkerchief and patted her eyes. "And now it's too late."

I patted her hand. There was no comfort I could offer, no words that would bring Charity back. A moment later the carriages ahead started to move. I clucked to Peaches to follow them.

We didn't have to wait long in the hospital foyer for Elias Swift to arrive. His haunted eyes were damp and the corners of his mouth dragged downward as if he might weep again at any moment. He was a tall, sturdy man with a silver chinstrap beard and normally lively blue eyes under dark brows.

Nurse Jeanne Peele led us down into the hospital's keeping room where more than one white-shrouded body lay on trolleys awaiting transport to their final resting place.

The air was chilly in the somber room. I noticed open vents high on the walls allowing the outside air of winter to naturally cool the bodies. The hospital must have to bring in ice in the summer despite the room being mostly underground.

The nurse gently folded back the cloth covering Charity's face, then stepped away, folding her hands in front of her. I was glad for Virtue's sake someone had smoothed back the dead woman's hair and wiped her face clean. At first glance one might think she was in repose, but a closer look showed her skin had taken on the waxen quality of a corpse. I had long thought that if anyone had any doubt about the soul persisting in the body after death, they had only to view a deceased person. The physical being was truly merely a shell once the life force departed.

But now the poor Swifts had to view the shell of their daughter. Virtue — with her rigid spine, ever-neat appearance, and strongly held views — was near collapse, as was her husband. Tears streamed down her cheeks as she bent over, stroked Charity's lifeless cheeks, kissed her brow.

"I'm so sorry, my darling. I'm so very sorry." Virtue murmured more words I couldn't catch. Elias stood behind her wringing his hands. As I watched, Virtue calmed herself, eyes closed, standing with one hand on Charity's forehead, the other on her heart. I sensed she was praying, holding her daughter's released soul in the Light. I closed my eyes and did the same.

After a scant minute, the door opened behind us.

"You wanted to see me, Nurse Peele?" a man's voice said.

I opened my eyes and turned to see John Douglass, a well-known doctor in town with a general practice, which meant he also cared for pregnant and birthing women. My heart sank. In the past he had not been favorably inclined toward my own practice — or that of any midwife, he had once maintained. On our way downstairs I had mentioned to Jeanne that I would like to talk to the supervising doctor about Charity's bleeding and death. I hadn't heard that John Douglass had moved from a private practice to here, but he must have. I glanced at Virtue, who paid us no mind and continued her prayerful vigil.

I moved quietly to the doorway. "It was I, John, who wished to speak with thee." I spoke as softly as I could and still be audible.

He shook his head, lips pursed, likely unhappy with my addressing him by his Christian name. His silver hair and full beard of the same hue showed his age as over sixty, but he was vigorous for that stage in life, with keen, clear eyes and a steady hand.

The nurse nodded, murmuring, "Doctor, this is midwife Rose Carroll."

"Oh, we've met, Nurse Peele," he said.

"Let us step out into the hall." I gestured toward the door.

The doctor frowned. "Very well."

"I'll remain in here with the parents," Jeanne said.

I waited until the door closed to speak. "Charity Skells summoned me this morning, saying she was taken ill. I brought her here because I was alarmed at the quantity of her bleeding. It seemed too copious for a miscarriage. Does thee know her history?"

"I do." He checked a piece of paper in his hand. "Under your care, she lost a prematurely born infant last November."

I pressed my lips together at the way he stressed the word *your.* "I believe she would have lost the baby no matter who was caring for her. None of us have the means to save an infant born two months before its time."

"The woman was malnourished, Miss Carroll. I dare say she wouldn't have given birth so early if she'd been eating the quantity and quality of food a pregnancy requires."

I kept my calm. "And would thee have moved her into thy home to feed her?" Why hadn't Virtue done exactly that? Could she not overcome her husband's objections to nourish her own daughter?

"Of course not." John dismissed my question with scorn in his voice. "There is assistance available. But maybe you don't offer that to your ladies."

How dare he? "John, I help my clients explore all their options for good health. In fact, Charity was receiving donations of food from our church, despite her reluctance to accept a gesture equaling her own name. As a caring mother, she likely gave most of the food to her children. It is her husband, Ransom Skells, to whom thee might better assign the blame for her condition." I smiled, despite feeling exactly the opposite of cheer and goodwill. "What I wanted to ask the attending physician was his opinion as to her cause of death. Will thee call for an autopsy?"

"What do you think she died of, if not the miscarriage of an early-term fetus?" He watched me, his hand fiddling with the chain of his pocket watch. He narrowed his eyes. "I hear you've been playing lady detective around town. Do you imagine Mrs. Skells was murdered?"

I gazed at him over the top of my spectacles. "Excuse me. I have not been playing lady detective, as thee puts it." And I couldn't imagine why someone would kill a struggling housewife like Charity. "A poorly executed termination is a possible explanation."

"An abortion?" he scoffed. "Surely not here in Amesbury. They're against the law, in case you didn't know."

"Of course I know." I sighed. Men had no idea the lengths to which women in difficult circumstances would go to avoid one more baby, or one at all. "I also know Charity was tired, impoverished, and with few resources to feed the children she already had. She might have sought out a way to avoid adding one more to her family. At any rate, as her midwife I would like to ask for an autopsy to be carried out. I imagine the police will want to see the results of it, too."

The door opened. Jeanne ushered out Virtue and Elias.

"We'll go now, Rose," Elias said.

"Thank you, Jeanne," I said. "And thee, John. Please send word when the results become available."

"I'll need Mr. Skells's permission." The doctor folded his arms.

It was a pity the autopsy had to be discussed in front of these deeply saddened parents. "I don't believe you will, not if the police request it."

"Permission for what?" Elias looked bewildered.

"The police?" Virtue asked. "Request what?"

I laid a hand on her arm to soften my words as I addressed her and her husband. "To perform an autopsy. We need to determine the exact cause of Charity's death."

"Autopsy? Where they cut the b . . . person open?" She blinked away the tears that had quickly filled her eyes.

"Yes," I said.

"And thee thinks this is necessary?" Elias asked me, his voice so low I could barely hear it. "Why?"

"I do." I knew many relatives felt it was a desecration to violate a loved one's body in any way after death. "It is the only sure way to ascertain the cause of her death." I would leave it at that. Talk of botched termination or even murder wasn't necessary. Yet.

"Elias?" Virtue looked to her husband.

He gazed at her with a tender look and took both her hands. "I think we should agree." Elias faced the doctor. "I am Charity's father, and if it matters, I find no objection."

"I am very sorry for your loss, Mr. and Mrs. Swift," the doctor said. "You'll get your wish, Miss Carroll, only if the husband or the police give the order." He turned and stalked toward the stairs, grumbling to himself.

"Elias, if thee pleases?" Virtue said, her spine no longer rigid. Her face looked like it had aged ten years.

He offered her his elbow. "We thank thee, Nurse Peele," he said to Jeanne. He and Virtue walked away as if they both wore shoes of lead, their heads bowed and shoulders slumped.

"I thank thee, as well," I said.

Jeanne nodded her head, then leaned closer. "Don't worry about Doctor. He talks big. But he'll do what's right."

In my experience, what John Douglass thought was right could be considerably different than my own views.

EIGHT

After I left the hospital, I finally directed Peaches to the house on Orchard Street where Orpha resided with her granddaughter Alma Latting, a dressmaker, and Alma's young family. My former teacher always had a wise word to offer about difficult matters in my practice. Her wit and insights on life in general made her a delight to be around no matter what was going on with my clients. And today I was eager to ask her what she had warned Charity against.

When Alma answered the door, a tape measure draped around her neck, she welcomed me. But a visit with Orpha was not to be. "I'm afraid my grandmother isn't in, Rose. She went out with some friends to a quilting bee. She's been gone since morning and won't be back until late. I will tell her you called, though."

I thanked her. "Please tell her I'll be by in the morning."

"I will. And can you tell —" She stopped abruptly and clapped her hand over her mouth.

"What?"

"I'm sorry, I got something confused. Goodbye, Rose."

I retreated to my horse and buggy. Despite being frustrated I still couldn't learn Charity's secret, I was glad Orpha was well enough to spend a day quilting. When she'd suffered an apoplectic seizure last summer, I'd been afraid her life would take a steep decline in quality or even end. But the event turned out to be a fairly minor stroke and not the end of her time here on earth at all.

Another of my mentors, the famous Quaker abolitionist and poet John Greenleaf Whittier, wasn't available to talk over my concerns with, either. He spent winters with his cousins in Danvers, several towns to the south of here. John was growing more frail with his advanced age and the family was happy to have the tall creative bachelor to feed and fuss over.

I parted my cloak to check the watch I kept pinned to my bosom. It was already half past two and I had clients coming to the house for antenatal visits beginning at three o'clock. The exchange about the autopsy with Douglass at the hospital had left a bad taste in my mouth despite the nurse's reassurance. I resolved to pay a quick visit to police detective — and my friend — Kevin Donovan. If he ordered the autopsy be done, neither John Douglass nor Ransom Skells would be able to halt it.

It didn't take long to reach the centrally located police station downtown. After I gave the lad at the stable around back a coin to watch Peaches, I hurried up the front steps. I greeted Guy Gilbert, the young officer at the front desk.

"Miss Rose, I s'pose you're wanting to talk with Kevin," he said, standing.

"Yes, please." The place smelled as it always did, of old wood, gun oil, and stale tobacco, with an overlay of burnt coffee.

"Is there a homicide I haven't heard about?" Guy scrunched up his nose and peered at me.

"Ah, that's the question, Guy," I replied.

Guy glanced behind me at same time as I heard Kevin's voice.

"My old friend Rose Carroll, is it?" The detective wore an open coat over his uniform, and his round cheeks were even ruddier than usual from being out in the cold. He was at least a decade older than my own twenty-seven years, but he always looked hale and youthful.

"Good afternoon, Kevin. May I speak with thee in thy office?"

"Certainly, but briefly. I have a meeting with our new chief in a few minutes."

"It shouldn't take long." I followed Kevin back and perched on the chair across from his desk as he shed his coat and also sat.

The office was in its usual tidy state, with a stack of papers neatly squared on the desk next to a wide blotter. I leaned in to examine a framed drawing on his desk. It was a pencil likeness of a barefoot boy leaning against the trunk of a leafy tree, an open book in his hands, an intent look on his visage.

"What a lovely picture, Kevin."

He beamed. "It's of my son, Sean. My wife drew it. She's quite talented, wouldn't you say?"

"Indeed I would. How old is he now? He looks about seven in this picture."

"On the nose. Had his birthday last month. Now, what brings you here, Miss Rose?"

"I'm hoping if you order an autopsy on one of my clients, we might better discern her means of death." I outlined my suspicions about Charity's death.

"And because this lady was bleeding more than she should have been, you want me to investigate, I gather." Kevin set his forearms on the desk and leaned forward. "Do you think it might be a homicide? Surely she could have had another ailment to cause such a hemorrhage?"

I leaned forward, too. "Maybe, but I never detected one."

"Then who would want to kill a wife and mother like her?"

"I didn't say it was a homicide, although I think that's a possibility."

"Where's the motive? You have to give me more than this, Miss Rose. You've been involved in enough homicide investigations to know how it goes."

"Kevin, I think she was desperate not to have any more children. Her bleeding could have been from a botched abortion." And she could have used Virtue's money to pay for it. Perhaps that was the money she'd referred to before she died.

"Sweet Mary and Jesus." He sat up straight as if I'd slapped him. He crossed himself, like the good Irishman he was. "What a thing to say! That kind of act is against the law. Both our law and the good Lord's, you know."

It was no use explaining even to this well-meaning man, just like it wasn't with Douglass, the extent of some women's desperation not to bear a child.

"And a botched termination" — he shuddered at the word — "still would not qualify as murder, Miss Rose. Malpractice, yes."

"We need an autopsy, Kevin. If thee investigates the death as a suspicious one, the autopsy will at least show what she died of. It remains to be seen whether the death was purposeful or accidental. Will thee order it?"

Kevin's gaze wandered to the open door. His eyes widened and he leapt to his feet. "I'm just coming along, Chief Talbot."

A tall, stern-looking man wearing a well-cut suit filled the doorway. "Why is this lady in your office asking you to order an autopsy, Detective Donovan?"

This had to be the new chief, whom I hadn't yet met. He'd clearly been at the doorway long enough to hear the end of our conversation. I stood and extended my hand.

"My name is Rose Carroll. I am midwife to a woman who died from hemorrhage this morning. I have reason to believe it wasn't natural bleeding."

The chief narrowed his eyes and his mouth puckered like he'd tasted sour milk. I expected he thought such talk was unseemly in the presence of men. He shook my extended hand but didn't return my smile.

Kevin rushed to say, in a nervous burst, "Miss Rose, this is Police Chief Norman Talbot. Chief, Miss Carroll has provided us with information in several homicide investigations over the past year. She's been quite cooperative."

"Is that so? We frown on civilian involvement in our work, Miss Carroll. It's dangerous and not the purview of the man on the street. Definitely not of the woman on the street. Detective, I'll thank you to show her out and come directly to my office. We have some talking to do."

"Yes, sir." Kevin saluted, but it was to Norman's back. He turned to me, whispering, "You have to go."

"I understand. I hope I didn't cause thee a problem with thy new supervisor."

He rolled his eyes. "I hope not, as well. But don't come in here again, please. I can't afford to lose my job."

NINE

While I was checking my client Lucy Majowski in my parlor an hour later, I tried to put Kevin's warning out of my mind. I wasn't very successful, despite this young *primigravida* — first-time pregnant — who deserved my attention. The new police chief had echoed Kevin's own prior cautions to me. Of course I hadn't gone looking for murder investigations with which to become involved. They had simply happened along. My knitting needle being used as a murder weapon, and one of my postnatal clients being brutally killed. An unmarried mill girl who had confided in me of her condition hours before her own death by a violent hand. And me being the one to discover the body of an outspoken woman suffrage activist during last fall's presidential election week. I had been the target of more than one villain, but I had always been able to use my brains and a dose of luck both to survive and to overcome my attacker.

Now I wouldn't be able to pop into the station when I learned a piece of important information or had a caution for Kevin to hear. I valued his intelligent thoughts on the investigative process, and his intuition that came from long years of detection experience. Our face-to-face discussions had often proved fruitful. It wouldn't be the same if we were reduced to formal communication via the mails. Kevin's previous chief had turned a blind eye to my presence in the station. He didn't condone it, but had never prohibited it, either.

The new chief was just doing his job, I supposed, but it made my life more difficult. Or, I mused, perhaps it made it simpler. I knew my David worried when my private investigating had put me in harm's way. And when we were ever able to marry and start our own family, I would need to take my personal safety and the use of my time much more into consideration. I didn't intend to close my midwifery practice, however. I had David's support in that regard.

I gave my head a little shake. It was time to focus on my client rather than on my personal problems or the mystery at hand.

"Thee is doing quite well, Lucy," I said

when I was finished with my examination. "The baby is of a good healthy size and its heartbeat is strong. Thee also seems in exceedingly good health. Does thee have any concerns or questions for me?"

"Other than that he's always kicking my ribs and it's hard to sleep? Not really." She pulled her green woolen dress back down over her belly. She swung her legs over the side of the chaise that doubled as my examination table, just as my parlor doubled as my bedroom, with a day bed tucked against the back wall.

"The baby is getting thee ready for not sleeping after it comes." I smiled gently. "I know that's not much comfort, is it?"

She batted away the suggestion. "It'll be fine. And you'll come to my house next week for your home visit, isn't that right?" The blond young woman's voice still held a hint of a Polish accent. She'd told me she'd come to this country with her parents when she was ten. Now, nine years later, she was married to Henryk, a young farmer and fellow Pole, and was expecting their first child.

"That's right. I think thee might give birth a little earlier than we'd first calculated, so I should come early in the week. I'll even try to get along there at the end of this week if my schedule permits. Will thee be home?"

"Of course. The cows don't milk them-selves, Rose!" Her laugh was a joyous peal. "This belly is too big to take anywhere besides here, anyway."

She had an irrepressible sunny outlook on life. I glimpsed movement through the front window and peered out. "It looks as if thy husband has come to fetch thee. And it's snowing. Let me ascertain thy address before thee goes." Henryk sat on the seat of a wagon in front of the house, white flakes powdering his dark brimmed hat. I checked her file on my desk. "It says here thy farm is a mile beyond Union Cemetery. On Haver-hill Road. Are there many farms nearby?"

"Only a handful, but you'll know ours by the white house and red barn. It's funny, Rose. I have a neighbor my age. She lives across the road." Lucy frowned. "We went to school together, but we've grown apart in the last few years. She's quite proud of her employment as a secretary at Lowell's Boat Shop."

"A Delia Davies? I met her just this morn-ing."

"Yes." Lucy went on, smoothing her dress over her bulging figure with both hands. "As for me, I'm a farmer's wife. I think she looks down on me a little. But I'm the one who's happily married and about to become a mother. I wouldn't swap my life with hers for a moment."

"Being content with one's life bodes well for thy birth and thy baby."

"How is that?" She tilted her head, waiting for me to explain.

"I have seen women unhappy with their husbands, or with becoming a mother, whose worries slowed the progress of their baby coming out."

Lucy nodded slowly. "That sounds likely."

"One client of mine with an overly long first labor confessed to me that she'd been beaten on the head as a child," I said. "She worried that her child would be similarly hurt simply by the process of being born. Once I assured her that her birth passageway would expand, and the baby's head would mold as it came through and not be truly harmed, those facts freed her to relax. Her little boy emerged within the hour."

"I don't think I have any such fears," Lucy said. "No one ever beat me, and Henryk is a good man. The silent type, but he loves me and looks forward to this child — boy or girl — as much as I do, perhaps even more." Lucy pulled on a large wool coat and laughed. "My husband insisted I wear his new overcoat. It's the only thing big enough to fit the both of us, the child and me."

TEN

At a few minutes before six, Faith and I were bustling about in the kitchen of the house I shared with Frederick Bailey, the husband of my late sister, Harriet, and their five children. Faith, the oldest at eighteen, had recently left her job in the Hamilton textile mill to write for our local newspaper. Betsy was the youngest of the family at eight years old, the twins Matthew and Mark were ten, and Luke had just turned fourteen. My lodging with them was a good arrangement for all of us, now two years after Harriet's death. I could help Faith with the cooking and housework, the children had another adult in the house, and some of the burden of being a widower parent was lifted from Frederick's shoulders. At times the chores were a burden on my and Faith's shoulders, instead. At least we now employed a kitchen girl and sent the laundry out to be cleaned.

The long farm table doubling as dining table was set for nine. I pulled a pan of buttermilk biscuits out of the oven, while Faith ladled a rich, thick beef stew into a serving bowl. Fat slices of golden carrots were mixed in with pale chunks of potatoes and tender shreds of meat. It was a perfect rib-warming dish for a snowy night. Our kitchen cat, the yellow and white long-haired Christabel, sat mewing expectantly. Faith had gotten her as a kitten last summer, and she'd turned into an excellent mouser. We now had a vermin-free home.

"She smells the meat," Faith said with a smile.

I fished out a chunk of beef and one of potato, and mashed them together in a small bowl for the cat's dinner, setting it on the floor for her after it cooled.

"Matthew, Mark, Betsy," I called into the adjoining sitting room. "Time to wash your hands and get ready to eat." I set the dish of stew in the middle of the table and counted the plates. "Faith, don't we only need eight places?" I counted again. Five children. Frederick, Zeb, and me. Eight. My brother-in-law Frederick had asked to use my parlor for a moment, and was sequestered in there with Zebulon Weed, Faith's beau.

"Father said to put on nine. So I did."

My heart lifted. Was my David surprising me with a visit in the middle of his meetings in Portsmouth? How I would love that.

The three younger children ran in and shoved each other to be the one who controlled the pump in the wide black soapstone kitchen sink. Betsy lost out, of course. Matthew, who'd had a recent growth spurt, now stood with his black curls a few inches taller than his towheaded brother. He pumped water for all of them to wash up with.

At that moment the front doorbell jangled. "I'll see who it is," Luke called in his newly gruff voice, which still cracked into a boy's higher pitch at odd moments.

"No, Luke. I will answer the door," Frederick said from the front of the house.

Odd. Usually Frederick ordered Luke around as if he was his personal servant instead of his teenaged son.

Slender sweet Zeb joined us in the kitchen. Beaming, he bestowed a kiss on Faith's forehead. He spied the basket I'd readied with a cloth for the biscuits and slid them into it, then brought it to the table. This Friend was not a man bound by the rigid tradition that says kitchen work is women's work.

71

A moment later Frederick escorted a short woman with a comfortable body into the kitchen. She entered hesitantly, almost shyly. So the guest wasn't my David, after all. My disappointment was palpable and I tried to keep it off my face. On the other hand, who in the world was she? The room fell quiet as we all watched.

"Family," Frederick began, his own voice hesitant, "I'd like you to meet my friend, Winnie Hanson. Winnie, this is my family." He placed his hand lightly on her back with one hand and gestured with the other.

A hush fell over the room as the family took this in. His *friend.* She appeared to perhaps be more than a friend. Frederick had always been difficult and had grown more so since his wife's death. I was glad if he had found joy in a companion. In truth, he had seemed somewhat less argumentative and disgruntled of late. But was Winnie also a Friend?

Betsy, always the fearless one, stepped forward. "I'm pleased to meet thee, Winnie." She extended her little hand. "I'm Betsy."

Winnie appeared to blink away a tear as she smiled down at Betsy and clasped Betsy's hand in both of hers. "And I am pleased to meet thee, as well, Betsy."

Apparently she was, in fact, a Quaker like

us. In turn we each introduced ourselves, me hanging back until the immediate family was named and greeted.

"And I am Rose Carroll, Winnie. I'm the children's aunt. My late sister was their mother."

"Rose has been good enough to lodge with us," Frederick added, "and help out around the house."

"She's a midwife," Betsy chimed in. "She helps babies get born."

Winnie, now appearing more at ease, smiled at me, her bright blue eyes a contrast to her nearly black hair. "I have heard of thee, Rose."

"Oh?" I asked.

"Yes. I am a member of Newburyport Friends Meeting. They were most supportive when I was widowed. Benjamin Lehigh has lauded your skills both in the birthing chamber and as an amateur investigator. And I believe I have met your betrothed."

"David?" I was surprised, but perhaps I shouldn't have been. Benjamin, the Quaker lawyer and also a widower, was a good friend of David's parents.

"Yes. I'm a nursing supervisor at Anna Jaques. David is one of our best physicians, and always respectful to the nurses."

"As well he might be, but I am not surprised to hear it. Welcome to our home, Winnie." I glanced at Faith, who nodded. "Dinner is hot and ready. Shall we sit?"

After we'd held hands for our silent prayer of gratitude and begun to eat, I asked the newcomer, "Does thee have children, Winnie?"

Her smile was a sad one. "I had two babies, but their souls were released to God in that outbreak of influenza some years back. And my husband died not long after. It was then that I trained as a nurse."

So she and Frederick had in common that they'd both lost a spouse, but perhaps I shouldn't have asked about such a painful topic. "I'm so sorry."

"Don't bother thy head about it, Rose," Winnie said. "I work primarily with sick children at the hospital, so I am able to mother them to my heart's content."

The conversation moved on to lighter topics, like the poem Betsy had memorized for school and Luke's opinion on the Arthur Conan Doyle novel he'd just read. Twenty minutes later the serving dishes were empty and our stomachs were full. Mark stood and said, "Father, may we be excused?"

"Not quite yet, son."

Zeb took Faith's hand. Her eyes gleamed. "We have some news," she said, gazing at her beau.

"Yes," Zeb said, looking at each of us in turn. "I have asked Faith to join me in holy matrimony. She agreed."

"And I have given them both my blessing." Frederick beamed. He reached under the table for Winnie's hand and didn't try to hide the gesture.

Betsy clapped her hands. She sprang up and ran around the table, climbing onto Faith's lap. "Do I get to be the flower girl? My friend at school got to be the flower girl in her auntie's wedding. And we're sisters, so that's even more important, isn't it?"

Faith stroked her little sister's hair. "We'll see, Betsy."

"Have you chosen a date?" I asked of both Faith and Zeb.

"That's the thing," Zeb said. "We proceeded a little backwards and have already been cleared for marriage by Amesbury Friends. My father has to travel to Chicago on business next week."

"And Granny Dot is going to Washington for a woman suffrage meeting as soon as he gets back," Faith added. "So we thought we would be married on First Day."

"This First Day?" I asked. I felt a pang of missing David amid these happy couples. How I wished he could have been here beside me at this moment. I was completely happy for Faith and Zeb, but this sharpened my unhappiness with my own as-yet unmarried situation. And it meant I would lose Faith's companionship and help at home, too.

"Yes, in the afternoon," Faith continued. "Granny and Grandfather said they can come. Will thee help me, Rose? Alma Latting is making me a new dress, and the Women's Business Meeting is arranging the food for afterward. But I do hope thee will —" Her mouth quavered and she gazed at me with full eyes. "I want thee to stand in for Mother, if thee will."

"Of course I will, dear Faith. Thee has my blessing." I pushed away my own feelings as I rose and went around to kiss her cheek. "And thee as well, nephew Zeb." I kissed his, too. My time would come. Theirs had simply come first.

ELEVEN

By eight thirty I was in my room, my head swimming with the events of this very full day. It had begun with Charity's apparent miscarriage, and ended with meeting Frederick's new love as well as hearing news of Faith's impending marriage. The middle of the day was the confounding part. Charity's mysterious message about the money, and her final inaudible words after her mention of Orpha. Bertie's tidbit about Ransom acting unpleasantly. The way Ransom had reacted to the news of his wife's death. Virtue's animosity toward him. John Douglass's displeasure with me at the hospital. Not being able to talk with Orpha. And being banned from the station by Kevin's new boss.

I resolved to visit Orpha first thing the next morning. At least that part I should be able to clear up, whom Orpha had cautioned Charity not to see. Or where not to go. If it had been an abortionist Orpha had warned against, who was it? I'd heard a name or two in town but never encountered any of them. Since the highly restrictive federal Comstock law was passed more than fifteen years ago, sharing information about abortion or contraceptive methods was now illegal, even though it hadn't been earlier in the century.

A self-appointed vice hunter, Anthony Comstock had sponsored a bill in the forty-second Congress effectively making dissemination of information about contraception and abortion illegal. I had read the wording, which prohibited "any article whatever for the prevention of conception, or for causing unlawful abortion."

Prior to that law, and several passed in states prior, inducing an abortion before the fetus quickened wasn't a crime at all. After the fetus began to move, terminating a pregnancy had been considered a misdemeanor, not a felony. Now advertising, mailing, or even talking about contraception or abortion could land one in jail. A number of states had also passed what people called "little Comstock laws," as well, many of which went even further than the original law. Massachusetts was one of them. My state's law sought to make even private conversations about contraception or abortion illegal by prohibiting verbal transmission of information. As a result, those offering services for preventing or ending pregnancy had been driven underground and forced to act out of the public eye.

Abortion by mechanical means, rather than from ingesting an abortifacient, was a very risky procedure. In the hands of a skilled and patient practitioner, a curettage of the uterus using one of the available metal tools could be successful. The tools included a slender rod with a bend near the rounded, flattened end that would be gently inserted into the pregnant uterus and manipulated. Inserting the rod was extremely painful for the woman, and the wielder had to exercise great caution not to perforate the uterine walls. There was a certain root that practitioners sometimes inserted into the mouth of the uterus, the cervix. Left there for a time, the root absorbed the body's fluids and expanded gradually, opening the cervix and making the tool's insertion less of an ordeal for the patient.

But impatient, less-skilled abortionists with primitive tools like knitting needles or long crochet hooks were dangerous in the extreme and often resulted in deaths like

Charity's.

And if Orpha had not warned Charity against attempting to terminate her pregnancy by mechanical means, what had she cautioned her not to do? There were also herbal and chemical methods to induce miscarriages, of course. But if not used correctly, women could become severely ill or even die from taking them. I'd heard of a death when a woman ingested an extract of foxglove, a toxic poison, and another when too much nightshade was taken.

I drew out paper and pen and began a letter to David. After greeting him, I started with Faith and Zeb's happy news.

I hope thee will accompany me to the Meeting for Marriage this First Day afternoon. My parents will be arriving on Seventh Day to join in the celebration, and the young couple is so joyful I could not help but feel the same.

I also mentioned Frederick's introduction of Winnie to the family, saying I was glad that he seemed to have found someone with whom to be happy. I rested my pen and sat back for a moment. At the dinner table I hadn't broached the subject of where the newlyweds would live, but I doubted it would be here. I didn't know if Zeb had saved enough money from his employment at the carriage factory to buy a modest home for the two of them. His father was of more means than Frederick, as he was a judge, so perhaps he would help them purchase a residence. Which would leave me as sole housekeeper here, a prospect I did not relish.

On the other hand, if the bond between Frederick and Winnie strengthened, they might well wed too, and she move in here. In that case, would she want me to stay occupying the front room? She seemed a sweet woman, but she could easily wish for the use of the parlor. Where would I go in that case? I had lived in a boardinghouse while I apprenticed with Orpha and in the first year of taking over her practice, but I'd had to do all my antenatal examinations in the pregnant woman's home, which greatly increased my travel and meant I had to cart client records all over town, too. I wouldn't like to return to that way of conducting my business if I didn't have to.

I knew at some point David and I would work through the obstacles thrown in the way of our own wedding vows and then I would be leaving the Bailey household, regardless. But when? It was really only David's mother Clarinda standing in our way now. Amesbury Meeting would neither let us marry there nor even let me remain a member of the congregation for a time after I wed my intended.

I wrinkled my nose. Would Amesbury Friends even allow David to attend Faith's Marriage Meeting for Worship? They had to. Non-Quakers always were welcomed to occasions such as weddings and Memorial Meetings for Worship.

I heaved a heavy sigh and returned to my scribing, turning to Charity's death. After I described the facts of it, I wrote,

I long to talk through the situation with thee. I cannot decide if she in fact suffered a miscarriage, or if a person did harm to her. Her last words were

I was so absorbed in my writing that I started at a knock at my door. "Come in," I called.

Faith poked her head in. "May I?"

"Of course. Come and sit for a bit. I was just writing to David."

"To tell him our news?" She smiled shyly and perched on the chaise with a tentative air.

"Of course, dear Faith. I am so happy for

thee and Zeb, and I want to be sure David is free for the service." I turned my chair to face her. "I had a few other things I wanted to share with him, but it can wait."

"I wanted to apologize for arranging our clearness and the wedding date without consulting thee." She twisted her hands in her lap. "I . . . I was so worried thee would feel hurt that Zeb and I were marrying before thee and David."

"It's all right." I reached out and patted her hand.

"Is thee sure?"

I nodded. "Thee has far fewer obstacles in thy path than we do, for which I am glad. We'll arrive at our ceremony as Way opens."

"And I eagerly anticipate thy union, as well. I have told Annie about our ceremony. She will be with us on First Day and said to tell thee she will do anything to help, it is only to ask."

Annie Beaumont, Faith's friend from the mill, had also left that grueling job and was my apprentice in midwifery. She had an excellent manner and was a fast learner. Right now she was attending a week-long training in Boston, but blessedly would return at week's end.

"I am glad of it. Shall I invite John Whittier back to town, as well?"

"Would thee? It would mean so much to me. After he introduced me to Lucy Larcom in the fall, my purpose to also become a writer became ever more clear."

"I'm not sure he'll be able to come, but I'll send him a quick note. Now tell me about thy new dress." Which must have been what Alma had been about to tell me earlier in the day before deciding it wasn't her news to share.

Faith's face glowed. "As thee knows, Friends are not to indulge in fancy wedding dresses. None of this virginal white for us, although of course I have never . . . thee knows what I mean." Her color rose.

"Of course. Go on." What a sweet innocent thing. And what a gift that her betrothed was as kind and sweet as she was. They would explore their sexuality together and learn from each other over time.

"I found a fine wool in the most beautiful blue. Alma is adding delicate shirring on the bodice, and it is in a simple version of the latest style. It's plain enough for the Women's Business Meeting to approve of, and nice enough for a wedding."

"And then thee shall have a new frock for special occasions thereafter," I said.

"Exactly."

I rose and extracted a flat package

84

wrapped in tissue from my armoire. "Here. Wear this with thy new garment. Don't they say the bride is to wear, 'Something old, something new, something borrowed, something blue'?"

She unfolded it and squealed, clasping the lace collar with both hands. "It's beautiful, Rose."

"Mother tatted it and sent it after we'd made our visit to Clarinda Dodge during her last visit. I think Mother hoped my marriage to David would transpire sooner rather than later. But thee shall have it now."

"I thank thee." Her face grew serious as she stared at the collar. "But I have a request of thee that gives me some trepidation."

"Better to come out with it, then, and we'll examine the issue together."

"All right. Both Zeb and I are eager to become fully intimate after we are wed. And we want to have children, create a family, by and by. But not right away. Are there methods to delay becoming with child?" She gazed at me with the most earnest face I'd ever seen on her and I almost laughed. "The girls at the mill would talk about such matters, but nobody really knew anything."

"Of course I can help thee, darling. There are pessaries thee can insert inside thy passageway." I couldn't help noting the irony that I knew how to help clients both prevent pregnancy and terminate an unwanted pregnancy, as well as how to birth a healthy baby. I continued. "Or a sponge treated with a spermicidal solution. French letters are an excellent solution for preventing the impregnating fluid to pass through. They're also known as rubbers." I ticked the methods off on my fingers. "And then there's the man withdrawing his member before —" I glanced up. Faith's earnest eagerness had turned to complete confusion. Now I did laugh. My niece didn't have a clue as to what I was talking about.

"What does thee know about the actual sexual act?" I asked gently.

She simply shook her head, her cheeks aflame.

"Then we'll start with the basic lesson. Orpha made it clear at the start of my training that if I was to help women with the consequences of having sexual intercourse, I'd better know how it all worked." I'd had one disastrous experience with intercourse when I was nearly Faith's age. But it was during a terrible assault — not exactly a lesson in love and intimacy — and I wasn't going to share that with my happy young niece. I turned to my desk, pushed aside

David's letter, drew out a blank sheet of paper, and beckoned her to share my chair.

"Here's what happens," I began. My niece had asked me to stand in for her mother, and stand in I would.

TWELVE

By the time Faith and I had finished talking last night, I'd been too tired to complete my letter to my beau. The delay was worth it, though. I was able to help her ready herself for her wedding night, and we'd grown even closer in the process. She was truly an adult now, no longer the little girl I'd watch grow up into this caring, thoughtful, intelligent young woman.

Faith had told me she and her husband-to-be were planning to move in with Zeb's parents. Sadly, the family had had an extra room available ever since Zeb's younger brother's death in the Great Fire last year. The couple would have two rooms in the large house as their own while they built a new cottage at the end of Orchard Street. At least they'd be close by. Orchard was only a few blocks from here.

The next morning after breakfast I wrote the rest of what I wanted to and readied

David's letter for the morning post, glad he'd given me the name of his hotel. He wasn't due home until Sixth Day, so the letter should reach him in plenty of time.

I spent the following hour reviewing my files and my schedule of client visits and due dates. I didn't want to pay my visit to Orpha too early, but I also had an antenatal visit scheduled at eleven. While I worked, though, the back of my mind still labored on the conundrum of Charity's death. Would I hear from Kevin about the autopsy? If he'd ordered it done, I longed to hurry the process. And if he hadn't, I wished I could go see him and try again to convince him it was necessary.

Finally the clock reached a decent visiting hour and I decided to walk. Orpha didn't live far and it was a sunny, albeit cold, morning, because the snow had ceased falling during the night. The clean fresh inch of white on the ground squeaked when I trod on it. Faith's happy news should have made me glad and given a spring to my step. Instead my feet were leaden. The sadness of losing Charity had made my body heavy, dragged down into sorrow. It felt more acute than yesterday, as if the truth had finally invaded my very bones.

Fifteen minutes later I sat opposite Orpha

in her small sitting room. We'd chatted for a few minutes about our respective families and I'd filled her in on David.

"But you're not here to ask me how my great-granddaughters are." Orpha was old and her eyes rheumy, but her gaze missed nothing, even my thoughts. "I heard poor Charity Skells crossed the dark river yesterday. Were you with her?"

"Yes, I was. She sent for me in the morning, saying she was ill. When I reached her house she was bleeding copiously, Orpha, so I took her to the Methodist Hospital."

"Did you try extract of ergot to stop the bleeding first?"

"I didn't think I had time. They administered some to her there, but it was too late and she expired from a grave loss of blood. In my calculation, she must have barely been pregnant, and I don't understand how such an early miscarriage could even hold that much blood. In any case, none of us was able to save her and I confess to feeling a heavy sadness."

"That's to be expected." Orpha nodded, rocking slowly. "She came to me."

"I know."

She cocked her head topped with grizzled hair. "Oh?" The lines in her face depicted canyons of experience and the wisdom she'd gained from it.

"Yes. Her last words were that she was sorry. That thee warned her not to do something or see someone. But her voice trailed off and that was it. I couldn't make out what she said." I clasped my hands in my lap and leaned forward, intent on her answer.

The old midwife nodded again. "She visited me last week. She said she had never gotten back her monthly, despite not having a baby to suckle, and that she was certain she was with child. Rose, she was desperate to end the pregnancy."

"As so many women are."

"Yes." Orpha strung out the word as if it fueled her rocking. "As so many are. She'd already tried the safe herbal measures by mouth to no avail."

"Did she say where she'd obtained them?" Virtue had mentioned giving Charity funds for such herbs. Had Virtue gone the extra step and obtained them herself?

"No, she refused. She insisted she needed to terminate her condition by aborting the fetus through mechanical means. You are correct, it was early days yet, which should have made it easier."

"Except as we both know there are no safe mechanical means."

"Which is what I told her." Orpha rocked back and forth, back and forth, then paused. "Would that it were safe, though. Women would be saved much grief. It would greatly help those who are not ready to become mothers. Those who have a husband unwilling to help them avoid carrying a too closely spaced child. Those who are victims of assault." She focused her rheumy but keen eyes on me.

I had told her I myself had been a victim of a terrible assault, but my resulting pregnancy had blessedly ended itself in an early miscarriage. Having gone through that ordeal was one way I knew Charity's bleeding had been excessive.

I nodded slowly. "Thee speaks truth. But why didn't Charity come to me?" I sat back, frustrated. "I would have helped her."

"In your heart of hearts you know why, Rose. I'm the old lady, her first midwife, and she knew I would not judge her. You are young yet, and wise beyond your years. But — and do not take offense at what I say — even you have things still to learn about how to go gently with our women." She peered at me over the top of her spectacles. Her gaze, one which I knew almost as well as my own visage in a looking glass from the number of times I'd seen it, was kind and firm at the same time.

I did not take offense, yet the criticism was the jab of a small but sharp needle. "Does thee think I am too quick to judge?" Had I perhaps judged Charity too quickly for staying with Ransom, for not being successful in spacing her pregnancies? I hoped I hadn't.

"We are given long lives so that we may continue to learn throughout them. Just keep doing the best you can, my dear."

It was my turn to nod. "In the end, thee gave her a name of an abortionist?"

"No, I refused to," Orpha said. "But I suspect she had already obtained one or more contacts. They are available if you know who to ask. She might have had a friend, an acquaintance, even a sister who'd undergone an abortion and survived with her health and her fertility."

"If, as I fear, Charity's death is the result of an improperly executed curettage, the person must be prosecuted," I said. "I need to discover the name and pass it along to Kevin Donovan. I knew it was too much blood," I added, murmuring.

Orpha raised a bony cautioning finger. "Rose, I want you to consider your path carefully. Many who study the best termination methods and offer them to women also provide contraceptive information and do our clients — your clients now — a great service in spacing their pregnancies to conserve the women's health. Let us not jump to prosecute with too much haste."

THIRTEEN

I made it home in time to wash up and ready myself for three client visits in a row. Lina Doyle, the hired kitchen girl, was busy scrubbing pots and readying to wash the floor. I greeted her and availed myself of a thick slice of bread and butter before heading into my parlor. I smiled, thinking of my lesson to Faith in this room the night before. She'd been a motivated learner, naturally.

I checked my schedule. One initial appointment with a woman I hadn't seen before. After that came a four-time mother with a rich husband. She was a woman who loved giving birth and had an easy time of it. And then a case not too different from Charity's, one which I prayed would have a safe and happy outcome. The family had no extra money, but the couple loved each other and their three children, and both worked hard to keep the young ones interested in learning and bettering themselves. After this birth I planned to convince the couple to try several methods to space out any remaining pregnancies. A woman with more than four or five births in a short period could become worn down physically and emotionally. It put a strain not only on the family's monetary situation but also on the sacred relationship between husband and wife, leading to arguments and sometimes even dissolution of the bonds.

First things first. I finished my brief repast, brushed the crumbs from my dress, and washed my hands again. I penned a note to the Women's Business Meeting of Amesbury Friends, a task I should have undertaken yesterday. I mentioned Charity's death, although not the details, and suggested that the family would appreciate the usual care. I knew the women would organize Friends to deliver a series of meals to Ransom, something he doubtless would be glad of at this time.

After my client arrived and we had filled out my questionnaire about her general health, her mother's and sisters' pregnancies and births, and the situation of her home, I asked her to recline on the chaise and began my examination. She was rather robust for her height. Sometimes carrying too much fat caused problems later in the pregnancy, and sometimes it provided a healthy buffer in case the first trimester brought so much nausea the mother-to-be had difficulty gaining sufficient weight.

"I notice thee has well-spaced children. I commend thee for minding thy health in this way."

"The mister would have a dozen if he could." She gave a little snort. "Not me. And this one, my third, will be my last."

"How does thee achieve this spacing?"

"I'm a firm believer in the water cure. I douche with a vinegar solution, and I also take herbs. But once . . ." Her voice trailed off.

Before Charity's death, I might have let such a comment go by, but I found myself curious. I paused my examination, waiting a moment, then gently encouraged her to continue. "Once?"

"Once all my methods didn't work, and my baby was only a year old. I was damned if I was going to have another so soon. So I did away with it." Moisture filled her eyes and a small tear rolled down her full cheek. "I visited Madame," she whispered.

"Who is Madame?"

She shook her head, hard. "A lady who takes care of such things. I promised I wouldn't tell a soul her full name. She could get in hot water with the cops."

I filed away this name of a Madame who "takes care of such things." That sounded very much like an abortionist, but since my client hadn't used that word, I wouldn't, either. "Thee was fortunate to have a competent person taking care of thee. I've heard of bad, even fatal results from time to time."

"I was very lucky." She nodded, crossing herself.

I thought again of Orpha's words and imagined a world where abortion would be safe and legal. Medical knowledge of the body was ever increasing in these modern times. Perhaps one day soon women would be able to truly control the size of their families without risking their lives in the process. I shook off my musings and resumed assessing my client's health. I was in the middle of taking her pulse when she spoke up again.

"I heard a lady in your care died a violent death yesterday and you were with her. Is it true?"

A violent death? Was that the word around town? Was I never to escape being associated with unnatural death?

"It is true that she lost her life from excessive bleeding. But it was an early miscarriage of her pregnancy. There was no violence involved." I hoped this was true.

"My cousin's wife's brother works for the police. He told her violent was what they were saying. They got some kind of test of her body after she died. An *auptosink* or something like that."

"An autopsy?" I asked. Her mangling the pronunciation was understandable. It wasn't a word the average citizen would be familiar with.

"That's it. She told us the results said the poor lady was killed."

I tried not to stare at her. Kevin had ordered the autopsy after all. It showed death by violence. Was he even going to tell me? Or . . . maybe he had.

As I showed my client out after we were done, the morning mail waited on the floor in front of the mail slot. On top of the other letters was a long envelope addressed to me in Kevin's sloppy sloping handwriting. So he had sent the news. A conclusion of a violent death changed everything. Or maybe it didn't change a thing.

FOURTEEN

It was one o'clock before my last client left and I had time to open the letter from Kevin. Sitting at my desk, I unfolded it and smoothed it out.

Before I could start to read, Lina popped her head into my office.

"I'll be off now, Miss Carroll."

No matter how many times I'd asked her to address me simply as Rose, the kitchen girl always refused, saying it wouldn't be right to use the lady of the house's Christian name. I'd stopped rolling my eyes — for one thing, I was certainly not the lady of the house, despite being the eldest female living here — and accepted her ways. Lina was not a Friend, but was a reliable fifteen-year-old who had left school to help support her large family. We were glad to employ her, and it had freed up both my time and Faith's.

"Thank thee, Lina. We'll see thee tomorrow."

She curtsied, another habit I had yet to break her of, and turned to go. Now for my letter.

Miss Rose,

Kevin had dispensed with the flowery opening salutations of most letter writers.

Upon your suggestion, I ordered the autopsy be done with all due dispatch. The medical examiner found that Mrs. Skells's womb had been pierced in several places by a sharp object, thus the excessive bleeding. Due to the nature of the internal wounds, he was not able to ascertain whether she had been with child.

My job now is to locate this dangerous abortionist and bring him or her to justice.

I am risking my job merely writing this to you, so please don't come here with information you might glean. However, based on our past collaboration and your extremely useful access to persons and places where I am unable to traverse, I would welcome communication addressed to my home.

Well, knock me into a cocked hat, as Orpha often said. Kevin was welcoming my investigatory contributions. He even gave his street address. I stared at it. He lived not a half mile from me on Boardman Street, two over from Clark.

I'll tell the missus not to worry if I receive a letter addressed in a lady's hand. I'd like you to meet Emmaline and my wee boy someday soon. I think you'd enjoy my wife's company, and her, yours.

I would like to say that I'm sorry about the Chief's admonishment. Obviously I couldn't tell you that in front of him.

Now duty calls. Will write again when I know more about this sorry turn of events. That poor woman.

Most sincerely yours,
Kevin

I sat back and stared at the paper. The report said Charity had been pierced more than once with a sharp object. No wonder she'd bled so copiously. And that the examiner wasn't sure if she was pregnant or not. Had she in fact been carrying an early-term fetus? She thought she had. Depending on the type of sharp object, her uterus could have been scraped clean. Or had her death been at the hand of a malicious person posing as an abortionist? Perhaps the Madame my client had mentioned? Except my client this morning hadn't spoken of Madame in a bad way at all. She'd wanted to protect her, in fact. What a confounding puzzle.

At least Kevin was still welcoming my help, as long as I wrote to him at home, not in care of the police department. And he'd apologized for the way the chief had treated me. That was kind of him, but independent women like myself were accustomed to men not crediting us with our own minds or expertise, with them not treating us as equals. We weren't even allowed to vote, for heaven's sake.

But that was neither here nor there. I too wanted to seek out whoever had killed Charity. I would heed Orpha's words, though, and keep my mind open to the person being a supporter of women and of family spacing. Based on the report, I doubted this particular abortionist was much in favor of women's lives at all, so it likely was not Madame Whoever She Was.

The loud and insistent *brring-brring* of the new telephone startled me from my thoughts. I hurried into the sitting room and picked up the hearing device.

"Hello, Rose Carroll here." Frederick and I had conferred when the telephone was installed and decided the members of the family would all answer similarly. With so many people available to use the device, it would be important to let the operator know who was speaking.

"A call for you from Mr. David Dodge," Gertrude's tinny voice said. "I'll put him through."

David? Calling me in the middle of the afternoon? My heart couldn't decide whether to soar with joy or sink in dread of bad news. This happened nearly every time I received a call. Using the communication box was still so new I hadn't become accustomed to the thought that a call might not be urgent or bearing ill tidings. Which was silly. A letter didn't prompt the same reaction at all.

I quickly thanked the operator.

"Rose, dear?" David asked after we were connected.

"Yes, David. Is thee well? Is everything all right?" The anxious words tumbled out of me.

My betrothed laughed, a delicious sound that even over the wires set me at ease and made me smile. "Yes, of course. I simply had a few free minutes and wanted to hear your lovely voice. And is life going smoothly for you, my sweet bride-to-be?"

I blew out a relieved breath. "Not completely smoothly, no. I am well, but I lost a client to bleeding yesterday morning. I sent thee a letter this morning about it, but thee wouldn't have received it yet. I just now learned the hemorrhage was not from a miscarriage." I cut myself off. I shouldn't talk on the telephone regarding the autopsy report. Which I had learned about in a somewhat illicit fashion.

"Does this mean you'll be starting up another investigation, as you have in the past?"

"No. Well, after a fashion, perhaps. I'll tell thee all the details when thee returns." By Sixth Day perhaps we'd have answers, even a culprit in custody.

"I look forward to that."

It occurred to me that David might know of doctors who provided abortion services, as illegal as they were. "And I might need a bit of help from thee."

"Whatever I can do."

"We had a happy announcement here last night. Faith and Zeb are also to be wed, and it will be this First Day."

"My, so soon. You're correct, that's very happy news." He fell silent for a moment. "Did this news make you wistful for our own vows, darling?"

"I confess it did."

"I will redouble my efforts with Mother upon my return. I think she might be softening."

Clarinda Dodge, soften? That I'd like to see. The woman was as brittle as a piece of frozen treacle. And as unyielding as steel.

"I don't want to run up your penny, David." Making calls from a public place was not inexpensive, even though I knew David and his parents did not want for funds. "Might thee come directly here on Sixth Day after thy train arrives?"

"I will plan to. It should be shortly past noon, and then I'll fetch a carriage and make my way across the river."

"Good. I'll make us a special soup."

"Only if you have time. I love you, Midwife Carroll."

"And I thee, Dr. Dodge." I depressed the hook and hung up the device. Two days seemed a long time to wait for my man, but wait I would.

FIFTEEN

I plunked down my coins for the *Amesbury Morning Courier* half an hour later in the Mercantile. I hoped to find advertisements for people offering health services to women. Such terms were sometimes a coded way to say the person actually offered contraceptive advice, treatments, and devices. I might find an abortionist among them. But could I get such a person to talk with me?

"Catherine isn't working today?" I asked the young woman behind the counter as I slipped the newspaper into my bag. Catherine Toomey was a congenial woman who'd assisted at a birth I'd been called to last fall. She'd also provided a critical piece of information about the murder of a woman suffrage activist, a killing which had taken place nearly across the street from Catherine's home.

"No, she's off visiting her kin," the clerk

responded.

I thanked her and headed for the door. I paused next to it. Tacked-up slips of paper filled a board. They seemed to be notices about all manner of news and services. *Best firewood in the county. Best price, too,* read one. Another advertised, *Weekly spiritualist sessions. Contact loved ones who went on ahead. Resolve unfinished business. First séance free of charge.* I snorted at that one. As if we could contact our dead relatives. Then my eyes went wide. In the bottom corner of the board was a neatly lettered card. *Ladies, are you feeling poorly? Babies wearing you down? Get help from Madame Restante. Female tonics made to order, and more.* That wording sounded a lot like family-spacing services couched in vague terms about women's health. And this might very well be the Madame who also provided mechanical abortions.

I grabbed the pencil and paper I'd added to my bag before leaving the house. I copied down the exact wording. Unlike the other notices, no home address was listed, no storefront, nor a mention of reaching her by telephone. The only way the card provided to contact Madame was a post office box. I jotted down that information and made my way out into busy Market Square, clutching my cloak about me against a bitter wind. This investigation might be looking up, because I knew precisely who to talk to next. My friend Bertie Winslow, that was who.

But the post office was bustling with customers picking up packages, buying postage for letters, and chatting about the events of the town. Furthermore, Bertie stood alone behind the counter. She normally had more than one employee working for her. Maybe they were out doing an errand for her or on a lunch break.

She spied me lurking at the back of the line. "Five o'clock?" she called.

Half the people in front of me twisted to see who the postmistress was talking to.

I nodded and waved, then turned to go, bumping smack into a man whose coat smelled of stale tobacco. "Excuse me." I took a flustered step to the rear even as I heard a snicker behind me. I pulled my bonnet back onto my head and glanced up to see Joey Swift.

"Well, well, Midwife Carroll, wasn't it?" His breath again reeked of spirits through his grin.

"Joe Swift. Please forgive me, I wasn't watching where I was going." On the other hand, why had he been standing so close behind me? I gazed at him. Up close I could see his bloodshot blue eyes and that he hadn't shaved since yesterday. I also saw that he would be a handsome man if he cleaned himself up.

"Not a problem, miss. You friends with the postal lady up there? Going to head out for a spot of sherry at five, are you? I could join you both, become acquainted." His grin turned to a leer.

What? I blinked. "Thank thee, but no. I don't imbibe, and we have personal matters to discuss between us. Good day, Joe."

"G'bye, Miss Carroll."

His mocking tone followed me out the door. My skin prickled as if he was watching me go, but I didn't turn to check. I walked a block, pausing to peruse the reflection of the street behind me in a storefront window. I wanted to make sure he wasn't following me. Relieved he was nowhere in sight, I hurried home. I'd learned over the years to pay attention to that still small voice within, as Friends put it. No matter if it was seemingly God's voice telling me an action was wrong, or the one nagging at me when I left home telling me I'd forgotten to bring something I needed. It always behooved me to listen. Right now the voice was telling me Joey Swift was a problem. I had no idea why, or what kind of problem he was. Still, I was listening.

Safely at home with the door locked behind me, I sat at my desk with paper, pen, and ink. I wanted to write to Madame Restante, but should I say I was a midwife — true — with a client wanting her services — false — or pretend to be a woman in need of help — also false? I chose truth, mostly.

Dear Madame Restante,
  I saw your notice in the Mercantile. I am a midwife and often have pregnant and postpartum clients interested in services such as yours.

In fact, I had prescribed herbal contraceptive teas and regulating pills available at the pharmacy in the past, pills sold ostensibly to help women become pregnant, but which could also help end a conception before its time. I didn't actually need Madame's knowledge about such things. But a slight mistruth in pursuit of justice did not seem like much of a transgression.

  Might I pay thee a visit in the very near future?

Sincerely,
Rose Carroll

Like Kevin, I didn't hold with the elaborate groveling salutations many used. "I remain very sincerely your humble servant," and so on. I wasn't even sure why I used such a word as *sincerely*. Why would I not be sincere? Why would a reader need reassurances that I was?

I included my address and that I was available via telephone, slipped the note into an envelope, and readied it for the afternoon post. It was now three o'clock and the children would be home from school soon. But Faith would also be along soon, having made an arrangement with the newspaper that she could do part of her work at home. Her younger siblings were certainly responsible enough not to need my presence, and today I wished to do my searching in quiet.

After leaving a note for the family saying I wasn't sure when I would be back, I grabbed my bag and headed out once again, this time to the public library.

SIXTEEN

I trudged through streets messy with slush and dirty snow to the post office at nearly five o'clock. My two hours in the library room on the grounds of the Hamilton Mills had been peaceful but not overly fruitful, at least in terms of looking for others who offered services like Madame Restante's. I'd perused the notices in my newspaper and jotted down a few, but they were even vaguer than Madame's, and hadn't included her reference to babies. I'd seen advertisements for Lamotte's French Remedy, Cullen's Female Specific, and Rimmel's Medicated Vinegar. The last was a douching solution that women used to wash away the products of sexual intimacy and thereby prevent pregnancy, although the product itself would never promise exactly that.

On the next-to-last page of the paper I found one more lead that looked promising. It was an advertisement for a Wallace Buckham, who described his herbalist treatments. *Gain relief from the tensions of a mother's life. Achieve regularity. Safe and effective treatments. Initial consultation at no cost.* The language made me wonder if he, too, was a clandestine abortionist, so I noted the name and address.

It was calm and quiet in the library, and sitting surrounded by high shelves full of books had always been one of my favorite things to do. So much knowledge, so many stories. I'd spent the last hour losing myself in a book of George Eliot's poems, finally rousing myself to venture out into the winter twilight toward the post office.

Bertie was just locking up. "Evening, Rosetta. Come along home with me and we'll talk. I could tell by the look on your face you had a crime to work through with me." She pulled a fanciful purple felt hat onto her head as I followed her to the nearby stable where she kept Grover during the workday. Together we walked him up Main Street to the cottage on Whittier Street she shared with her lover, Sophie. Once Grover was settled and we were inside with lamps and fire lit, Bertie fixed me a cup of tea and poured herself a sherry.

"Now, what's up?" she asked, settling into

one of the cozy armchairs in the sitting room.

A giggling snort slipped out of me from my chair opposite hers. "It's not that what I want to discuss is funny, but a man named Joe Swift was behind me in the post office and I bumped into him by accident. He proposed he join us both at five o'clock for a spot of sherry. In a bar, no doubt."

She cocked her head. "Do you know this fellow?"

"He is — was — Charity's cousin. I met him briefly when Ransom and I went to inform Virtue of the death."

"I'm always happy to partake in a spot of sherry," Bertie said. "Even though neither of us happens to be in need of one Joe Swift to drink or otherwise consort with." She clinked her glass with my teacup and took a sip. "So?"

"So I told thee yesterday about Charity's demise, as well as her mention of money, and of Orpha's caution which Charity hadn't heeded. Thee talked about Ransom Skells's behavior. Now I've learned more." I told her what I'd observed of Ransom. "His mother-in-law, Virtue Swift, doesn't care for him at all and he told me Charity's father likes him even less."

"Swift. Related to this Joe in the post office?"

"Yes, his aunt and uncle. Something about Joey nags at my inner voice. Virtue herself said he was a drunken gambler who has fallen away from being a Quaker. His father, also Joseph, apparently made quite the fortune in rum but is recently deceased."

"Joseph Swift," Bertie said, furrowing her brow. "Now where did I hear that name? I'll have to ask Sophie. Maybe his was the complicated will she's been executing. Something about trusts, too."

"Joseph was Charity's uncle. And she mentioned something about money as she was dying. I wonder . . ."

"I'll get the whole story for you from Sophie."

I thanked her. "There is a Delia Davies who is a secretary at the Lowell Boat Shop."

"Where Skells now works?"

"Exactly."

"She seemed a bit protective of Ransom when I went to give him the news about Charity's death."

"Delia Davies," Bertie said, brow furrowed. "I say. If memory serves, Mr. Skells mailed her a package last week sometime."

"I wonder why he would do that. Was it big?"

She tapped her finger against her glass. "No. Not much bigger than a shirt box. Maybe he's getting a bit of sugar on the side. Maybe he mailed her some fancy undergarment."

"It's possible. He called her a chippy and then claimed he didn't intend to say she was a prostitute, but was just a girl who means nothing to him."

"Isn't that what they all say?" Bertie swung a foot up and over the chair's arm, splaying her bloomer-clad legs. "Sakes alive, my pins are beat from standing nearly all day. Do go on, Rose."

"Today I learned the results of the autopsy. As I suspected, Charity's excessive bleeding was not the result of a miscarriage, but rather her womb had been perforated more than once by a sharp object."

Bertie sucked in a breath. She swilled the rest of her sherry. Her posture was more relaxed than when we'd arrived home, likely due to the effect of the alcohol, but her face was knit into a somber expression at the autopsy news.

Once in a while, now being one of those times, I envied Bertie her life. Not that she was carefree, exactly. She held a position of some responsibility as postmistress, a job she'd had to fight for. Her love of a bit of drink, her ability to live without care for society's strictures? These things appealed to me in a theoretical way. I knew I was unlikely to cut loose like she did, but it was fun to live her life vicariously on occasion. Except for the parts where townspeople spat at her and openly disapproved of her living arrangement with Sophie, and especially her situation of being estranged from her mother, something she didn't like to discuss. If it were me, I would hate not having my mother's comfort, wisdom, and humor in my life.

"So it was a botched termination?" she asked.

"She died of a poorly done abortion, whether intentionally or by accident," I said.

"Do you mean murder?" She sat up straight, both feet on the floor. "Now this is a horse of a different color."

"I doubt it, but Charity's womb was perforated. That point is beyond dispute. Let me lay out the rest of the facts as I see them."

Bertie held up a hand. "I think best with a pen in my hand. Wait a moment." She moved quickly to a desk at the side of the room and opened a journal to a blank page. Pen inked and ready, she gave me a nod. "Go."

"Someone killed Charity. I want to discover who."

"You want to? What about your darling Kevin?" Her expression was full of mischief. "He was the homicide detective, last I knew."

"He's not mine and he's not darling. More important, his new chief doesn't want me working with him anymore."

"A pity, that." Bertie looked genuinely rueful.

"But yes, I do seek to get to the bottom of Charity's death. Kevin was able to send me the autopsy report. Any information I gather I'm to mail to him at home. I believe our collaboration will continue, just along the alleyways, not in his office." I cleared my throat. "Shall I go on?"

"Sorry, didn't mean to interrupt." She scribbled in the journal. "We now have a Suspects heading. Please proceed."

"Fine. I guess the simplest case is an incompetent provider of criminal abortions, who meant to terminate Charity's pregnancy but instead killed her."

"All right. The anonymous fumble-fingered practitioner."

"Thee might write down the husband, Ransom. He never seemed particularly loving toward Charity."

"To the extent of murdering her?" Bertie asked.

"I don't know how he could have managed, or why, really. I mean, he would have to take over the care of a passel of children, as is now the case. But he might have inadvertently steered her toward an incompetent practitioner."

"Got it. What about this Delia element?"

"I met her briefly and that's the extent of my knowledge. I'd say go ahead and add her to the list. Ransom was rather too vehement with me that he had no connection to the girl."

"Which probably means he does." Bertie bent over the sheet. "If he's poking her, she might have wanted to eliminate the wife."

"And inherit six little ones?" I batted away a look from Bertie. "I know, we're just throwing out ideas. I have a client who knows Delia and lives across the road from her. I'm going there tomorrow or the next day for a home visit and will try to glean more facts."

"Who else?" Bertie asked. "Do we know anything else about Joe the younger?"

"No. He knows Ransom. He would, of course, as Charity's cousin. When I saw them together Ransom didn't seem a bit happy to see Joey. I don't know what's going on between them." I took a sip of tea. "By the way, I actually wondered if Joey followed me into the post office today. Dark messy hair, blue eyes, yesterday's beard, smelled of drink and tobacco. Did he stay and buy stamps or mail anything?"

Bertie thought, but finally shook her head. "No. And I was alone there, as you saw. But he could have checked his box if he has one, of course."

"Of course."

"Anyway, I'll write him down. Now, do you think any of these types would have done the actual deed?" Bertie asked. "Or would they have hired an abortionist to kill Charity for them under the guise of ending her pregnancy? Which she would have had to agree with, of course."

That was quite the sticking point. "It's awfully complicated, isn't it?" I drained my tea. "First, there is the question of whether Charity was in fact pregnant. The medical examiner couldn't tell."

"What do you mean? Didn't she think she was?"

"Maybe. She'd not gotten a monthly after her premature baby was born only three months ago, but that could have been due to her being malnourished. What if Ransom put it in her head she was with child and hired an unscrupulous person to kill her under the guise of an abortion?"

"Then he's a very wicked, disgustingly bad person." Bertie's lip curled in disgust. "And that seems unlikely even though I know such humans exist. Also, it would mean he'd have all those babes to look after by himself. No, I think we should look at the money, instead. That's a more likely cause of murder, isn't it?"

The money. "I suppose." I smoothed my hair back off my brow despite it being tidily in place. "Except we don't know which money."

"Now, what about the purpose of your visit this afternoon?" Bertie asked.

"I found a public notice from a Madame Restante when I was at the Mercantile." I dug in my bag until I found the paper I'd written on and read out the text. "I think that's a coded way of saying she'll help women avoid pregnancy, or end it if it's already underway."

"Coded because of the Comstock Laws, I'd wager."

"Exactly. Bertie, as postmistress thee must be obliged to enforce those laws. How do the authorities expect thee to do that? Open every parcel, inspect every missive?"

She made a *psh* sound and tossed her

head. "As if anyone has time for that. I am obliged to post the official summary of the federal law on the notices board in the post office. You know, the board where the Wanted posters are, and the rates for the postal boxes."

I nodded. "Does anyone actually check to make sure materials to contravene pregnancy aren't being conveyed through the post?"

"They might inspect a parcel at some point in its travel through the system on its way to the addressee. I've had an inspector visit unannounced only once. He spent an hour opening parcels. Didn't find anything illegal of any sort and left." She rolled her eyes.

"I just had a thought," I said. "Thee said Ransom mailed a package to Delia. If the two are having illicit relations, I wonder if he mailed abortifacient herbs, or French letters he didn't want to keep at home for fear Charity would come across them."

Bertie nodded. "Possible. The parcel wasn't too heavy, as I recall."

"This Madame Restante has a post box. I wondered if thee knew her, or at least knew of her."

"Let me see that." Bertie held out her hand for the piece of paper on which I'd written. "Box 89. I know this lady."

"Thee does?"

"Yes. She claims her name is Savoire Restante and she puts on a fake French accent. *Tu parles français, non?*"

"*Oui, un peu.*" I agreed that I did speak French, a little. "So she says her name is Knowledge Remaining, with an extra *e* on *knowledge.* That's an invented name if I ever heard one."

"I know. But most around here would have no idea what the name means. She wears shades of purple and blue and flowing scarves, with a black turban. Very mysterious. Or at least that's the image she wants to project."

"I mailed her a note, saying I often had clients needing services like those she provides. A client I saw this afternoon has well-spaced children. She confessed that one time her pregnancy control methods failed, and she visited a Madame who 'took care of it,' in her words. I believe she meant she underwent a mechanical abortion performed by Madame." I tapped my fingertips together. "Does thee think this Madame might be our culprit?"

"I've never visited her for any of her products, of course." Bertie was in need of neither contraception nor criminal abortion.

"But despite her sham name — someone I met whispered she's really called Sally Davies — she doesn't strike me as a criminal nor someone that incompetent."

"Certainly Lucy survived her abortion, so the woman must be skilled. I'll see what I think when I meet her, I guess. But Davies? That's Delia's surname. Perhaps they're related."

"Stranger things have happened, Rosetta."

SEVENTEEN

The morning dawned bitterly cold once more. A wicked wind crept in through the cracks of the house and chilled me to the core. I made a big pot of samp, the nutty cornmeal porridge the family loved. I heated milk to go with it so breakfast wouldn't cool in the bowls. Topped with sugar and cut-up fall apples, it was a hearty first meal that warmed us all.

After everyone made their way out for the day, I carried a second cup of coffee to my parlor and checked the day's schedule. On top of it lay Bertie's Suspects list, which she'd sent home with me last evening. She'd persuaded me to stay for supper, since Sophie had to work late, and had given me a ride back to my house behind her on Grover so I didn't have to walk.

I read through the list again. Abortionist, Ransom, Delia, Joey. I knew very little about Delia except where she lived and where she worked. Neither of the men was the nicest I'd met, but murderers? An anonymous abortionist wasn't much help, either. I sighed and laid the sheet aside, turning to my schedule.

Oh, my. My client Genevieve LaChance was coming at nine this morning, and it was already past eight thirty. How had I forgotten? Clearly Charity's death was pushing business concerns out of my mind, which was not the way I liked to conduct myself.

I quickly tidied my room and pinned up my hair, making sure I was presentable. Genevieve trudged with a heavy step up the path at five minutes before nine. I was about to go and greet her when I saw the Suspects list face up on the desk. This would never do. Talk of homicide suspects had no place in a pregnant woman's visit. I hurried to stash it in the top drawer, and then did my best to reorder my brain before greeting one of my favorite clients.

After she was in my parlor and out of her coat and hat, I asked her to sit. "What can I help thee with, Genevieve? Is thee with child again so soon?" She'd given birth to her fourth child and first daughter only ten months ago. She'd said at the time her husband Jean was worried about providing for the family with that many children, as his job at the Walkers Shoe factory did not pay well. Genevieve herself took in piece work to bolster the coffers, but they lived in a small tenement down on the Flats where many French-Canadians resided, and space was already tight.

"I tink I am," she said in accented English. "After four times, I know the signs, even so early, even though I miss only the one monthly."

"Congratulations, Genevieve."

Her face fell. "Do not say it, please, Rose. The family, we barely make it now. How can I have one more? And little Elsie, she has only ten month, she still drink my milk." Genevieve clasped her hands in her lap. She was a full-figured woman who'd always had an easy time giving birth. Last year she'd tied the baby to her back the day after the birth and returned to her washing and cooking. "Can you help me, you know, be rid of it?"

How did my world suddenly revolve more around preventing children rather than bringing them into the world? Still, it was all in the same realm — my realm — and my mothers' health was predominant. If helping Genevieve space out future children or even not have any more was what she wanted, it was my responsibility to do what I could.

"I can offer thee no sure measures, because they don't exist. But especially if thee isn't too far along, I can recommend several things to try. Thee must take the dose I suggest and no more, though. These things can be dangerous in excess."

"I will do whatever you say, Rose."

I rose and fetched a package of dried tansy from the top shelf in my armoire where I kept my herbs. I never wanted the Bailey children to be able to get to them. I slid a portion into an envelope and folded it over.

"This is tansy. Make a cup of tea with a teaspoon of it twice a day and drink it down." I handed her the envelope. "It will be more effective if thee adds alcoholic spirits to the tea. Whiskey, brandy, whatever thee has."

"We always have a bit of wine in the house." She smiled broadly. *"Nous sommes Français, non?"*

"Yes, I know you French love your wine, even French Canadians." I smiled back. "Wine will do just fine."

"And that is all I will need?"

"No. Thee must also buy these pills." I jotted down E.L. Patch Number Two on a pad of paper. "This contains several herbs

129

in a chocolate pill. Directions will be on the box."

"Where do I find them?"

"I recommend the druggist Nayson on Main Street over druggist Merrill. The latter can be a bit, shall we say, obstructive when it comes to female matters. I am not sure he even stocks these regulating medicines."

"Regulating?" She scrunched up her nose.

"All of these can also bring on a woman's monthly if she is irregular in her cycles. Most ladies who miss monthlies have difficulty conceiving. That's why druggists can legally sell such medicines. But if one wishes to bring on the periodic bleeding for another purpose . . ." I spread my hands.

"I see." She turned the envelope of tansy over in her hands, frowning. "The pills, are they . . . um . . . ?"

I knew Genevieve and her husband were of very modest means. "They are not the least expensive medicine in the store but I think thee can afford to give them a try."

She nodded. "I have my small hidden can of coins from my piece work. I save out a little every time a lady pays me. I will use those monies. Much as I love my babies, my boys and our sweet Elsie, that's enough.

Jean, he agrees. He will not argue about this."

"I cannot guarantee that this prescription will be effective for thee. But it's all I can offer." Under no circumstances would I advise her to go looking for a person to terminate the pregnancy by mechanical means. It was simply too dangerous. "I am afraid I also must ask that thee not tell anyone other than thy husband about our conversation. It is a dangerous topic in these restrictive days."

"I understand, Rose, and I promise. Now I will pray the teas and the pills do what I need them to do." She crossed herself. "I know the priest would put me out for such a prayer, but the Virgin Marie, she watches over us all, especially *les femmes.* She will help me, I know it."

I hugged Genevieve before she left. "Send for me if thee has any problems at all, please. And I will pray for thy success." I watched her make her way back down the path the way she'd come. Her feet seemed lighter now. And mine? I did not feel lighter for prescribing a method to expel the tiny but growing fetus from her body. But it was her body and her choice. My mission was to help my mothers. That was all I could do.

EIGHTEEN

After my second and last client of the morning left, I picked up the morning post from the floor inside the door. Amid letters for Frederick, one addressed to the children from my mother, and an envelope for me including payment from a recently delivered client, I found what I was hoping for.

"Perfect," I said aloud. The small blue envelope bore my name and address on the front, but the back was sealed with old-fashioned wax in a shade of lavender. The initials MR had been stamped into the wax. Bertie had said the woman dressed in colors and scarves in an unconventional fashion. It looked like her stationery followed the same pattern. If this wasn't from Madame Restante, I would be very surprised.

I sat at my desk to open the missive.

My very dear Miss Carroll,

Please come to my office at your earliest convenience so that we may discuss matters of mutual interest.

Ever your humble servant,
Madame Savoire Restante

At the bottom was a printed drawing of a woman sitting in a field of flowers, with the words *Provider of Ladies' Health Products and Services* below. The picture certainly brought to mind ladies, health, and herbs. An address on Clark Street followed, with the notation Second Floor appended.

Madame didn't make claims, at least not in writing, that her products and services had anything to do with women's reproductive health. Still, I wanted to pay her a visit. If she hadn't helped — or rather, had fatally harmed — Charity Skells, she possibly knew of others who might have.

I bundled up against the weather with my warmest wool scarf wrapped around my neck and head, and the hood of my woolen cloak pulled up over it. I donned my heavy gloves, passing through the kitchen on my way out. I paused. Lina didn't come in on Fifth Day, and Frederick had said this morning he was dining out with Winnie tonight. What could I fix for five young people's dinner that was easy and filling, too? When I had the chance, I liked to prepare the repast to relieve Faith of the burden. On Lina's days, we often asked her to chop and prepare ingredients for our evening meal so the assembly at the end of the day wasn't so burdensome.

I checked the cold larder in the entryway. In winter there was no need to add ice to the thick box. Yes, enough beef stew remained to serve as filling for several big meat pies. I could add more carrots and potatoes to stretch it out. That and a loaf of bread would do, except making the lunches this morning had finished the bread. I slid out of my warm wraps.

Five minutes later the sourdough sponge was mixed and covered with a damp cloth. I set it to rise on the shelf above the stove, which I'd damped down until I returned, and suited up for the cold once again.

Clark Street was less than a ten-minute walk for me. It led down a steep hill from Market Street just north of the square and ended at the bridge over the Back River. The river itself drained Clark's Pond, then emptied into the Powow, the Merrimack, and the Atlantic Ocean in turn. As I walked, I slowed my pace and held my search in the Light, that the information I needed would flow like the river, and that I would stay safe while searching for it.

When I reached Clark, the biting air shot straight up the roadway, which was lined with buildings on either side so that it formed a kind of wind tunnel. I shivered even in my woolens as I searched for my destination.

I located the address in a building featuring a row of small shops on the street level and flats above. Was this also Madame's home? I'd find out soon enough. A door next to the end shop opened to a staircase. On the wall at the bottom of the stairwell was another version of the ideograph that was Madame's business mark plus her name, although not the description of what she offered. Next to it had been painted a hand with its index finger pointing upward on a slant matching the angle of the stairs. A stab of trepidation hit me halfway up. Could I couch my questions in a way that wouldn't make her suspect I was looking for a criminal abortionist who had ended my client's life? If Savoire was the one, was it even safe for me to be alone with her? No one knew where I'd gone.

My palms grew sweaty and I wiped them on my cloak. I scolded myself. How could I be in danger? It was broad daylight. I smelled onions frying from somewhere in the building. Shopkeepers were downstairs and surely people were at home in the other flats. I was a tall, strong, healthy young woman, and I'd gotten myself out of dangerous situations before by means of my wits. Madame's letter, including her address, was sitting in plain view on my desk at home. If something untoward should befall me, sooner or later I would be found.

And really, although I was indirectly looking for information about Charity, I would appear as simply a midwife looking for recommendations for my clients. Madame didn't know that I myself sometimes prescribed abortifacients to my clients when asked, and had done so this very morning. Such prescriptions were rare, but I didn't turn down a needy mother. I couldn't.

I squared my shoulders and knocked on the door bearing her name and yet another copy of her mark. She seemed to have a degree of business acumen, using a consistent visual representation for her enterprise. If she distributed printed materials, I was sure the same illustration would head the paper. It made me wonder whether I should advertise to solicit clients instead of relying on women telling other women about my practice. So far I'd had no lack of business.

A bolt snicked and the door opened to a woman both taller and broader than I. She was backlit by tall windows on the street side of the office and the hall was so dimly lit all I could make out was a dark rounded shape atop the head and the silhouette of scarves flowing about neck and shoulders.

"Savoire Restante?" I asked.

"*Oui.*" The timbre of her voice was lower than one usually heard in a female, but perhaps it went with her height.

For a brief moment I wondered if this was a trap, if the advertisement had been a ruse to lure customers wanting contraceptive medicines and devices only to arrest them for buying the same. Perhaps she was a man in disguise. But I told myself not to indulge in fears and forged ahead.

"I am Rose Carroll, midwife. Thee invited me to come and converse."

"Ah, Meese Carroll." She pronounced the *r* sound in her throat in the French way and made an emphasized long *o* out of the second syllable. "Please come in."

She stood back, gesturing. I stepped into the room, where colors and rich fabrics predominated. I faced Madame, extending my hand. Now I could see her plainly.

"I am pleased to meet thee, Savoire."

Her eyebrows, drawn in high arches with

black grease pencil, went even higher. She pursed her reddened mouth, etching small lines in a heavily powdered upper lip. She shook my hand. "People address me as Madame."

I smiled, relinquishing her large hand, with its nails painted a shade of dark maroon. "I'm a member of the Religious Society of Friends. We don't believe in using titles for anyone." I kept my voice light and friendly.

"I see. A Quaker, are you?"

I nodded.

"And that's why you don't talk the same as we do. Well, please sit and tell me your purpose in coming." She nodded at a small sitting area and an armchair upholstered in a dark purple and forest green brocade. Her accent seemed to be fading with each utterance.

"It seems we both trade in women's health," I said, sitting. "Sometimes my pregnant mothers come to me with maladies brought on by too many births in a short span of years. I was curious about the products and services thee advertises."

Savoire sat across from me in a large chair with ornately carved hand rests and legs. The top above the back cushion featured her same business mark carved into it. She had neither the skin of a recently shaven beard nor the protuberant Adam's apple of many men. This was most certainly a woman, not a male outfitted as a lady. As Bertie had mentioned, Savoire sported a black turban completely covering her hair. She wore the same kind of waistless gown Sophie favored. It was cut in the new style of the Aesthetic Dress Movement, which let the wearer move about easily and didn't require a binding undergarment of any kind. Despite the dress not revealing her figure directly, the flesh about her neck and the puffiness of her wrists suggested a woman carrying quite a bit of extra weight, possibly to an unhealthy level. Her dark eyes were lined with painted-on soot.

"I do nothing against the law, you understand." She waved a hand vaguely as if dismissing the idea. "But surely you know that sometimes a lady requires assistance regulating her periodic bleeds. I am an experienced herbalist and I offer solutions tailored to the customer's needs."

I glanced around the room. An oriental screen hid one area from view. A long table against another wall held dozens of jars of dried herbs, all labeled with numbers instead of names. A small scale sat to one side, and a box was filled with plain brown envelopes.

"Does thee grow these herbs?" I asked. I obtained my herbs from a local farmer, those I couldn't grow myself.

She lifted her chin in pride. "Yes. They are pure and dried at home."

"Does thee send these solutions through the mail?" I hoped she would answer truthfully.

"Yes. I do quite a good business all across the country."

"Thee has never gotten hauled up on the Comstock laws?"

Her eyes narrowed but she only shook her head.

"I'd like to see thy catalog. May I have a copy?"

"Certainly." She reached for the top one on a stack nearby and handed it to me.

I perused the brochure, also headed by her business mark. Without looking up, I said, "I had a client, Charity was her name. Did she come to you for an extreme solution recently? She wanted to terminate an early pregnancy, and I believe she sought mechanical means." I lifted my face and watched her as she sucked in air with a rasping sound.

"No! Of course not. I've never met Mrs.

Skells. Who are you, anyway?" Her French accent had now melted away entirely, and she sounded as much a New Englander as the rest of us who were born and raised here. She stood, towering over me, her eyes dark.

It was time for me to leave. I stood. "Thee is positive? She was thin, the mother of six already. At most two months along. Maybe she used a different name."

"No. I don't dabble in terminations like those. Why would I lie to you?" She folded her arms. "And why do you speak of her as if she is no longer among us?"

I shrugged. "It's good you didn't treat her. Because she died two days ago of perforation to the uterus."

She stared at me, then eased back into her chair with a heaviness to her movements. "The poor woman. May she rest in peace." She knit her brow, in a sad look that appeared to my eyes not quite genuine.

"I hope she does." I gathered my cloak about me. "I'll be going now. I thank thee for the information."

She didn't budge, so I opened the door myself. After I went out, I glanced back. The sad look was gone. She glared after me with flushed face and heaving bosom, her lips pressed together in a thin line.

NINETEEN

My walk home was a slow one, and not only because of the cold and the hill I had to ascend. This Savoire was certainly not French. It seemed she certainly offered "solutions" contrary to the Comstock laws, much as I did. But wasn't her reaction to my mentioning Charity overly extreme if she didn't know my client? If she was telling the truth, I imagined she considered my questions insulting or as if I was besmirching her trade, so perhaps her glare was justified.

For one thing, I hadn't mentioned Charity's last name. Yet Savoire — or Sally Davies, as Bertie had said she was actually named — referred to her as Mrs. Skells. Also, Savoire had stood, acting indignant that I'd asked if she offered her clients an extreme solution, even though she'd said solutions were her trade. At the end, she'd acted shocked and sad in a way that made me doubt the sincerity of her reaction.

Was this the criminal we sought? Or was she simply frightened at being discovered for the kind of products and services she offered? And if she was innocent, I was the guilty party for badgering her. I reached home deep in thought, barely seeing where I put my feet.

When Bertie said my name, I jumped, looking up to see her laughing at me from the back stoop of the house.

"You're a funny one," she said. "Lost in thought, are you, Rose?"

"I'm afraid I am." Sure enough, I hadn't even noticed Grover tied to the hitching post.

Bertie trotted down the steps. "I was just leaving you a note. Come for dinner again tonight, will you? Sophie will actually be home at a decent hour and she promised to tell you all about that complicated estate deal. I think you're going to be interested."

Tonight Friends gathered in midweek worship. I discerned on the spot that God would be better served by my following up every lead on the matter of Charity's death rather than sitting in silent worship. "I would be delighted. Thanks, Bertie. What time?"

"Six would be good."

"I shall be there."

Bertie waved, flung herself onto Grover's back, and rode off. I unlocked the door, catching her envelope before it fell into the snow. I still meant to prepare dinner for the family, even though I wouldn't be at home to eat with them. Before long the shape of the household would change. Very soon Faith would move out to join with Zeb. One of these days, months, or years I would do the same and create a household with David. I hoped that would happen sooner rather than later. And it was looking very much as if Frederick might invite Winnie to be his wife, which meant the Bailey home would once again have a real lady of the house.

It was all as it should be, once one accepted that life is always in flux. If I didn't embrace that philosophy, I wouldn't be able to be a midwife. It had been a bitter pill to swallow, though, accepting my sister's death just two years prior. She had been a healthy, intelligent, loving mother to her brood, and the best older sister I could imagine. She'd also been in what I regarded as a difficult marriage, but she'd never confessed any desire to end it. She'd said she loved Frederick deeply. I didn't think he'd been as difficult at the beginning of their marriage, and his moods and tempers were simply something she put up with and learned to manage, although they had intensified since her death. I wasn't as skilled at managing them as she had been.

I had a pang of trepidation. My dear David had always been a kind man of level moods. What if he also changed after we were wed? What if some quality in his personality bumped up against my own once we were in constant proximity? Would my feelings for him be strong enough to help me continue loving him in the face of difficulties? I had to pray they would.

Meanwhile, I had a batch of bread to manage and my lunch to eat before I ventured out again. I removed my wraps, washed my hands, and donned an apron. The dough needed more flour and a good kneading. I greatly enjoyed using my hands to work with the warm living lump that was bread dough. As I turned and pushed, turned and pushed, all the way around the clock, over and over, my mind was freed to muse on Charity's death.

How and where could I learn what Ransom had been up to in the last week? I could return to the boat shop and ask the kindly supervisor if Ransom had missed any shifts. Would he tell me, though? I supposed I could query the oldest child in the family, but it didn't quite seem fair to ask a girl who had just lost her mother questions that might lead to exposing her father's culpability in wrongdoing. Last autumn I'd been responsible for uncovering two killers whose actions, once they were apprehended, left their children essentially orphans. I didn't favor a repeat of that experience one bit.

Speaking of wrongdoing, I glanced at the back door with alarm. Had I locked it when I came in? I dusted off my hands and hurried to turn the latch. It wouldn't do to leave myself vulnerable. Just in case. Christabel darted by, nearly getting stepped on, likely in pursuit of a mouse come in from the cold.

As I resumed kneading, Charity's lifelong membership with Friends came to mind. It hadn't occurred to me when her Memorial Meeting for Worship would be. I was sure the family would want to schedule it soon, despite the actual burial being delayed until spring. Memorial meetings never included a body in a coffin, anyway. The service was likely to take place in two days on Seventh Day. I could ask Ransom about the details, or perhaps Virtue.

Once the bread was rising again and I ate something, I planned to visit Lucy Majowski out on Haverhill Road. After my home inspection I could poke around to learn what I could about Delia Davies. Neighbors who knew her and her family could possibly be convinced to share information. And if I visited Ransom at work I might be able to speak with Delia there, as well.

But what about the suspicious Joey Swift? Was I falsely reading malicious intent into his actions, or was he simply untrustworthy because of his unhealthy habits of strong drink and tobacco?

I finished kneading. Back into the bowl went the dough, now sitting up in a good ball, shiny and elastic to the touch. Back onto the bowl went the cover of damp dishcloth, back above the stove went the bowl. The dough should be perfectly risen once I returned from my afternoon foray. Pie crust was easy to assemble and roll out, and I could ready the pies for baking while the loaves cooked.

A great bang on the back door sounded. I started, turning, staring at it. Did thinking of a killer actually make one appear? Of course not. But who came to the back door other than close friends and family? None of them would raise such a racket. The hairs on my arms raised, even under my sleeves, and on my head, too. A window was next to the door, but I'd drawn the curtains against the cold before I'd gone out this morning and never bothered to reopen them. At least the window didn't look out on the landing, so a bad person couldn't break it and climb in. The house was built well up off the ground, too. One would need at least an eight-foot ladder to reach the bottom of the glass.

A second bang resounded and I jumped again. An idea sprang into my head. I dashed into the sitting room and raced up the stairs while trying to keep my footsteps quiet. From the bedroom directly above the kitchen, I slid open the sash. The house was only nine years old and well built, so the sash neither squeaked nor creaked. I leaned my head out and looked down.

The very same Joey Swift I'd been thinking about stood with fists at his sides. He gave one more mighty bang on the door, this time repeating it four times: *bam, bam, bam, bam.* The building shook with his force.

"I know you're in there, Midwife Carroll," he shouted. "I need to speak with you. If not here, if not now, you can believe it'll be later."

The next-door neighbor poked her own

head out her kitchen window. "Keep it down out there, mister. I got babies napping in here." She glanced up, catching sight of me, and opened her mouth. I put a finger to my lips and shook my head fast. She smiled, looking down again.

Joey whirled. He shook a fist at her, but his yelling and hammering at least ceased. I couldn't see his face from up here and expected his expression was a furious one. I waited in silence until he stomped down the stairs and away toward town. I shut the window and sank onto the bed, stunned. I wished I had thought to call the police while he was here, but I was still so unaccustomed to our even having a telephone in the house it hadn't occurred to me. That didn't mean I couldn't call them now. I hurried downstairs and a moment later Gertrude had put my call through.

"An exceedingly belligerent man was just at my house pounding on the door," I told the officer who answered after I gave my name and address. "Of course I didn't let him in. But I thought I should report it."

"This man's name, please?"

"Joe Swift."

"Do you know where he lives?"

I searched my brain. "No, I'm afraid I don't." As much as I didn't want Joey to return, it didn't feel right to trouble Virtue in her grief and have the police — or me — asking where Joey resided. "Can thee have someone patrol our lane from time to time in case he returns?"

"I'm afraid we're short on men at present, Miss Carroll, but I will note your call in the log. You should lock the doors and windows and be careful when you go out."

He hung up, and I did too, with somewhat more vigor than was entirely necessary.

What did Joey think I knew? What did he want from me? If he hadn't been so angry, I would have gone out and spoken with him. Me alone here and him in such a state? Confrontation would not have been a wise move. I worried a bit about going out alone to visit Lucy in half an hour's time. But no, I'd be taking Peaches and the buggy. I'd be safe. If I let angry men stop me from doing my work, I'd have given up long ago.

TWENTY

"What a bucolic setting thee has, Lucy, even in the dead of winter." I'd arrived at her farm twenty minutes ago without mishap. She'd shown me the house, including a sunny bedchamber upstairs, and all looked suitable and in order for an impending birth. I didn't think she'd have any problems with her delivery.

Now we stood at the back door looking out at a faded red barn, a small grove of fruit trees, and the snowy expanse beyond. A few forlorn and wizened apples clung to the bare branches of the trees, and the snow was halfway up their trunks. A shoveled and much traveled path ran between house and barn, with a rope strung along the walkway.

"Is the rope in case of a blizzard?" I asked.

"Indeed it is. Henryk's papa near got lost in one once, and all he was doing was going out to the barn to feed the cows. That's why they moved south, his father hates the winter so. Henryk and I, we mean to connect the house and barn with an enclosed passageway by and by."

"A good idea."

"We have ideas aplenty about how to improve the place. It was Henryk's grandpa's, and he left it to my husband when he passed on two years ago." She gestured at a good-sized fenced section of the yard near the door to the left. "That's my kitchen garden, and just here is where I grow herbs." She pointed to a patch to our right, where humps of snow indicated the woody remains of perennial herbs. "I love growing things. Even this one." She smiled, cradling the bottom of her belly with one hand and the top with the other.

I prayed we wouldn't have a blizzard during her baby's birth. That was in God's hands, not mine. "Does thee have any concerns, any worries about the delivery? Thee can tell me anything. Sometimes women have strange dreams close to the birthing time but they hesitate to mention them to anyone for fear they will be thought odd. I can tell thee they are more common than one imagines."

She led me back inside and shut the door. "I do, Rose, in fact. Last night I dreamed I gave birth to a turtle and a seven-year-old girl, except she was only a foot tall." Her laugh was a peal of amusement. "It seemed perfectly normal in the dream, of course. Not a nightmare at all. But once I awoke? I didn't even dare tell my husband."

I laughed with her. "That kind of dream is not unusual in the least. It only shows that thee is feeling a degree of perfectly normal anxiety about the birth. After all, this baby is a person thee has never met who will proceed to change thy life irrevocably. I promise thee will deliver neither a turtle nor a schoolgirl of any size."

"Would you like a cup of tea?" Lucy asked, one hand now in the small of her back.

"Yes, but thee shall sit and I'll fix it." I pointed to the kitchen table. "Soon enough thee won't be able to sit every time thee wishes to."

"All right." She fetched a plate of sugar cookies from a pie keep and set them on the table before she sat.

Henryk pushed through the door from outside, stomping his feet on the mat and removing a knit cap. "Hello, Miss Carroll."

We'd met on Lucy's first prenatal visit when he dropped her off. "Good afternoon, Henryk. Please call me Rose. We don't need titles among us."

"It don't seem right, quite. But I'll try. How's my bride?" He stood behind Lucy's chair and laid meaty hands tenderly on her shoulders.

"She's doing exceptionally well, and all is in order here for the birth," I said in my most reassuring voice. "Thee should have no concerns." First time fathers-to-be were often far more anxious than their wives.

"If you say so." A small frown still creased his forehead.

"Tell her about the mare, dear." Lucy twisted her head to smile up at him.

"Our Bella is about to have her first foal, too. The vet came and said she's due any day." He picked up his cap and twisted it in his hands, looking worried. "I hope she don't have no problems. Do you know much about animal births, Miss . . . Rose, I mean?"

"I grew up on a farm in Lawrence. I have seen many foal and calf births. Those large animals know what they are doing, Henryk. I wouldn't worry."

"If you say so. I'll be getting back to work, now. Even in midwinter a farmer's work ain't never done." He smoothed Lucy's hair with a gentle touch. "You fetch me if you need me, Lucy Lu."

Her love for her husband was evident in

her face as she smiled up at him. "You know I will."

After the door closed behind him, I stirred up the fire in the big old stove and put the kettle on, then joined her. "Thee mentioned thy former classmate, Delia. Where does she live, exactly?"

"It's the purple house on the other side of the road and just a bit farther west."

"Purple is an odd color for a residence."

"Indeed. I'm not surprised, though. Her mother is an odd bird."

"Is Delia's father alive?" I asked.

"He might be alive, but he doesn't live with them," Lucy said. "There's another man been by the house a couple of times. I set eyes on him once when I was sweeping snow off the walk, and one other time, as well. I don't know if he's calling on Mrs. Davies or Delia. Acts kind of furtive, like he doesn't belong there. Henryk saw him, too, when he was mending the fence in the front."

Ransom Skells, perhaps? "That's unsettling. Does the man come when they are at home? He's not trying to rob the place, is he?"

"I don't know. Delia has an older sister who's married and lives in Newburyport with her brood of babies. Six at last count, but I don't think this gent is her husband, either."

"Thee can always summon the police if the man seems to be up to no good." When would Ransom have time to visit Delia, what with his job and his family? When the kettle whistled, I got up to remove it from the heat. An earthenware teapot sat on a shelf next to the stove along with a square canister labeled *Tea.* "How is Delia's mother odd? Besides the color of the house, I mean." After I brought the steeping pot and two cups to the table, I sat again.

"She wears the strangest garb. All purples and blues. Plus shapeless dresses, scarves that make her look like an Arab lady, and that turban."

So Madame Restante was definitely Mrs. Davies. "A black turban?"

"Yes. I don't know why. It's not for warmth, because she wears it in summer, too. Maybe she's bald. I've never seen her without it." She munched on a cookie. "How did you know about the turban's color?"

I poured us each a cup of tea. I had no intention of telling Lucy about my encounter with Savoire Davies. "I've, uh, seen her around town. What's her Christian name, does thee know?"

"It's Sally." Lucy giggled. "She looks about as far from a Sally as I can imagine."

TWENTY-ONE

When I left Lucy and Henryk's farm after we'd had our tea, I turned west instead of east back toward town. I pulled Peaches to a halt just before the purple house. An aproned woman with slate-colored hair swept the new snow off the front porch and walkway at the next house, a coat thrown over her housedress. She straightened when she saw me.

"Can I be helpin' yeh, miss?" she asked in a brogue. She swept back and forth across the walk toward me until she neared the road. She stopped, holding the straw broom upright with one hand and setting her other on a generous hip.

"Good afternoon. I noticed that brightly colored house and was curious about its owners."

"Them," she scoffed. "Some crazy lady and her daughter."

"Crazy? Does thee mean she should be in

a lunatic asylum?"

"Nay, not that kind of crazy. She's odd, like. Has some business downtown, she does. And the daughter, she's after going off every day to work, too. Not a one of them to keep the house." She made a *tsking* sound and shook her head.

"Surely one of the ladies is married, though."

"No. Nary a man in the place except the sneaky one." She narrowed her eyes at the purple abode.

"Sneaky?"

The woman leaned closer and lowered her voice, even though not a soul was in sight. "He comes by when the girl's here but the loony one isn't. He might be a courtin' her, but he doesn't act proper and polite about it. Yeh should see him. He comes in one of them conveyances for hire, looks around to see if a body might be spying him, then goes in by the back door. The back door, I tell yeh!"

"What does this man look like, Mrs. . . ."

"Lord a mercy, Miss. I'm Mrs. Sheila Burke, I am."

"I am pleased to meet thee, Sheila. I am Rose Carroll."

"Likewise, I'm sure. You one of them Quakers, then?"

I smiled. "Yes. Thee was about to describe this man." Was it Ransom?

She squinted her eyes, peering over at the house as if conjuring him up. "Ruddy cheeks. Built sturdy. One windy day his hat flew into the air and I saw his hair. Reddish, and curly-like."

Most assuredly Ransom. Sneaking in the back door. Only came when Savoire — that is, Sally — wasn't home. He was consorting with Delia, who wasn't married, but he certainly was, with children at home and an unhappy wife, now dead. I felt sick at the thought. Was he also giving money to Delia? She had certainly been stylishly dressed for a secretary.

"Interesting. Well, it's been lovely to chat with thee, Sheila."

"Hold on, there. I thought yer name seemed familiar, like. Yer the midwife, aren't yeh?"

"Yes, I am. I'm in this neighborhood because I'm attending Lucy Majowski across the way there."

"She's going to pop any day now, she's that big. Listen, Rose Carroll, I am so happy to meet yeh. Me daughter, she's been going to this man." She nearly spat the last word. "Her baby should be coming along in April, mebbe May. But this Dr. Douglass, he wants her to go to the hospital for her delivery. I told her no! A woman's place is in the home. She was birthed in the bedroom upstairs just like all me other wee ones, and me myself before them back in the old country. A hospital's for sick folk, not for a healthy girl. 'Twas her husband who wanted her to go to Dr. Douglass. What does a man know about women and babies, anyway?" She shook her head again with even more feeling. "I'll tell her to come along and see yeh, if I may?"

"If thy daughter is in agreement, I would be happy to take over her care. Thee can learn my address from Lucy. But perhaps she prefers the care of a medical doctor, despite his sex, and the comfort of a modern lying-in hospital."

"Well, I know what's best for my girl. She won't object to coming to see you instead of that man." Sheila held out a strong farm woman's hand and pumped my hand with vigor. "I'm that glad you stopped by, lass."

I wasn't sorry, myself. I'd rather it not be true that a married man was visiting Delia on the sly. I couldn't change what was, though. And if Sheila's daughter wished, I might have saved a woman from a physician treating her like an object to be studied and manipulated as if she were an invalid instead of a normal thriving farm girl who happened to be pregnant.

TWENTY-TWO

As Peaches plodded up the packed-down pathway that served as the street on which the Bailey house was situated, I spied a man striding down the walkway next to the house. He was headed toward the back door, which was actually on the side of the house. Was it our house he'd approached? Three identical homes had been built for the Hamilton Mills workers a decade earlier, and ours was the one in the middle.

We grew nearer. Peaches naturally began turning in the direction of her stable behind the house, her oats, her straw, her freedom from bit and traces. I clucked to her. "Go straight," I murmured. We passed by the walkway at the same time I heard a banging sound. Sure enough, Joey Swift stood hammering on the door again.

"Midwife Carroll, I need to talk to you. Come out, will you?" He was just as loud and angry-looking as he'd been earlier in the day. I clucked to Peaches to pick up her speed before he saw me and we drove on by. I wasn't going home until others were about. But where to now? And what if Joey was still there when the children arrived home from school? It was between two thirty and three o'clock now and they would be home by four, with Faith arriving about that time, too. She was a wise young woman, but she was only eighteen. I'd have to return before the family did. If we all arrived at the same time, we'd have safety in numbers.

Before this week I would have driven directly to the police station and reported Joe Swift's second incident of aggressive behavior. Now? I didn't want to imperil Kevin's job by even showing my face around there, and I'd already telephoned the station to no avail. Once I'd turned the corner onto Center Street, I slowed Peaches again and tried to picture the home address he'd included in the letter with the autopsy results. As I recalled, it was on the other side of Market Street somewhere in the Clark Street area. Was it Fruit Place, or Tuxbury Street? Neither rang a bell in my memory.

The carriage factory to my right had a door propped open at the back and sounds of saws and hammers working floated out into the clear winter air. Boardman Street. That was it. I laughed out loud at the sounds of carpentry making me think of boards, which made me remember the street name. I'd go to Kevin's home and leave him a message. I always carried a pad of paper and a pencil in my bag. I'd leave my note with his wife, or on the doorstep if she wasn't home.

Five minutes later I stood on the front stoop of the small two-story house, one as modest as mine but looking older and in need of minor maintenance. I doubted a police detective earned a luxurious salary, although I'd never asked Kevin. What I did know was that he was devoted to his wife and son, Sean. So what if the house looked a bit shabby?

A petite woman opened the door. Dark tendrils escaped her long braid and framed a heart-shaped face anchored by brilliant green eyes. "Yes?"

"Emmaline Donovan?" When she nodded, I went on. "I am Rose Carroll. I've worked with thy —"

"Miss Rose, the midwife-detective?" Her face lit up. "You wouldn't believe how often Kevin speaks of you. Please come in. It's freezing out today."

It wasn't until she took a step back that I

noticed she was well along in a pregnancy, possibly around six months. Kevin hadn't told me. That dedicated family man must be delighted to have another child on the way.

"I thank thee. I won't take much of thy time."

"Don't be silly. Come and sit." She spied Peaches. "Wait, we'll need to provide for your horse. Seannie!" she called.

A sturdy child hurried in, a toy police wagon in one hand. "Yes, Mama?"

"Sean, this is Miss Rose, of whom Papa speaks."

"Pleased to meet you, miss." The boy extended his hand to me.

"And I, thee, Sean." I shook his slender hand.

"Please be a good boy, put on your coat and cap, and watch her horse out front," Emmaline directed the boy.

"The horse's name is Peaches," I added.

A broad smile split his face. "Yes, miss." He ran off, and a moment later I heard a door slam from the back.

"He loves having jobs." Emmaline gazed after him with affection writ large on her face.

"What a polite lad." I thought back to my conversation with Kevin. "Thy husband told me his age, but I can't recall. Is he around six?"

"He turned seven in January. You're probably wondering why he isn't in school."

I had been, but didn't like to say.

"Our boy seems to be very quick in his mind. I am schooling him at home for the present. We didn't want the classroom to hold him back. Now, do come along and we'll have a good chat."

I was liking this woman more with every passing minute. I followed her into a comfortable, family-centered sitting room with book-lined walls and a toy chest in the corner. Five framed pencil drawings like the one I'd seen on Kevin's desk hung on the walls depicting what looked like Sean at year intervals. They were as good as photographs at capturing his essence. Better even, because the subject wasn't stiff and poised.

"Emmaline, thee is very talented. I saw one of thy drawings in Kevin's office."

"Thank you." She blushed. "It's rather a passion of mine. I'd fancied myself becoming a famous artist before I was married. Now it's more of a hobby."

"Who's to say thee won't still be famous? Thee has thy life ahead of thee."

She brushed away the idea. "Please sit."

I chose a comfortable armchair as she

lowered herself carefully onto a nearby chair.

"I apologize. This baby is making me work." Emmaline laughed.

"Is thee about six months gone?"

Her eyes widened. "Exactly. You're good, Miss Rose."

"Please just call me Rose. I can't seem to break Kevin of the title, but thee doesn't need to use it, truly."

"Very well, Rose. How can I help you today?"

My own smile slid away. "A man, a Joe Swift, has been bothering me at home. He's possibly involved in the death of a client of mine, and I wanted to let Kevin know. But . . ." I wasn't sure how much Kevin had told her about his new chief's strict policies.

"But his new boss doesn't want you around. He told me all about it."

"That's it, exactly. I put in a call to the station earlier today, but they said they have no men to spare and I should just be careful. I have also learned a few new facts and have some thoughts about the case that I wanted to share with Kevin. If thee could possibly let him know, I would so much appreciate it."

She pushed up to standing and pointed to

the telephone on a desk in the corner. "I'll call him right now, tell him to come see you on his way home. How does that sound?"

"Splendid. I thank thee." I hadn't noticed the phone when I came in. Some detective I was.

"Gertrude, this is Emmaline. Put me through to Detective Donovan, please." Several moments passed, then, "Kev, yes, everything's fine. Your tailor is here, and he wants you to stop by for a fitting on your way home. Can you get there before five?"

His tailor? I waited for her to give him my message.

"Lovely. He also said a difficult customer had come by twice today acting in a threatening way, so maybe you could send somebody by sooner to investigate."

I watched Emmaline. She saw me and winked, holding up an index finger in a *wait* gesture.

"Perfect. I'll see you for supper, then. Thanks, darling." She hung up, smiling from one ear to the other.

I could see where Sean got his broad smile. "His tailor?" I asked. "Was that code referring to me?"

"Yes! Isn't it fun? When Kev said he was disappointed he couldn't work with you on this case, I suggested we make up some code words. He told me you might be writing to him here, so I said if I needed to relay a message, I'd call you his tailor." She rolled those green eyes. "Gertrude is a competent operator, but she listens to every last word she can get away with. And her brother is an officer in the force. There are no secrets where Gertrude is involved." She returned to her easy chair.

"It's a brilliant solution, and I thank thee greatly, Emmaline. I suppose I should get along home in case an officer does stop by. I was worried about Joey Swift being there and accosting my young niece and nephews when they arrived home from the Whittier School."

"That would be terrible."

"Tell me, how does thee school Sean?"

"We have the arithmetic and mathematics books from the school, and I let him work through them at his own pace. He's already up to the eighth-grade level. But he's interested in everything. He likes to puzzle out how Shakespeare's words would have been expressed in today's English, and learn about cloud formations and the life cycle of frogs. He's already surpassed my knowledge level in many areas, so I just learn along with him. I suppose in a few years we'll need to get him an advanced tutor, but for now it's glorious to give him his freedom to soak up whatever he can."

"He must have a remarkable intelligence," I said. "Kevin hasn't mentioned it. He's told me about playing ball with the boy, and how good he is at jokes."

"Kev doesn't like to brag, and he doesn't want other officers or strangers regarding Sean as if he's an oddity. Because he's not. He's a regular boy who happens to have an extra-keen mind." She caressed the mound of her growing belly. "I hope this one will, too."

"Who is thy midwife, Emmaline?" I stood.

She peered up at me, new lines between her brows. "I don't have one yet. I know I should have been seen already. We have been hoping for this baby for five years, Rose. I am finally with child and terrified something will happen to the baby, to us during birth, to the newborn. Just terrified. So I haven't sought care, which doesn't make sense at all. Except that . . ."

"Except thee is afraid a midwife might find something awry?"

"That's it in a nutshell. I have been meaning to pay you a visit and haven't drummed up my courage yet."

"If thee wants my care, I would be more than happy to provide it. Please don't worry.

The most dangerous period for the pregnancy itself has passed, the first twelve weeks. Now thy job is to eat well — meat and vegetables — and drink clean milk. Make sure thee rests when thee needs to, go out in the fresh air, and let this baby grow well inside thee. Thy body is made for this work. We'll work together to bring a living and healthy baby into thy happy family."

She clasped my hand. "It's what I want more than anything. Kevin and I always planned to a have a passel of Donovans. We have one child we love, but two would make us all very happy."

TWENTY-THREE

After I realized how close I was to the Skells' flat, I decided to pay Ransom a visit before I returned home. I wondered how I could get him to acknowledge visiting Delia at home. The flat was located on the second floor in a house that had been converted to apartments. As I pulled Peaches to a halt in front, a girl in braids trudged up. She kicked snow with her foot, her shoulders slumped, and her strapped books nearly dragged on the ground.

"Priscilla," I called to Charity and Ransom's eldest child and Betsy's friend. I climbed down from the buggy, holding the reins. "Has thee just come from school?"

Priscilla glanced up. "Hello, Rose." A smudge of dirt marred the delicate skin of her cheek and a long strand of hair escaped from its braid hung listless next to her ear. "Yes, I have. Why is thee here?"

"I wanted to see how thee and thy sisters

and brother were doing." A pang of guilt made me realize I should have come earlier to check on the motherless brood. I knew them all from Meeting, of course, and Priscilla had played with Betsy at our house before.

"The little ones don't hardly know Mama's gone, and my sisters cry all the time now. They are only seven, six, and five, though." Priscilla sounded scornful of such babyish ways, despite being barely nine herself.

"And thee?" I stroked the top of her head. "Thee must miss thy mother very much."

She sniffed, swiping at her eye and smearing the dirt on her cheek. The original patch must have come from tears, too.

"I'm mad at her, Rose, and at Father, too. It's all rotten now." Her mouth turned down. "Why'd she have to go and die? Why couldn't Father save her?"

How much had Ransom told the children? I gentled my voice. "I was with her, my dear. There was nothing anyone could do to save her. I'm so sorry."

"I want things back the way they were." She kicked a chunk of ice into the street. "A boy at school said somebody killed Mama. I had to beat him up to make him take it back."

I slid my hand over my mouth. Talk of Charity's death had reached the schoolyard. And this sweet Quaker girl had to resort to her fists to defend her mother's name. Peaches snuffled and an idea arose.

"Does thee want to pet Peaches? He's very friendly." I'd seen the calming effect horses could have on distraught people before. In fact, my father had started a program for children who resided at a special school for the feeble-minded and disturbed. They came regularly out to the farm, because he'd seen how taking care of large animals provided children with solace and a kind of inner peace.

"May I?" Priscilla asked, her eyes lighting up.

"Of course. He won't hurt thee." I watched her stroke the gelding's neck and run her finger down his long nose.

She looked up at me with a small smile. "He's so soft."

"I know. Priscilla, I'd like thee to wait with him here while I run up and check on thy father. I won't be long."

"Me?"

"Yes, thee is big enough. And I know thee will do a good job."

She squared her little shoulders. "Take all

the time thee needs, Rose. I'll watch over him."

I lifted my skirts and made my way up the steps, being careful on icy patches. Ransom, holding the youngest girl on his shoulder, let me in with barely a word of greeting.

"I wanted to see how thee is faring, Ransom." As I stood in the sitting room, it appeared he wasn't faring very well. Toys, clothes, and papers were in every corner. Little Howie's nose ran unwiped, and the baby smelled like she needed a change. The five-year-old sat on an old rocking horse sucking her thumb as she rocked, with the next oldest in a chair frowning at a picture book, her lips moving as she read. She sniffed more than once, and wiped a tear from her cheek.

"Have you come to help, then?" Ransom asked. His short red curls stuck up every which way, his ruddy skin had turned pale, and his shirt was rumpled.

"No, I'm sorry, I can't at this time. Have the women of the Meeting been bringing meals for thee and the children?" Maybe the women should also organize home care, but that might be beyond the extent of what was normally done. After my sister died, the food was plentiful, and Frederick had had

Faith and me to help out with the household.

"Yes, at least we're well fed. I am appreciating all my wife did around the house, I'll tell you. I don't know how she managed." The skin around his eyes looked as if he hadn't slept in days, and he probably hadn't. "It makes me want to get back to my job at the Boat Shop."

"What will thee do with the little ones when thee does?"

"My mother-in-law will take them. She said she doesn't mind, and she's already got the nursemaid hired." He looked around the room. As if the thought just occurred to him, he said, "Sissy, where's Priscilla? Didn't she come home from school with you?" His expression turned from fatigued to alarmed.

The reader looked up with reddened eyes. "She's mad at the world. She said she was coming later." Her lower lip wobbled.

"Not to worry, Ransom," I said. "She arrived when I did. She's downstairs watching my horse."

"I'm glad to hear it. If I lost one of these on top of Charity, well, I don't know . . ." His voice broke and he turned away. The baby began to whimper.

"Give me the little one, Ransom. Go wash

thy face. I can stay for a few more minutes."

He handed me the stinky baby silently and hurried into the kitchen.

"Come on, baby. Let's find thee a clean diaper." I'd come in part with the intention of questioning Ransom about visiting Delia. Now clearly was not the time. He was distressed and it didn't seem like an act. Perhaps he'd had a change of heart now that his wife was dead. Instead of seeing Delia on the sly, this father was going to have to learn how to care for his children.

Twenty-Four

I arrived home by four o'clock to no Joey. I had no way of knowing if Kevin had found an officer to pass by, or if Joey had just given up on me. The old adage, "All's well that ends well" ran through my brain, although I rather doubted this particular episode had actually ended.

Collecting the afternoon mail, my eyes widened at a note from Virtue Swift. It was brief, saying only that the Memorial Meeting for Worship for her daughter had been scheduled for Seventh Day at two o'clock in the afternoon. She did not mention her son-in-law. I set the missive aside and washed up. It was time to bake.

I set to work shaping loaves of bread, heating up the oven, and cutting lard into flour for a big batch of pie crust. By the time the children clattered in, all red-cheeked and talking over each other, the bread was baking and I was filling the bottom crusts with the thickened stew.

I'd saved out the crust scraps for pie cookies, as we called them. It was just the extra rolled-out dough topped with cinnamon and sugar, and baked for a few minutes until they crisped up, but the children loved them. I did, too. I popped them in the hot oven next to the bread.

"Wash up, now, and we'll have a treat in a couple of minutes." The normality of a busy family life soothed me for the moment from my thoughts of suspects, criminal abortion, and homicide.

Faith returned in time to snatch the last cookie off the plate. She removed her outerwear and hugged me, eyes agleam, but her cookie-holding hand shook.

"Rose, how ever can I wait until First Day to marry? I am a nervous wreck. I alternate between pure joy and terrible worry that something will go wrong. What if we get a big snowstorm? What if my dress isn't finished in time? What if —"

I took her by the shoulders. "Faith, all will be well. We've walked to the Meetinghouse in the snow before, remember? When did Alma say thy dress will be ready?"

"Tomorrow. I'm to pick it up tomorrow."

"She is a reliable seamstress. It will be ready. And aren't the women handling the refreshments?"

"Yes, but . . ." She wrung her hands.

"No buts. I know thee is anxious, and anxiety never helped a thing. Thee and Zebulon will have a lovely worshipful welcome to your new life together and that's that. Now, help me roll out these top crusts and tell me about the latest story thee is writing for the newspaper."

By five o'clock the bread was cooling and the pies had just gone into the oven. I was in my parlor jotting down everything I knew about Charity's death when Kevin knocked at the front door. I let him in.

He stepped into the hall but stayed standing. "I can't stay long, Miss Rose. I sent a man over earlier to check on Swift, but he must have already gone. What did Swift say to you?"

"He didn't actually say it to me. He shouted at the house that he needed to talk with me. I'd be happy to do so, but it was the way he approached the house. Banging on the door in anger, yelling for me. Thee can ask the neighbor next door. She stuck her head out and told him to quiet down, that her children were napping. The way he acted felt quite threatening."

"We'll see if we can run him down for you." A little smile crept over his face.

"Heard you met the missus and my boy."

"I adored both of them. Sean was very polite and helpful. You both are doing a good job raising him. And I think I convinced Emmaline to come and see me about her pregnancy."

"I appreciate that. I've been telling her to for some time now. I'm grateful for your help, Miss Rose." Kevin's grateful expression echoed his words. "You had information about the case for me, did you?"

"Yes, quite a bit. But first, has there been any progress in discovering the killer? Does thee have a suspect in custody?"

He gave a little shake of his head. "Indeed we don't, and the lack of forward movement is more than frustrating. For me and my chief, too, as you can imagine."

"Thee hasn't learned anything?" I asked.

"I didn't say that. We're checking the husband's alibi. And if Joseph Swift the younger is bothering you, we'll add him to the list."

"I think thee should."

"Very well. Now, your news?"

"Where do I start?" I thought of all I'd learned.

He tapped his foot.

"Thee is in a hurry. I'll go fast." I grabbed the sheet of paper from my desk and read from it. "A woman going by the name of Madame Savoire Restante deals in contraceptive solutions. Her office is on Clark Street, but she lives on Haverhill Road and her actual name is Sally Davies. I think Madame either was involved with Charity's death, perhaps being the incompetent abortionist, or she knows something. A client of mine confessed that a Madame helped her end a pregnancy. This Savoire lives with her adult daughter, Delia Davies, who works at Lowell's Boat Shop. I believe Ransom Skells has been stepping out with Delia. Or stepping into her house when the mother was absent, according to the neighbor, Mrs. Sheila Burke." I took a breath and looked up.

Kevin gaped at me. He shut his mouth, then opened it again to say, "I am not even going to ask how you learned all this."

"Good." I returned to the list but spoke softly in case one of the children ventured near. "Joe Swift — who goes by Joey — is the recently late Joseph Swift's son. The father made a fortune in rum. Charity is the elder Swift's niece. Charity's mother, Virtue, says Joey is a drunk and a gambler. Virtue and her husband also do not care for Ransom in the least. I have a number of ideas about the web of these people, and who might have killed Charity, but these are some facts I unearthed." I handed him the paper. "Tonight I'm dining with Bertie Winslow and Sophie Ribeiro. Sophie has apparently been working on a complicated estate for Joseph Swift involving trusts. Bertie wants her to tell me about it. Perhaps he is Charity's uncle. I'll let Emmaline know tomorrow what I learn, shall I?"

"Please. This matter of the Madame concerns me greatly. Isn't she aware her kind of work is against the law?"

"Of course she is. Kevin, thee knows as well as I that some women simply aren't in a position to bear children, or to bear more. What are they to do? There are reasonably safe herbal preparations that can help them."

The detective was pressing his lips together, an expression I'd seen before when he strongly disapproved of my words or actions.

"I know thee thinks it's against not only the law but God's sacraments. But doesn't thy God want women to be healthy and have good lives, instead of bearing ten children they can't afford in as many years or having to give birth to a baby created by a violent act? Shouldn't we able to help them?" I suspected part of his opposition was also due to Kevin and his wife living with the opposite problem, not being able to have as many children as they wished.

"We disagree on this matter, as you well know."

"Auntie Rose," Betsy called from the front. "I need help with my 'rithmatic."

"Just a minute, my sweet," I called back. I continued with Kevin. "I would never recommend a mechanical abortion. It's far too dangerous, as Charity's demise shows."

"Unless her perforations were deliberate." His expression was grim, and now not directed at me.

"Unless it was homicide. Yes, unless that."

But why? Who stood to benefit from Charity's death?

TWENTY-FIVE

Sophie, Bertie, and I sat sated at their round dining table. Two ivory-colored tapers were halfway burned down, and remnants of a lamb dish decorated the edges of our plates. They'd said the dish was a Moroccan recipe.

"Morocco, I love you. Let me count the ways," Bertie declared.

"Has thee been there?" I asked.

"No, but the lovely Sophie has." She smiled tenderly at her partner.

Sophie nodded, her messy knot of dark hair bobbing atop her head. "My Portuguese father took me all over the world when I was a child." Her dark almond-shaped eyes and high cheekbones gave her face an exotic look.

"Who stayed home from work today to prepare this dinner?" I asked.

Bertie laughed. "Neither of us. We hire a cook for special occasions like today. Sophie gives her the recipe and she makes it and leaves it hot on the stove for us. It's quite splendid."

"That's a worthwhile service. I am not sure I can even move, I ate so much." I shifted in my chair. "I've never consumed such a divine mix of flavors."

"Come sit somewhere more comfortable and I'll tell you a story." Sophie divided the rest of the bottle of wine between her own and Bertie's glasses. I followed them into their luxuriously comfortable sitting room, with bright lamps illuminating colorful paintings on the walls — which were all painted by women, Bertie had told me previously.

I picked a chair into which I knew I wouldn't sink down a foot, unlike some of them in the room. The coal stove provided a comforting warmth, and the vibrant colors in the room glowed. "I'm all ears."

Sophie sat at one end of an upholstered lounge sofa. "Be aware what I'm about to tell you is confidential for the moment, but it will become part of the public record within a week, or maybe sooner."

She sat straight and I could imagine her in a court of law, holding her ground, not allowing anyone to treat her as lesser because of her status as a female. Sophie had a sharp intellect and no doubt had memorized tomes of legal precedents.

"If any of these facts pertain to the case Bert has told me you're working on, I suppose you may share them with your police friend," Sophie added.

"I thank thee. He has been welcoming the bits of information I give him of late." I pushed up my spectacles. I hoped the information would be pertinent and help us solve the conundrum of who killed Charity Skells.

"Joseph Swift was a rich man when he died a month ago," Sophie began. "Of natural causes, as far as anyone can tell, although he did have several enemies. Believe me, the family brought in an independent medical examiner to be sure someone didn't bump him off. Mr. Swift was married, but his wife died eight years ago. They had two daughters. The youngest child was a son, Joseph the third. The daughters are both married and have children, at least two apiece."

I sat, hands in my lap, eager to hear what she had to say about the belligerent Joey. Bertie lay on the same couch as Sophie with her eyes closed and her small stockinged feet in Sophie's lap.

Sophie continued. "When the younger Joseph, whom the family has always called

Joey, reached the age of consent, it became clear he had acquired not only an insatiable thirst for drink but an incurable addiction to gambling. He spent through his allowance every month in the first week and was given to begging anyone and everyone for more funds with which to support his dual habits."

"His aunt Virtue hinted at that to me," I said.

"Yes. Virtue is a stalwart Friend, as you must know, but rather a judgmental one, unlike you, Rose." Sophie smiled at me. "Her husband converted to the faith before their marriage, but has never been very keen on it, as I understand."

"Virtue told me the late Joseph Swift was not a fellow Quaker. Dealing in rum would be an odd enterprise if he were."

"Exactly. Now, for the meat of the story."

"Spiced Moroccan meat?" Bertie piped up in a lazy voice, eyes still shut, lips playing with a smile.

"Hush, my darling, and sleep." Sophie stroked Bertie's foot. "Mr. Swift came to me to write his will last year. He knew he was ailing. He wanted to leave his considerable fortune in trust for his grandchildren and to his great-nieces and -nephews — Charity's children and those of her sister.

But he decided he didn't want Joey squandering one more cent of his money, and asked me to draw up a revised will. I am to be the trustee and administrator of the money for the children, not their parents."

"Because Joseph didn't trust Charity's husband, Ransom?" I asked.

"Yes, that was one consideration. And Mr. Swift the elder also questioned the motives of one of his sons-in-law."

"Does Joey know the terms of the will?"

"We tried to keep the entire agreement confidential until it was finalized, but somehow the news of the youngest generation being the inheritors slipped out." Sophie sipped her wine. "Not, however, the fact that I am to administer the funds."

Bertie murmured, "The butler did it."

I snorted but then grew sober. "And the news no doubt got around the family. Both Joey and Ransom must think the children's parents would have access to the money."

"I think that is an accurate assessment," Sophie agreed. "For Mrs. Skells and the Swift daughters, this wouldn't have presented a problem. None of them would have abused their power, but would have used the money as Mr. Swift intended, for good food, decent housing, schooling, clothing, and the like."

"Things Charity desperately needed."

Sophie nodded.

"So Joey could have killed his cousin, thinking he could share the funds with Charity's husband," I said.

Bertie sat up in one smooth move, not asleep at all. "But why would Skells share the money?"

"I learned today of Ransom's indiscretions," I said. "He's been visiting Delia Davies, the young secretary from Lowell's Boat Shop at her home out on Haverhill Road, but only when her mother wasn't at home."

"Blackmail." Bertie put on a deep dramatic voice. "Joey would threaten to make the affair public if Ransom didn't split the pot."

"It's possible," Sophie said. "Or Mr. Skells killed his wife himself, thinking he'd get all the inheritance. He could marry the sweet young thing —"

"I called her a chippy two days ago and he took a bit too much offense."

"The chippy, then." Bertie grinned. "He could marry Delia and . . . wait a minute. Where do all the children fit in? Is the chippy going to want to be become an instant mother to another woman's passel of tykes?"

"I couldn't say. Ransom acted quite loving toward his young son earlier this week," I said. "Their grandmother, Virtue, seemed willing to take them all in. Delia might be counting on that. Or maybe she's only seeing Ransom because he told her he'd be coming into some sizeable funds."

Sophie nodded. "Many a young woman has entangled herself with an older married gentleman purely for the financial gain."

"But the sticking point I think is the actual death," I said. "Maybe Joey or Ransom hired an abortionist, but I can't see either of them doing the deed themselves."

"So who did?" Sophie asked, looking intently at me.

Twenty-Six

I yawned as I steered the buggy lazily down Whittier Street toward home at nine o'clock. The evening with Bertie and Sophie had been delicious, luxurious, and full of information, but I'd already had a long day and was ready for my bed. I let Peaches lead us — she knew the way. Clouds covered the waning moon. After we turned right onto Sparhawk Street, the night was especially dark. The road was a new one in town. When I'd first moved to Amesbury, the area was just a pasture. The town had constructed the road a few years ago and named it for Thomas Sparhawk. He had lived at the other end of the way, the same Sparhawk who had been John Whittier's friend and physician until the doctor's death fifteen years earlier.

Ahead of me was a quarter mile with nary a house on either side. To my left lay fields and a row of trees lining the way, to my right more of the same. The road was built up over a small stream that ran down to the Locke & Jewell factory and to Pattens Pond beyond. The stream was frozen and snow-covered at this time of year, of course. The night air was crisp, smelling of chimney smoke and warm horse.

I might have dozed as we clopped slowly over the stones. I jerked upright when a clatter rose up behind me. What was it? Was a horse out of control? It grew louder and my heart slammed against my ribs. One summer night last year as I walked, a criminal had nearly run me down. Maybe it was happening again. Maybe my sleuthing around town, asking questions wherever I went, had raised Charity's assailant's ire. Maybe the killer had followed me to Bertie's, had waited patiently, and was determined to put an end to me.

Peaches was not known for speed. We could never outrun an attacker, even though the big Catholic church was not far away. I pulled the gelding as far to the right as I could, though the road was not a wide one. "Whoa up, Peaches. That's a good boy." We stopped. My palms sweated inside my gloves and my hands shook so I could barely hold the reins. The horse tossed his head, snorting in worry passed down along the reins from my nervous hands.

The hoofbeats grew louder, closer. I leaned toward the middle of the road. Would I be able to see who was driving in such a reckless manner, and if they aimed at us or were simply in an enormous hurry? A closed black wagon, pulled by an equally dark galloping horse, charged toward us at full speed. I screeched and pulled back into the safety of my buggy.

I had no time to act. I heard a thud and a crunch, felt a powerful bump. The jolt knocked the reins out of my grasp. It threw me out of the buggy. Peaches trumpeted shrilly. The vehicle sped past as I crashed down the snowy embankment. My hands found nothing to grasp and I slid down on my side, half upside down. When I was almost to the bottom, my hip hit a rock concealed by snow, which did nothing to cushion the blow. I choked back a cry of pain, not wanting to give away my location. I prayed Peaches was not harmed.

Stunned, I lay for a moment where I landed. That wagon had come at me with fierce purpose but had kept going. At least . . . I thought I'd heard it speed past. Had Peaches, with no one holding his reins, followed in pursuit? Or was the horse waiting for me up on the road? I didn't dare call out to him in case my assailant was waiting to see if I was conscious or not.

The snow melting beneath my body heat was dampening my cloak, my skirt, my stockings. Snow had been forced into my gloves. I had to extricate myself from my plight before I froze to death. My fingers were already losing sensation. I hoisted myself up to my knees and then to standing, wincing at the pain in my right hip. I crawled up the embankment, digging in my toes for a foothold on the rocks under the snow. When my head reached the level of the street, I peered cautiously over the snowy berm, my pulse racing.

My heart sank when no familiar shape loomed above. No buggy, and no Peaches waiting patiently to take me home. What a blessing he hadn't been knocked over the embankment, though. He wasn't a fast horse, but he was sure of foot. I blew out a breath. A dark wagon wasn't in sight, either. Unless a second person had jumped off to follow up the attack on foot, I was safe. Cold, aching, and fearful, but safe — for now — I began my trudge the remaining distance home.

As I walked, I began to doubt everything I was undertaking. Not my calling to care for pregnant women and help them birth healthy babies safely. Never that. Nor my future with my beloved David. But my delving into the mystery of who killed Charity must be the cause of tonight's attack. I was lucky I hadn't broken a leg in my fall, or cracked my head on that rock instead of my hip. I wouldn't be alive at dawn if that had happened, stranded on the dark, snowy slope where I'd been tossed.

It wasn't the first time my sleuthing had gotten me into trouble, either. I'd been tricked into being a hostage, and I'd been threatened with a gun. I'd been hit on the head and left to die in a freezing carriage house. Kevin had been warning me about getting into dangerous situations. Who would have thought driving home from a friend's house in a buggy with the top up would be dangerous? Anything I did, anyplace I went could be treacherous if a criminal was feeling trapped, or about to be discovered, and thought I was the reason. And I didn't want to die. I had mothers to care for, nieces and nephews to help raise, and a life to build with David.

My walking raised thoughts of who could want me dead or injured, of who drove that wagon or hired it to do the deed. Joey Swift? Savoire or Delia? Ransom? My thoughts were a jumble as I reached St. Joseph's. The enormous brick church was dark, and the convent and rectory windows behind were, as well. My steady, rhythmic plodding, or maybe it was the presence of another faith's sanctuary nearby, reminded me to hold my problem in the Light of God. I needed to prayerfully discern whether I would continue my investigation or would cease my efforts and return to following only my primary occupation.

As I continued, images flooded my mind. Charity's pale face, the life force slipping out of her. Little Priscilla's anguish at losing her mother, expressed as anger. Virtue's barely contained grief. I prayed Kevin and his team would find the killer with all due speed. Could I abandon Charity and her family to the official investigation?

By the time I arrived home, my way was clear. I'd discerned, with God's help, that I must continue my efforts, although I would exercise extreme caution wherever I went.

My face lit up and my heart filled to find Peaches and the buggy waiting patiently in front of our small stable. As I walked, I'd feared perhaps the black wagon had absconded with him, but here he was. Despite my condition, I took the time to free him from the traces and remove his harness. I fed him and put the buggy away.

"Good boy, Peaches." I stroked his neck. "You kept your feet and your calm under threat. More than I can say for myself."

He whuffed his response, and I left him to his rest.

TWENTY-SEVEN

Dawn had not yet brought light to the sky the next morning when a loud knocking on the door awoke me. I groaned, having slept only fitfully, with dreams of sharp objects, stacks of money, and attack wagons floating through my slumber. I lit a lamp and threw on a wrapper. Stiff and with aching bruises from the night before, I hurried to see who was there. I had resolved to be more careful. But killers did not come knocking, and this might be the call to Lucy Majowski's labor I'd been expecting. I didn't think I had any other mothers expecting so soon. Sure enough, Henryk Majowski stood in front of the house with a frantic look on his face, a horse and wagon behind him.

"Miss Carroll, you've got to come."

"All right. When did Lucy's pains start?" I spoke in a low tone so as not to wake the family.

"No, not Lucy."

"What?" I peered at him. "What does thee mean, not Lucy?"

"It's my mare. She's foaling, but I think she's stuck. And the vet had to travel to Vermont." His thin face looked like a scared boy's. "I don't know what to do!"

I thought Henryk was not over twenty, so a boy he still was, despite being married and owner of several large animals. "I will help thee. Step into the hall and keep warm. I'll need a minute to get ready."

"Thank you, but I'll stay with the horse."

"Very well." I shut the door and hurried to do what was necessary. I dressed, put my hair up, scribbled a note to the family, and slid into my warm things. At the last minute I grabbed my birthing satchel. I hadn't helped a mare give birth in a decade, but in my younger years I had certainly witnessed and assisted my father with more than one foal having trouble entering the world and a few calves, too. It was just part of life on a farm.

I didn't attempt to speak as we bumped over the paving stones in the dark, my warm breath making little clouds in the frigid air. At least we had moonlight to guide our way, but the wagon was a simple one. Unlike some of the fine carriages made in Amesbury, this transport didn't provide cushioning against an uneven road. I gripped the side so I wouldn't bounce out, and winced when my bruised hip was the target of several uneven spots in the road. Still, this traveling in the dark was a familiar journey for me, and I took comfort in the quiet early hours as I went to help yet another laboring mother.

Just before we turned into the farm, I spied the Davies home a little farther down the road. No lights shone in its windows, a dark house keeping its secrets. Henryk opened the barn door and drove right in. He jumped down again, closed the wide door, and secured the horse, leaving it harnessed to the wagon. He lit a lantern and I climbed down, following him to a stall, where he lit another lantern and hung them both on hooks.

"There's our Lady." He pointed, quite unnecessarily.

The mare was a chestnut brown with one white foot and a white blaze between her eyes. She hadn't given birth in the time Henryk had gone to fetch me, but the sac was bulging out of her birth canal. She was still on foot.

"How long has she been laboring?" I asked.

"I'm not sure. I checked on her before I

went to bed last night and she was fine, then I got up around three and she was groaning."

"Has thee observed a foal birth before?"

"Only when I was a lad of five. After that we didn't have a horse."

We stood in silence, watching, waiting. Lady groaned as her swollen belly contracted, her coat damp and steaming in the cold air from the exertion of her labor. Henryk started to take a step forward but I grabbed his sleeve.

"Let's leave her be unless we have to interfere," I said. "It's better that way." So far I didn't see any reason why I needed to be here. The mare had been having a long labor, but she wasn't thrashing about or rolling over repeatedly, and stood quietly between contractions. As with humans, sometimes horse babies take a while to come out. Henryk was inexperienced, though, and didn't want to lose his cherished and necessary horse, or the baby, either.

"Is it her first birth?" I asked.

"Yes." He twisted his cap in his hands.

"So her body hasn't done this work before. Women's first labors can be long, too." I hoped Lucy's wasn't overly long. Both mother and baby can suffer when the birth takes days.

Henryk glanced at me. "I heard about that lady who died this week. She was one of yours, wasn't she?"

"Charity? Yes, she was my client. It was a very sad morning."

"They said one of those babykillers did it." His nostrils flared. "Babykillers. They should be killed themselves. And ladies who go to them? They deserve what they get." He turned and spat in a corner of the stall.

I stared at him. Clearly we held different views on this matter. Henryk, like Kevin, was opposed to the very idea of terminating a pregnancy, although the detective didn't express his opinion with such venom. I opened my mouth to argue with Henryk, then shut it again. Not here, not now, not with a man whose wife I was about to attend in her own birth.

"My crazy neighbor is one," he went on. "I don't know why the police let her keep operating."

"What neighbor is that?"

"Mrs. Davies. She goes by some ridiculous Frenchie name. And then there's the so-called doctor." He rolled his eyes while saying the last word. "Doctor Wallace Buckham. That's a ridiculous name, too. My wife thought he was a real doctor and went to him for some lady problems last year. She saw through him right away. She would never go to an abortionist, not if she had fifteen babies, she wouldn't."

Oh, she might, I thought. She certainly might. "Where is Doctor Buckham's office?"

"In one of those fancy houses up near Highland Street. Calls himself an herbalist. He ought to be arrested. It's plum wrong to mess with nature like that."

I made a note of the name and location. I might just pay this Buckham a visit later in the day.

A hoof appeared in the silvery translucent sac. I was relieved to see the sole pointing down. Hooves pointing up can indicate that the foal is in the wrong position for an optimum delivery. Lady bent her front legs and lowered herself to the straw-covered floor. Another hoof followed the first into the sac in short order, breaking the membrane. As we watched, the nose appeared between the legs. It retracted, but came out again with the next contraction.

"She's doing a splendid job," I murmured.

"Should I pet Lady?" Henryk asked.

"No, leave her be. Her body knows what it's doing. We don't want to distress her in the slightest."

One more contraction and the entire head followed the nose. But when it came to the shoulders, progress stalled. Lady panted after each contraction. A minute passed, then another. Usually the front legs coming out staggered like that helped cock the shoulders for easy birthing, but these seemed hung up. Lady was tiring. I'd had to free up a human baby's shoulders once. In that case it presented a much more urgent situation, because the baby could suffer a starvation of blood to the brain if the head was born but the rest of the body remained inside for too long.

"I'm going to help her." I folded back the sac and grasped the foal's legs at the fetlocks. When Lady's uterus contracted again, I pulled. To my relief, the neck and shoulders slid out. The torso appeared a little at a time with each contraction until the hips. Progress stalled again.

Henryk started toward Lady. "I'll pull this time."

"Leave it, Henryk. The hips often take a couple of minutes." Lady seemed less tired now, just waiting it out.

Sure enough, the hips emerged before long and the foal began to stir. The baby turned its head and gazed at its mother. Once the rear legs emerged, the foal lay still on the hay. Lady reached over. She bit at and licked the membrane until it fell away from the newborn's body, revealing a curly coat moist and glistening.

I mused on how different this birth was than the ones I usually attended. We humans paid a price for our big brains. Women experienced labors that weren't always easy and birthed babies who were helpless for their first year and in need of care and protection until they were at least ten or even fifteen. We had sensitive skin that needed covering and we were prone to infections. We humans carefully tied off the umbilical cord and cut it with a clean blade, and we washed the baby with water. This mother horse didn't need a speck of help. She didn't mind that her baby was born on straw. The extent of the newborn bath was Lady licking him — and it was a male, as I'd just seen. The babe would be able to walk and stand up to nurse before an hour had passed.

"Is it all right, Miss Carroll?" Henryk's fingers fluttered at his sides, a gesture of a man not used to being idle. "The foal isn't moving."

"He's fine, Henryk. And it's a colt. See his chest moving, his eyes focusing? He is breathing and healthy. Thee only needs to wait."

After a few more minutes, Lady pushed herself up to standing, groaning with another contraction, needing to expel the placenta. The foal tried to stand but collapsed in a legs-akimbo heap. The attempt to stand severed the umbilical cord, which was not a problem for equines. The placenta plopped onto the hay with a small amount of blood. I was glad to see that Lady didn't continue to bleed.

The tiny colt tried to stand again, but was still too wobbly. Lady nickered at him, a sweet sound encouraging his efforts, and I smiled. I knew before long the infant horse would be stable.

I turned to Henryk. "Lady wants to be alone now. She might become aggressive if thee goes near. The colt looks well, and the afterbirth came out without a problem. We are done here."

He pressed a hand to his chest. "Thank you for coming, Miss Carroll." The worry lines between his eyebrows slid away as he swiped a hand across his forehead. "I wasn't sure if I needed you, and it's good you were here to help."

"I was happy to assist, and I'm glad to see that all is well with Lady and her baby boy.

What will thee name him?"

He held up his thick farmer's hands. "I'll let Lucy handle that. I wouldn't have the first idea on what to call him. Do you want to go home now? And what do I owe you for your services?"

Morning light now streamed in the high window facing east. "Thee doesn't owe me anything. I was glad to help. And yes, I would like to return home, if thee pleases." I had a few calls to make this morning, but they would be better done with Peaches and my buggy. Wallace Buckham had been on my list before, but now I had an extra reason to visit him.

TWENTY-EIGHT

By eight thirty I'd had coffee and eggs on toast at home, and was in my own transport, heading down Main Street toward the Merrimack River. I wanted to talk with Ransom's supervisor at Lowell's Boat Shop while Ransom was still out, and maybe have a little chat with Delia Davies, too. I drove slowly and carefully, and had brought a cushion to sit on. At least this buggy was built in a way that absorbed the bumps and bounces that came with any of Amesbury's roads.

A lad outside the boat shop took Peaches across the road to a stable while I picked my way along an icy path. The north-facing sides of buildings often received no direct sunlight on these short winter days, so packed-down snow turned to treacherous ice after enough feet had trod it. The last thing I needed was to fall and acquire yet more bruises. When I entered the office,

Delia Davies again sat at the front desk.

"Good morning, Delia," I said.

She blinked, her eyes as dark as Savoire's. "Yes?" Delia was as tall as her mother and bore her wide shoulders. Unlike Madame Restante, she carried no excess weight at all.

"I was in several days ago, to speak with Ransom Skells." I watched her.

She didn't react in her expression, but her throat moved as she swallowed. Nerves? She kept her back straight and shoulders back.

"The poor man, now a widower and father to motherless children." She shook her head in apparent sadness.

"I was with Charity Skells when she passed."

"I liked Charity, God rest her soul. We had become friendly recently." Delia blinked again. "Why were you with her? Were you also a friend of hers?"

Was she feigning a lack of memory? "No, I was her midwife, as I mentioned the first time I came in. I recently had occasion to speak with thy mother, as well."

"My mother?" she asked after a pause. "Why in the world would you see her?"

"Just some business I was conducting. She goes by Savoire Restante, if I'm not mistaken."

Delia straightened the already impeccable stack of papers in the center of her desk and lined up three pencils by size like a mini regiment. She finally raised her gaze to my face. "Was there something you needed here this morning, Miss Carroll?" She smiled with her mouth only.

Neither deny nor confirm. An interesting tactic. "I was hoping to speak with thy supervisor. It's about Ransom."

"Mr. Sherwood is occupied just now." She set her mouth as if daring me to challenge her, the gatekeeper.

"I can wait." I moved toward the chair facing her desk.

"No, he's out." The words came out in a rush. "Won't be back until this afternoon sometime."

"I see. I'll come back, then." I had turned to go when the outer door flew open with a rush of cold air. "Ah." I smiled at the newcomer. "The very man I wanted to see."

"Oh? And you might be?" the supervisor asked. He removed his now fogged-up eyeglasses.

"I'm Rose Carroll. I was Charity Skells's midwife, and I met thee briefly when I came to give Ransom the news of his wife's tragic demise." I shot a sideways glance at Delia, who busied herself with the items on her desk again, lips pressed tightly together.

"Yes," he said. "Forgive me for not re-membering you, Miss Carroll."

"I wondered if thee might have a moment to speak with me about Ransom."

"Certainly. Poor man. Come through to my office, will you?" He gestured toward an inner door. "Miss Davies, please don't let anyone disturb us."

"Yes, Mr. Sherwood." She folded her hands primly in front of her.

I followed the supervisor into a bigger office, but all the extra space was taken up with model boats, schematic drawings posted on the walls, and piles of magazines and books wherever the eye looked. He closed the door after us and asked me to sit as he shed his hat and coat. The desk also bore a carved name plate, his reading *Jonathan Sherwood.*

"I thank thee for seeing me, Jonathan." I eased myself into a chair, protecting my sore hip.

His head pulled back in surprise at my use of his first name.

"I am a member of the Religious Society of Friends. As we are all equal in God's eyes, we don't believe in the use of titles." I smiled to soften my words. "And please address me as Rose in return."

"I see. Very well, Rose." His surprise turned to amusement with a small smile creeping into the corner of his mouth. "That's fine, then. How is Mr. Skells faring?" he asked, taking a seat behind the desk.

"I saw him again yesterday afternoon. He is stricken with grief and overwhelmed with his situation, I believe."

"I myself am the father of five. I cannot begin to imagine losing my children's mother and what that would have done to the poor tykes when they were younger."

"The baby doesn't really know, but the rest of them are having a very hard time of it, especially the eldest, who is acting out her sorrow with anger."

He nodded. "She'll have to grow up before her time now that her mother is gone."

"I expect so. Was Ransom regular in his appearance here? Did he ever have any unexplained absences?"

"I'm not sure why you are asking." He waited for my answer.

"Jonathan," I began in a low tone, "thee must have heard by now that Charity's death came at the hands of another." When he nodded, I continued. "I am assisting the police detective in gathering facts about the case."

"Very well. Yes, Mr. Skells did have a number of absences and tardy arrivals. Several times he appeared late and made up an explanation that sounded rather implausible to me. But he's a good worker and I wanted to give him a chance."

"I thank thee. I also wanted to be sure thee knew of the memorial service tomorrow afternoon," I went on. "It will be held at the Friends Meetinghouse at two o'clock in the afternoon. I'm sure the family will welcome thy presence." What I really wanted to do was steer the conversation in the direction of any dalliance between Ransom and Delia, but I wasn't quite sure how to accomplish that.

"Yes, in fact Mrs. Swift sent me a notice about it. I have asked Mr. Lowell to join me if he is able. You know, of course, that I am only a supervisor here. I work for the Lowells."

"A fine family who has done much for our town. Thee also did a great service to Ransom by offering him bereavement pay for this week. Many managers wouldn't be so generous."

"Thank you. We — the Lowells and I — believe treating our employees with kindness and respect is paramount in running an effective business. They work hard for us in return and turn out high-quality boats."

"Admirable." I spied my opening. "And I assume the workers treat each other well, too. Thee has a single lady working here, Delia Davies. Do Ransom and the other men get along with her?"

He cocked his head, regarding me. "That's a curious question."

I waited in silence.

"Of course they all get along. Skells in particular has been quite, shall we say, solicitous of Miss Davies." He lowered his voice from previously and raised one eyebrow.

"Solicitous?"

"Helping her onto the trolley, eating dinner with her, that kind of thing."

"Does thee think perhaps Ransom's solicitude toward Delia went beyond that of a friendly fellow worker?"

He turned and looked out the window. My gaze followed his to see a snow-covered tree, the iced-in river, and an enormous dark eagle beating its wings, its keen eyes boring out of the white head in search of prey.

Jonathan faced me again. "If you are thinking what I imagine you are, I would say that you may well be correct about the degree of their friendship. However, I have seen nothing egregious, nothing to reprimand either of them about. It's just a sense I have, glances of a certain type they have exchanged, that kind of thing." He cleared his throat. "But surely you can't think that either of them would kill Mrs. Skells over such matters."

"It doesn't matter what I think. I'm simply gathering facts for the official investigation." Which was getting more interesting by the hour.

Twenty-Nine

I stood in front of an impressively large house on Moody Street fifteen minutes later. It was new and featured a round tower on one corner of the building topped by a conical roof reaching above the rest of the house. This sort of residence was becoming popular around town. I'd always imagined the charm of the very top room, that it could hold a comfortable chair and table, that one could while away the hours reading and gazing over the countryside in all directions.

I checked the slip of paper in my hand again, which bore the address for Wallace Buckham. This was the place, and what a place it was. Did his herbalist business do so well he could afford to build such a big abode, such an elegantly proportioned house? I shrugged, tying Peaches to a hitching post. I stroked his neck.

"I won't be long," I promised. I glanced

up and down the street. It ran between Highland and Hillside Streets and was just off Greenwood, two blocks from where I had discovered a body on my way home from a birth some months ago. Despite my resolve last night to exercise renewed caution in my investigations, here I was alone on a road with only one other house nearby. But that building was directly across the street. The day was full of light, despite it being the weak cold light of winter, and I had a horse and buggy at the ready. If I let myself be cowed by fear, I'd never find out anything.

And I doubted this herbalist was Charity's killer, anyway. I simply needed to follow up all leads, and he was one. I marched up to the door and rang the bell. The brass plate next to it read DR. WALLACE BUCKHAM. His advertisement hadn't mentioned that he held a medical degree. Henryk had said Buckham called himself that and had implied he was a sham physician. With a spacious, fancy house, it looked very much like he earned a bona fide doctor's pay. I'd have to ask David this afternoon what he knew about Dr. Buckham.

The door was opened by a lean, dark-haired man with a pointed beard extending from his chin. He wore spectacles over dark eyes. His collar was the color of fresh snow and his suit and waistcoat of a fine wool. I was surprised he'd opened the door himself.

"Good morning, miss. I am Dr. Buckham. May I help you?" He didn't smile, but his voice was a gentle one.

"I am Rose Carroll. I'm a midwife, Wallace, and wanted to speak with thee about thy herbal offerings. It seems we might have a common goal of helping women regain and maintain good health." I smiled. "But thy advertisement in the newspaper didn't mention thee also practices medicine."

If he was surprised by my use of his Christian name, he didn't show it. "Please come in, Miss Carroll. Your skills as a midwife are well-regarded in the community."

So he knew of me. "I thank thee. Please call me Rose." I followed him into an airy and tastefully decorated foyer, with a wide staircase curving gracefully upwards. A stained-glass window on the landing softened the light with color.

"I am with a patient just now. Please have a seat and I'll be with you in a few minutes." He disappeared into a door to my right, the latch clicking behind him. An engraved plaque on the door read simply, OFFICE. The room was one that in other homes of this size might be the library or perhaps a sitting room.

Instead of taking him up on his invitation to sit, I wandered around the foyer. On the walls hung several paintings of families, whether his or of others I did not know. Something seemed similar about all of them. I studied each in turn. At the third I murmured, "Aha." To a one, the portraits featured families with well-spaced children. There were no stair-stepped six in a row, each a year apart. With the linen-suited father and summer-dressed mother in one family stood a boy of about fifteen, already towering over his mother, and a girl of eleven or twelve, her hair not yet put up and her skirts not yet let down. A younger girl of Betsy's age was a miniature version of her sister, and a toddler wore a little sailor suit. Another family of five were similarly spaced, and the third painting showed more of the same. Was one of these families Wallace's? Either way, the pictures taken together looked very much like advertisements for Wallace Buckham's women's health services. Finally I took a seat.

After ten minutes the office door opened again. The doctor ushered out a woman, who clutched a small paper sack and wore a grateful expression. He showed her the door and then turned to me. "Thank you for waiting, Miss Carroll." He made a little bow as he gestured toward the office. "Please come in and make yourself comfortable."

Inside I perched on an upholstered chair, careful of my hip, and folded my hands in my lap. The office, much larger and more well-appointed than Savoire's, featured some of the same items as hers. A long table with dozens of canisters labeled with the names of herbs from pennyroyal to black hellebore to savin. A scale. A stack of mailing envelopes. An ornate oriental screen blocked a corner, as in Savoire's office. But Wallace also had an examination table positioned near the half-curtained windows, and another counter containing metal instruments, one of the new flexible binaural stethoscopes, a rubber triangular reflex hammer, and other tools of a physician's trade. A telephone sat on his wide desk in front of a set of medical texts, including the one I most frequently consulted, Leishman's *A System of Midwifery.*

"I see thee has Leishman's on thy desk. Does thee include deliveries in thy practice?"

"No, I leave that to expert midwives such as yourself. But it's a good reference volume on women's health, wouldn't you agree?" He sat in the wooden arm chair in front of his desk, swiveling it to face me.

"Certainly." How could I ease into my questions? His seat gave me an idea. "Does thee know Thomas Jefferson invented the swivel chair?" I asked. "A brilliant invention."

"Indeed? I did not know that." He narrowed his eyes ever so slightly. "But you didn't come here to talk about furniture."

"No. Thy advertisement was for an herbalist, but it appears thee practices conventional medicine, as well. Does thee have a specialty?"

"Yes, I am an orthopedic surgeon. I primarily correct deformities in children's feet and legs."

"That's good and needed work," I said.

"I believe so."

"I came here not to talk about orthopedics, though. I noticed the portraits in your hall feature families with nicely spaced children. Sometimes my pregnant mothers visit me bringing maladies brought on by too many births in a short span of years. I was curious about the products and services thee advertises." I didn't see any reason not to use the same phrasing I'd used with Savoire.

He tented his fingers. "I see." He seemed to ponder for a moment, and then came to a decision. He swiveled back and selected a red pamphlet from his desk. He half rose to hand it to me. "This is my catalog."

A little bell rang at the back of my brain, but I couldn't think why. I thanked the doctor and leafed through it. The listings were very much like Savoire's. "Has thee been able to steer clear of the Comstock laws?"

"I offer only legal remedies, Miss Carroll." His nostrils flared and he blinked. "It's important for women to be able to regularize their systems."

"I agree. But what if a patient comes to thee early in a pregnancy bearing an unwanted child? Often women are forced to bear babies they cannot afford to care for. They could be unmarried and fear society's approbation, or be pregnant because of a violent assault. Does thee ever assist a woman like that in reversing her situation?"

He stood. "Our interview is over, Miss Carroll. I have heard not only of your reputation as a midwife but also of your repute as an amateur assistant to the police. I sense your purpose here is to learn whether I caused that poor woman's death this week. I did not, and I'll thank you to leave." His voice was no longer gentle, his expression no longer kindly and welcoming.

Within a minute I was down the front

stairs, the thud of the door slamming behind me resonating in my ears. That certainly had not gone as planned, although I wasn't sure how I'd expected him to react. Should he have said, "Why, yes, I do perform criminal mechanical abortions with one of these probes here on my table"? I glanced at my hand. I still grasped the pamphlet he'd given me. He must have been too angry to notice. I hurried down the walk to Peaches to make my getaway before the good doctor came back out to demand it. I thought Kevin just might be interested.

THIRTY

With my ban from the police station in effect, I made my way to Kevin's home once again. The church bells all over town tolled eleven, so I would make this visit brief. I still needed to get home and make a nice soup for David's visit, although he was unlikely to arrive before one o'clock. I had time so long as no black wagons came after me. The thought rippled a shudder through me and Peaches tossed his head. The shudder must have transmitted through the reins to him. How much did he remember from last night? I wished I could question the gelding. *Did you recognize the horse pulling the wagon? What did you see of the driver? Was anything written on the side of the wagon?*

I laughed out loud, my balance restored. Lore had it animals could speak between midnight and dawn on Christmas Eve. This being Second Month, that night was a long way away. I didn't believe the myth, anyway. It was going to be up to me to answer those questions, not the docile and dependable Peaches. Who now obediently pulled to a halt in front of the Donovan family home. Sean crouched out front, adding to a pile of several dozen snowballs near the wall of the house. I climbed out and hailed him.

"Is thee stockpiling ammunition, Sean?"

"Yes, Miss Rose."

I smiled at his use of his father's appellation for me.

"When Jimmy gets home from school we're going to have a snowball fight," he explained. "He's my friend, but he has to go to regular school."

Clearly, Jimmy had the worse end of the stick in Sean's view. And what child wouldn't prefer to stay home and make snowballs? Jimmy probably envied Sean his freedom, not realizing his friend was learning at a more rapid pace than Jimmy was ever likely to.

I held the gelding's reins. "Would thee mind watching Peaches again while I speak with thy mother? I won't be long."

He stood, his face a glow. "Don't worry about a thing, Miss Rose. I'll take good care of him. And if anybody tries to steal him, I have my weapons ready." He saluted like a miniature soldier. No Quakers in this family.

I thanked him and rang the doorbell, the red pamphlet securely in my bag. After Emmaline greeted me and said to come in, I replied, "I can't tarry. But I have a few more bits of information to relay to Kevin."

She frowned but led the way to a desk. "Why don't you sit and write down the facts? I don't want to forget anything, and I don't want to telephone Kevin at work today." She set out a sheet of paper and a sharpened pencil.

"Why the frown, Emmaline?"

"Oh, that new chief of his is on the war path about the death. Wants the case solved yesterday. Doesn't he understand these things take time? He's threatening to demote Kevin if he doesn't make an arrest by the end of today."

"I'm sorry to hear that." I sat at the desk. "And that's why thee doesn't want to call him?"

She nodded.

"Perhaps what I've learned will help him avoid his superior's threat." I began to scribble. I touched on the trust arrangements I'd learned from Sophie and what they meant. I wrote down a summary of my attack last night, assuring him that I was

228

fine, and added what Henryk had said about Wallace Buckham. What else? I relayed what Jonathan Sherwood mentioned about Ransom and Delia's friendship, and his alluding it might have been more than that. And finally Wallace's reaction to my inquiries. I appended a suggestion.

Thee might want to check into Wallace Buckham's reputed medical practice. I don't understand why a successful surgeon, and he appears to be one by the size of his new house, would conduct an herbalist business for women on the side.

I jotted down the doctor's Moody Street address, then glanced up at my hostess. "It's fine if thee reads my notes, Emmaline."

She glanced at the sheet and gasped. "You were attacked?"

"Yes. But I'm fine," I added in haste when I saw the horrified expression on her face. "Truly I am."

"Kevin won't be happy to hear about it." Her tone took on a touch of scolding.

"I know he won't." I stood and held my arms out to my sides. "I look fine, don't I? Tell him." I turned from side to side, but winced when my neck and upper back protested.

"I suppose," she said slowly. "You should be careful, Rose."

"I am." I laid the pamphlet next to the paper. "I was given this by Wallace Buckham. Please make sure Kevin gets it."

"I will. What is it?"

I hadn't even leafed through the pages and did so now. "Buckham claims to be an herbalist who helps women regulate their monthlies. I wonder if he might do more to, ah . . ." I glanced at her. She likely shared her husband's view on controlling family spacing. "To help women who are pregnant but don't wish to be."

She gave me a level gaze. "To help them abort?"

"Yes."

"Interesting. Even though that's not a service I'll ever need, I think there are cases where it is well justified."

I smiled at her. "I am in agreement with thee, although only using herbal methods. Mechanical abortions are simply too dangerous. To wit, we have to find the person who perforated Charity's womb. Of course Buckham denied it, but I want Kevin to investigate him. The doctor reacted rather too virulently to my suggestion that he was an abortionist, I thought."

"He protested too much?" she asked,

pointing to a volume of Shakespeare's work on a nearby bookshelf.

"Exactly."

THIRTY-ONE

I rested my cheek on David's chest in the front hallway of my house at a little past one. "I have missed thee so," I murmured into the smooth cloth of his shirt as I inhaled his delicious smell of healthy man, today with a slight air of soot added from his train trip.

He stroked my hair, which I'd unpinned and let flow loose down my back before he arrived. "And I, you, Rose," he said with an accompaniment of growling stomach.

I pulled away and laughed. "It sounds like thee is ready for a good home-cooked meal."

His eyes twinkled at me. "Almost nothing could sound so alluring. You can fill me in on your busy week as we eat."

I'd made it home in time to put together a thick ham and potato soup, which, with fresh bread and butter and glasses of sweet cider, were going to be our meal. I'd already set the table for two and sent Lina home early so I could have a rare hour alone with my betrothed. I had no antenatal appointments scheduled for a few hours, and as long as I didn't get summoned to Lucy's birth, we could cherish our time together.

David sat at the table. I was ladling soup into deep bowls at the stove when I twisted my neck to glance at him.

"Ow," I said at a sharp pinch in my neck.

"What is it, Rosie dear?" He stood and hurried to my side.

"It's nothing. My neck is a bit stiff from a little accident I had last night."

His eyes went wide. "An accident?"

"Yes. Here, let's sit and have our blessing before I tell thee." I handed him one bowl and took the other to the table. We sat and held hands in silence, holding this moment and our meal in the Light of God. I squeezed his hand and opened my eyes.

"Now, fill thy grumbling stomach." After a good mouthful of soup and a bite of bread and butter, I related what had happened on my way home from Bertie's. "It was a deliberate hit. Whoever it was, was definitely aiming for me. I only wish I'd had a chance to see the driver's face or check the wagon for markings. But the night was too dark and it all happened so fast."

"And you were knocked down the embankment?" he asked, concern filling his voice.

"Yes. But what a blessing that Peaches was neither harmed nor lost his head. He brought himself home and waited for me here. I'm afraid the buggy has a bit of a dent in the back left side, though. I'm sorry."

"I don't care about the buggy! I care about you, my Rosie. I'm so glad you weren't hurt. Your neck muscles are sore as a result of the buggy being hit. Your neck will likely become more stiff throughout the day. It's from your head being whipped forward and back after the impact." He savored a bite of soup before going on. "I worry for you constantly, darling, when we are apart." Lines etched his brow.

"I know. Thee worries even when only the Merrimack separates us." I suppressed a smile.

"Rose, it isn't funny. You're investigating the death of the woman who bled out. Let me guess. It's a homicide."

"Apparently so. I didn't want to tell thee on the telephone, but the autopsy showed that her uterus was perforated in several places." I was no longer smiling.

He frowned. "It could have been an incompetent abortionist who killed her without intent."

"That's possible. But there are several people and circumstances that make me think — and Kevin Donovan agrees — that it might have been a purposeful homicide."

"So you're investigating and someone found out. You know I hate it when you put yourself in danger like that."

"I'm aware of that." I took a sip of cider, careful not to move my head too far in either direction. "And I vowed to be very careful, but I can't not ask questions."

He sighed. "I know you can't. Who are the suspicious people? Let me guess. The husband?"

"Exactly. Father of six, he wouldn't hear about family spacing. And now it appears he is stepping out with — and yes, that's a euphemism — a young single woman at his place of employment. Whose mother is possibly an abortionist. She certainly deals in abortifacient herbs."

"That's a messy can of worms."

"Indeed. In addition, there's an equally messy situation with an inheritance coming to the children of the victim and her cousins' children. The husband and another cousin might have thought they could lay their hands on the money, but Bertie's sweetheart Sophie told me she is the administrator of the trust, not the parents."

"What a confusion." David shook his head. "Although is it any less of a web of suspects and lies than the other cases you were involved in?"

"I don't suppose so. But now I can't even go to the police station to speak with Kevin." I told him about the new chief's new strictures. "So I've been going to Kevin's home and leaving messages for him with his wife, a delightful woman named Emmaline."

"I hope you told him about the attack last night."

"Yes, I did." I popped the rest of my bread in my mouth. I loved the sour flavor, the chewy texture, the crunchy crust. I almost could live on bread alone. I sometimes did when at a prolonged labor after I'd been summoned without the chance to eat a proper meal.

"David, does thee know a doctor named Wallace Buckham here in Amesbury? He says he's an orthopedist."

He nodded slowly. "Why do you ask?"

"He advertises himself as an herbalist who treats women, and his notice in the newspaper did not mention the title of doctor. I thought he might be providing abortion services, and went to speak to him this morning. My questions were apparently too direct, because he showed me the door in high dudgeon."

"He has a less than stellar reputation."

"Oh?"

"I'll have to check the details, but I seem to recall some incident with the mother of one of his pediatric patients. It's possible he was censured by the AMA's Judicial Council and has ceased practicing medicine."

"What's the AMA?"

"Sorry. The American Medical Association. It's the national governing body for my profession, and ethical issues are in their purview. I'll check on Buckham and let you know what I learn."

"I'd appreciate that. So if Wallace's pediatric orthopedic practice is closed, then maybe what he calls his women's health offerings are his only source of income. The husband of one of my clients told me his wife had gone to Wallace last year for 'lady problems,' as he put it, but she didn't like him. The husband called him a babykiller." I pictured the foal coming out. "I was at their farm early this morning to help birth a foal, David."

"You're expanding your practice, my dear?" He covered my hand with his.

I laughed. "No, this farmer is young and inexperienced. I grew up seeing horses and cows born. It's a mammal's birth, after all. Even though large animals have certain issues different from humans, much of the birth process is the same."

"It's good you could help, then." David finished his soup. "Is Faith excited about her impending wedding?"

"She's beside herself, full of excitement vying with anxiety. I told her all will be well on First Day, but she can't quite believe it." I giggled. "David, I had to give her a basic lesson in the sexual act and how to avoid pregnancy. She didn't know the first thing, but wanted to learn."

He set his chin on his palm and gazed at me. "Come here, you beautiful woman." When he opened his arms, I flounced onto his lap with a grin, throwing my arms around his neck.

"Yes, handsome man?"

"You know how eager I am for our own wedding night." His voice was low, husky, as I imagined it would be in our bedchamber one day soon.

I closed my eyes and pressed myself against him, moving, luxuriating in the sensations even through a half dozen layers of cloth. "Mmm. I am, too." My breathing grew rapid and shallow. Warmth flooded me from my intimate parts outward. I slid off and kissed him hard and deep. I took his hand. "Come with me."

His dark eyebrows rose nearly to his hairline as he stood. He kissed me, murmuring, "Are you sure?"

"Come."

THIRTY-TWO

I pinned up my hair again after David left an hour later, smiling to myself at what a special reunion we'd had. I had a pregnant client coming at three. It was time to fix my mind on my business, not on my sweet love nor the mystery of this week's confounding death.

I tidied my parlor, washed up, and reviewed my client's history. I'd seen her for only one visit so far and needed to refresh my memory about her health and her prior births. I didn't have to worry about dinner. Faith and I had agreed yesterday on a simple dinner tonight of Indian griddle cakes and what *Clayton's Quaker Cookbook* called a Quaker Omelette. The two of us always shared a laugh at the term. What did this man know about Friends? The book, published five years ago in San Francisco, mentioned only that the author grew up cooking with his mother, not that he was a

Friend. It didn't matter, because the omelette was a delicious, nourishing, and easy dish. Plus there was plenty of soup left over from our lunch.

My client was late. The clock read three fifteen and she still hadn't arrived. I paced the short length of my parlor and back. Last year I'd lost a client's business because her husband hadn't allowed her to use the midwifery services of someone associated with violent death — me. I hope that wasn't happening again. A minute later the doorbell rang and I hurried to answer it.

"I'm sorry, Rose," the woman said, her cheeks flushed from the cold. "I tried to hail a conveyance but none were to be had, so I walked as fast as I could."

I greeted her, the first Scottish client I'd had, and added, "It's not a problem. I'm glad thee made it. Please come in." I hung up her coat and hat and showed her into my parlor. "How has thee been feeling since our last visit?"

"I felt the wee thing move! You know I have already the two bairns at home, but it's such a glorious thing to sense the wee new being come to life." She shook her head in amazement.

"I'm glad of it. Thy baby will be born in the warmer weather, which is pleasant for

241

both it and thee."

She frowned. "Rose, I had a wee natter with one of your other wifies, who tossed some blether about Charity Skells. She said it was" — she lowered her voice to a near-whisper — "murder. Is it true? My man, he told me not to come today, but I said, nonsense. Rose didn't kill that poor wifie, I told him."

"I thank thee for that, and I certainly didn't kill poor Charity. It's true that she died of unnatural means. I don't believe the police have yet ascertained whether it was a homicide or not."

The telephone bell commenced to ring in the sitting room. I jumped to my feet. "Please excuse me. I'll be right back."

My client nodded, so I hurried into the next room. I lifted the hearing device and spoke. "Bailey household, Rose Carroll, midwife, speaking."

"Miss Carroll, there's a lady in labor," Gertrude said.

"Please put her through." I waited until the sound changed. "Hello? This is Rose Carroll." But there was no response. I heard breathing, and a tapping sound. "Hello? Is there a laboring woman in need of my services? Who's calling, please?"

More near-silence. More breathing. I

frowned at the telephone. Could this be the woman herself and she wasn't able to speak? Then who had told the operator a laboring lady wanted to talk with me? "Who's there?" I queried anew.

"You need to lay off the snooping," a hoarse voice said.

The snooping. My heart dropped like a weight in my chest. "What? Who is this?" I realized I was almost screeching. I didn't want to alarm my client so I lowered my voice. "Is there a woman in labor?"

"Maybe. Maybe not. Quit nosing around where it's not your business. Or you'll end up in the same place as Charity Skells."

What? A click followed and the sound in my ear turned dead, as if the connection had been severed. I pulled the listening device away from my ear and stared at it, my hand shaking. My throat was so thick I could barely swallow. Goosebumps stood erect on my arms and the back of my neck. The caller could be Charity's killer, or someone close to the killer. Maybe he — or she — was the same person who had attacked me last night. Maybe my threatener was . . . I suddenly remembered I could talk to Gertrude again. I depressed the lever twice.

"Gertrude, is thee there?"

After a brief moment she came on the line "Yes, Miss Carroll?"

"Who put that call in?"

"I don't know. He didn't give a name."

"It was a man?" I asked.

"I actually don't know. The voice was too raspy to tell. Could have been a lady, I s'pose."

I hadn't been able to tell, either. "Does thee know where the call originated?"

"Hang on."

I heard switches, clicks, and women's voices chattering in the background, saying things like "One moment, please," and "A call for you, ma'am."

Gertrude came back on the line. "No, I can't tell. It might have been one of those telephone cabinets they have in the fancy hotels, where you pay fifteen cents to make a call."

I'd heard about telephone cabinets. Did Amesbury have any? "Thank you." I hung up and took a few deep calming breaths until my heart rate had returned to something approaching normal before rejoining my client.

"Rose, what's to do? You sounded feart there." Her eyes were wide.

"I'm not scared. It was a prank call." I tried to laugh. "Now that telephones are becoming more commonplace, apparently lunatics and scoundrels are paying money to bother innocent people. It's not a problem." I swallowed, thick though my throat remained, and inhaled deeply. "Let's listen to that wee heartbeat, shall we?"

THIRTY-THREE

By five o'clock the house was full of female voices. Faith was home, as were the younger children. Faith's friend — and my apprentice — Annie Beaumont had come straight from the Boston & Maine train. Alma had just arrived with Faith's dress, and Betsy, Faith, and Annie were cooing over it. My last client had just left, so I joined them in the kitchen. This company would help greatly to push worrisome thoughts of threatening telephone calls out of mind.

"I thought I'd save you the trouble of coming to fetch the dress," Alma said.

"I thank thee," Faith answered, running a finger along the shirring.

Betsy clapped her nine-year-old hands. Her eyes gleamed. "I want one just like it when I get married."

"That day's a long way off, Miss Betsy," Alma said, stroking Betsy's hair. Her older daughter was only a couple of years younger than our Betsy. "Faith, run and try it on, will you? I want to be sure I don't need to alter it."

"Use my room, dear," I called after her as she swept away with the dress over her arm.

"Alma, sit and tell me how Orpha fares," I said. "I saw her this week and to my eyes she seems recovered." I had found Orpha on the floor of Alma's house last summer. My teacher had been incoherent from apoplexy and dehydration.

"She is well. Her mind remains clear, a blessing."

I nodded.

"She grows more frail," Alma went on, "but that doesn't stop her from going out and doing as she pleases."

"And thy children keep her spirits up, I dare say."

"That they do." Alma smiled.

I turned to Annie. "Annie, I want to know how the course went."

"It was excellent, Rose. I learned so much." She covered her mouth as she yawned. "Please pardon me, I didn't get much sleep last night. We midwife-trainees stayed up late sharing stories. I made some good friends there."

"I'm pleased."

"How has the practice been this week?" Annie asked. "Did I miss any births?"

"No, although I think Lucy Majowski will go any day now." I opened my mouth to tell her about Charity's death and shut it just as promptly. Not here, not now, especially not with both Betsy and Alma in the room.

Annie nodded as Faith shyly appeared in the door. The dress fell perfectly on her slim figure, and the slate blue flattered her fresh skin and dark eyes.

Betsy jumped up and down, her hands clasped in front of her. "Thee is so pretty in it, Faith!"

"Come in and give it a turnaround," Alma said.

Faith obliged, lifting her arms to the sides. She turned slowly under the seamstress's critical gaze.

"No, I think it's perfect," Alma said. "Doesn't need a bit of altering."

"That's a relief." Faith sank into a chair. "I'm not sure I can stand even one thing getting in the way of my marrying Zeb."

"I'll be going, then," Alma said. She picked up her quilted bag.

"I hope thee will join us on First Day for the marriage, Alma."

"I would be honored, and that way I can accompany Nana Orpha. Thank you for inviting me, Faith."

Faith rose and retrieved an envelope on the sideboard. "Here is thy pay. I'm exceedingly grateful thee was able to finish the dress in such short time."

"Thank you. But the rush, it was nothing. It's better than having to make mourning attire in a hurry, I can tell you."

Annie gave a little shudder and crossed herself.

"Alma, please give my love to Orpha," I said.

"I will do that. She asked to be remembered to you, too."

Faith showed Alma to the door and went to change out of the wedding dress.

"Is everything set for Sunday?" Annie asked Faith once we were all seated around the table again. "For the wedding?"

"I think so," my niece said. "Zeb is in charge of the certificate of marriage."

"What's that?" Annie looked puzzled.

"When Friends are married," I began, "they prepare a large sheet of parchment that includes their wedding vows, the date, and other details. After they pronounce their vows to each other, the man and woman sign it during the Meeting for Marriage. At the end of the Meeting, everyone present also signs the certificate as witnesses to the union. Often the couple frames the certificate. They hang it in their house in a place of honor."

"That's beautiful," Annie said with a wondering look on her face. "We Catholics don't do anything of the kind."

"Do I get to sign it, too?" Betsy asked, looking hopeful.

"Thee can sign thy name already, can't thee?" Faith asked.

"Of course I can! I'm not a baby."

"Then thee will sign the certificate, too," I assured my younger niece.

Faith frowned. "I'm just so afraid something will —"

I interrupted. "Faith, it will all go smoothly. We had this talk, remember?" I stroked her hand.

"I remember, and thee is my rock to be so calm, Rose. I can't wait for Granny and Grandfather to arrive tomorrow, too."

"When is their train due in?" I asked.

"At seven in the evening. Zeb and I will fetch them at the station."

"You know Granny will calm thee, too," I said. "Thy wedding will be perfect."

"And I get to be the flower girl?" Betsy asked.

"Betsy, dear," I said. "Friends don't have fancy things like flower girls at our Meetings for Marriage."

Her face fell. Her lower lip quivered, but I knew she wouldn't cry. She was too old for pouts even though I knew she was disappointed.

"But thee and I can greet the guests together at the door," I continued. "Would that make thee happy? It's a very special job."

She sat up straight. "I'll help thee, Auntie Rose. I'm a very good greeter. John Whittier said so himself."

I tried not to smile. "I know he did." I spied Faith and Annie also working hard to keep from laughing, but it was true. Last year when I'd been assigned the job of welcomer in the hall outside the worship room, Betsy had stood with me, and John had said exactly that to her. "Now go play in the sitting room until dinner, will thee?"

"Thee can always ask for my help," Betsy said. "I'm getting very big now that I'm nine." Off she ran.

"Thank thee, Rose," Faith said. "She's been asking nearly every hour if she can be my flower girl."

"We could have had her give thee a nosegay to carry if it weren't winter," I replied.

Faith rose and fixed us each a cup of tea. Annie cocked her head. "Rose, they're talking about you all the way down in Boston." She kept her voice low.

"They are?" I asked.

"Indeed. The news of the woman with the perforated uterus was quite the topic of conversation among the midwives this week."

I scratched my head. "I didn't realize Charity's death had made the newspapers."

"It must have."

"And how was my name associated with the news?"

"Simply that you were the woman's midwife. Except it wasn't that simple, really. Some whispered you had attempted to perform the abortion yourself."

I gasped at the same time as Faith set the hot mugs on the table. "I never would! Who said that?"

"I don't know. It was whispers in the corner, like. But our teacher, who knows you well, defended you. She asserted to everyone, as you just did, that you would never perform a mechanical abortion, and that none of us ever should, either."

"Did the gathering believe her?" Faith asked. "About Rose, I mean?"

"It helped her case, certainly," Annie replied.

This was not the first time my practice

had been imperiled by gossip. What if those new midwives spread the word that I'd expanded my practice to include abortions, and that I was dangerously unskilled? Besides losing my existing customers, I might also be arrested for violating the Comstock laws. I could only pray the teacher's words had convinced the whisperers.

THIRTY-FOUR

Lucy Majowski leaned both forearms on the dresser in her bedroom, moaning her way through a contraction. Her flannel nightgown was faded, but mended and clean.

"Thee is doing very well, Lucy." I used my most soothing voice and rubbed the small of her back.

Henryk had come to fetch me two hours ago at nine o'clock, just as I was about to go to bed. Worry carved fresh lines in his face as he said his wife was having regular pains and wanted me to come. I sent him along back home, saying I would follow right away. The night air was cold and smelled of snow, but I hurried out and harnessed Peaches to my buggy. I didn't want to make Henryk leave home after the birth was accomplished, whenever that ended up being.

Now the gas light in the upstairs farmhouse bedroom was a steady beacon. Henryk kept the big kitchen stove going down below, and a vent in the floor let the warm air rise into the bedchamber. Lucy's pain finished and she plopped back on the bed. I noted the time on the watch I pinned to my bosom.

"How much more of this will I have, Rose?" she asked in plaintive tone.

I smiled gently. "You'll be in labor until your baby is born. I can't predict exactly how long it will take, because every woman is different and so is every newborn. When I arrived thee was about six fingers dilated, and thy cervix must open to ten before thy baby's head enters the birth canal. But remember, thy body is made for this work. Women have been birthing babies for all of time. The child will come out, fear not."

Lucy closed her eyes. Good. She needed to rest while she could. I surveyed the room. Lucy had followed all my recommendations and the space was nicely prepared for the delivery. A towel was spread on a low chest of drawers, and a stack of clean folded cloths sat atop it next to two empty basins. When Lucy got closer to pushing the baby out, I would ask Henryk to bring up recently boiled water. The dresser she'd been leaning on had a drawer full of baby blankets and tiny clothes, and another held a sufficient number of diapers. This couple was ready to be parents.

Lucy eased down onto her side. When another pain set in, I checked my watch. Ninety seconds since the last one. Things were progressing. When I'd arrived the contractions were two minutes apart. I moved to her head.

"Sit up more, Lucy. I'll put pillows behind thee."

She obliged, but halfway through the contraction she slid her legs onto the floor and stood. "It hurts when I lie down," she muttered.

"It's good to stand. Gravity will help the baby come down. Put thy arm around my shoulder."

Her weight was heavy, but I was tall and strong. I could hold her. When the pain finished, she removed her hand and placed both on the back of her hips in the classic late-pregnancy stance. She stood swaying, rocking from side to side and rolling her hips in a figure eight. I'd read about the ancient art of belly dancing, and that it was originally a dance for pregnant women to strengthen their abdominal muscles. Once in labor the dance movements helped relieve their pains. Lucy seemed to have an intuition that these kinds of movements would help her.

"Rose, did I ever tell you about when I visited that quack doctor Buckham last year?"

My ears perked at that. "No, although Henryk mentioned it yesterday. Why does thee say this man is a quack?"

"I saw his advertisement in the newspaper. Henryk and me, we wanted to have a baby right away. I thought Dr. Buckham's ad said he helped women. But when I talked with him, it was clear he wanted to help me not have babies, or to rid myself of one if I was with child." A groan escaped her lips. "Here's another pain." Her rotating movements slowed but she kept her body moving in the same way.

I wiped the moisture off her brow when the pain was through.

"I stood up and left that instant." Lucy picked up where she had left off. "I told him he ought to be ashamed of himself."

"Family spacing isn't a bad thing, but it was clearly not what thee wanted. Now I'd like thee to lie down. After the next contraction I'll check thy progress."

I led her to the bed and had her sit again with pillows boosting her up. "There," I said. "Is thee comfortable?"

"As comfortable as a person can get with

a blooming watermelon trying to get out of her bottom."

I laughed. "Tell me, what did Buckham want to give thee to prevent pregnancy?"

"Some herbs, I don't remember which. But Rose, he also hinted at a way to remove a pregnancy if the herbs alone didn't work."

As I suspected.

"That's when I walked out," Lucy continued. "He's a babykiller and I didn't want any part of it." She pushed her hair back off a brow glistening with sweat. "And I'm fairly certain I saw Delia leaving when I arrived. Remember, the girl you asked about? I do hope she isn't getting herself into trouble." She let out a low moan. "Here's another one."

I waited through her next contraction. So Delia had visited Buckham last year. Why? If she needed contraceptives, she could simply ask her own mother. Unless she didn't want her mother knowing that she, an unmarried woman, was being intimate with a man. Or perhaps she'd asked Buckham to terminate a pregnancy.

"Remember," I told Lucy when the contraction was over. "Breathe into my hand if this is uncomfortable." I slid two fingers into her passage and felt the soft, opening cervix, but it wasn't much more open or thinned out than when I'd arrived. I removed my hand and wiped it on a cloth.

"How am I doing?" she asked, eyes widening as yet another pain set in.

"Not quite ready, but things are moving along." They weren't moving along very fast, but she didn't need discouraging news like that. First labors were often long affairs. A *primigravida* woman's body had never done birthing work before. The connective tissues, while loosened by the processes of pregnancy, were still as yet unstretched. I had palpated the baby when I first arrived and it was head down as well as face down, in the optimal position for birth. Lucy and Henryk's baby would be born before dawn, I expected. But how long before I wouldn't dare to predict.

Meanwhile, she'd possibly given me another piece in the Charity death puzzle. It sounded very much like Wallace Buckham performed mechanical abortions. But had he done Charity's?

THIRTY-FIVE

Sure enough, the baby delayed his entrance until the small quiet hours, as so many do, not emerging until after four o'clock in the morning. Lucy was tired but summoned enough energy to push her newborn out into the world. It wasn't without a good deal of work on her part, though.

When her cervix was finally fully open and she felt the urge to bear down, she threw off her nightgown and maneuvered herself onto a hands and knees position on the bed. I piled pillows high under her head so that between contractions she could rest her head and muster energy for the next wave.

The pains came fast and furious, though, allowing her almost no respite. During the contractions she alternated between mighty grunts, weeping, and uttering words I was pretty sure were curses in Polish. I didn't care. Whatever got her through this short but intense stage was fine with me. Women dug deep into their resources of strength at this last stage of labor, becoming nearly primitive beings. I'd seen it many times and marveled at our gender's ability to endure the most difficult physical test humans go through.

"Thee is doing so well," I encouraged when she wept. "Thee is strong and the baby will be here soon."

I laid a basin of warm water and a bowl of oil on the foot of the bed, and knelt behind her. After I spied the top of the baby's head, I pressed a warm folded cloth to her opening. When it cooled, I dipped two fingers in the oil and slid them just under the rim of skin and over the head to lubricate the baby's passage. Alternating these two bits of assistance helped ease out the head without the mother tearing delicate membranes.

The baby's head was nearly born. "Give me all thy effort with the next pain, Lucy."

"I can't," she wailed.

"Of course thee can."

And she did, exerting her entire torso down into her pelvis with a great growl of effort. As soon as the head was out, the baby opened its eyes, gazing at its new world, and made sucking sounds. With Lucy's next push, out slithered the tiny body, a boy. He gave a hearty cry of complaint right away. I grabbed a clean cloth and wiped his eyes and nose clear.

I sniffed away the emotion that always overcame me at this miraculous moment and swallowed. "Thee has a healthy baby boy, Lucy. Carefully now, roll over to thy right and lift thy left leg." I handed her the baby, still attached by the tough silvery cord. This stage was always easier with a helper, but I hadn't wanted to disturb Annie last night after her long week in Boston.

Lucy, instantly smiling, received her newborn son with both hands and leaned back into the pillows. I covered him with a soft baby blanket and rubbed his back for a moment, then stepped back.

"It's so sweet to meet you, little boy." She touched her son's cheek with a finger. His dark eyes gazed into hers, as they would for years to come.

THIRTY-SIX

I stayed until I was sure the newborn was nursing well and that his mother's uterus was firming up, returning to a non-pregnant state. I'd told Lucy I would be back the next morning to check on her and the baby. That and attending births was the only work I did on First Day, God's day of rest. I figured He created both the mother and baby, and I was doing God's work to make sure they both were safe and well.

Henryk offered me milky coffee, bread and butter, and a warm section of Polish sausage, which I gratefully sat and consumed.

"I wanted a boy, but I didn't dare say so," Henryk said from across the table in the farm kitchen. Tears dampened his eyes. "A son. Henry. Lucy insisted on naming him for me. Now, you're sure my Lucy is well?"

"Yes, have no fear, Henryk." I swallowed the last of the coffee. "It took a while, but both she and the babe are as healthy as they come. Do be sure she drinks plentiful clean water, milk, and eats goodly portions of meat and vegetables for the next month or two to build up her strength." I dusted off my mouth and stood to don my cloak, hat, and gloves. "How's the other baby boy, the foal?"

"Thriving, thanks be to God. And to you, Rose. Lucy named the colt Ambrose, after you." He pressed money into my hand. "Here is thy payment. I wish I had enough to give you ten times the amount."

I laughed. "There's no need for that. I'll be back tomorrow to check on Lucy and the newborn."

Now, an hour after sunrise, I clucked to Peaches. I had fresh snow to traverse as I left the Majowski farm. The snowstorm had moved on, and sun glittered in the three inches of fresh white crystals all around. I glanced down toward Delia and Savoire's home and shook my head. I had no reason to call on them, and it was too early, anyway.

I yawned, but was determined to locate a telephone cabinet before I returned home. I thought the hotels would surely keep records on who had paid money to make a call. And if my threatening message yesterday had been made in public, I wanted to know who spoke those words.

I headed up Main Street and out Friend Street, past the Meetinghouse, to the turn that led up Whittier Hill. David had taken me to dine last summer at a luxurious hotel that sat atop the hill. It was the kind of fancy place that might well host a telephone cabinet for its wealthy patrons. As I drove, my mind sorted through everything I knew about Charity's death. When had I decided she was murdered and not simply killed by a sloppy, incompetent abortionist? Had Kevin used the word? Was I mistaken in my thinking? Having not slept in the night, I was too fuzzy in the head to make sense of anything, although the crisp air did much to revive me.

Finally I reached Le Grand Hotel. I left Peaches in the care of the stable man and made my way carefully on the neatly shoveled path to the wide front entrance. A liveried doorman held the heavy door open for me.

Inside, the ornate glamor of the place stunned me as much as it had the first time. I was not accustomed to such rich trappings. Gleaming carved wood. Heavy gilt-edged mirrors. Velvety maroon curtains. Even tropical-looking potted plants. From the dining room to my left came the clink of silver on porcelain as diners tucked into eggs, potatoes, ham, biscuits, and other delectable breakfast dishes.

At the mahogany front desk, polished to within an inch of its life, the same man as last year looked up from his ledger. His formal black suit was the same, and his greased hair hadn't changed, either, nor had his obsequious manner. He pressed his lips into a little rosebud and blinked like he'd smelled something distasteful. He looked me up and down, from my gray bonnet to my black cloak to my gray dress. It was the garment I wore to deliveries in the winter and was by no means of a fine cloth nor in a fashionable cut.

I was certainly not the elegantly garbed kind of customer he was used to, but I wasn't going to let that fact either bother me nor distract me from my mission. "Good morning. I wondered if this hotel has a public telephone cabinet."

He looked me up and down. "We do, but it costs fifteen cents per call."

"I'm aware that is the going price. My concern is a person who made a threatening telephone call to me yesterday at approximately three thirty in the afternoon. Does thee keep records of who made calls?"

"We do. Are you some kind of detective?"

"My name is Rose Carroll. I am a mid-wife, but regardless of my occupation, I find receiving anonymous threats quite disturbing. I'd like to find out who did it."

"Rose Carroll. I've heard of you." He scowled.

"I dined here with my friend David Dodge last year." I kept my voice level and expression calm, waiting for his reaction.

Light dawned in his eyes, as if he'd just realized he'd been rude to a friend of one of his regular — and well-off — customers. He cleared his throat. "Welcome back, Miss Carroll. Welcome back." He beamed.

"Might I inspect the call register, please?"

"Yes, yes, of course." He reached under the desk and turned an open ledger to face me atop the counter that stood between us. "Here you are."

The ledger was open to only the fourth page in the book, and it had a sole entry on it. "Has thee not had the cabinet long?" I asked. Either that or they'd filled a previous book and had started afresh on this one.

"Indeed we haven't."

I flipped back one page to yesterday's entries and checked the numbered lines. Twenty-three people had availed themselves of the telephone cabinet. But there were no calls made anywhere near three thirty.

Someone had placed a call at two o'clock which lasted three minutes, and the next wasn't until half past five. I glanced up at the concierge and shook my head. He must have noticed my disappointment.

"Too bad, Miss Carroll. You could try the Mechanics Hotel down by the rail depot. They have a cabinet, too."

"I thank thee very much."

"But you might wish to bring a companion. It's not exactly the kind of place nice young ladies frequent, if you catch my meaning." He gave me the kind of scolding look I often received from conventional people who didn't approve of my going around town without an escort.

"I shall take that under advisement. Good day."

Thirty-Seven

The environment in the vicinity of the
Mechanics Hotel was indeed very different
from that on top of Whittier Hill. Drays and
hacks and carriages vied with each other on
the now slushy road. Men shouted to be
heard over the din. A fellow unloaded
trunks, valises, and three hat boxes in front
of the depot. A train whistle pierced the
morning air, and the smell of manure was
everywhere. Did I really want to make my
way into this busy, rude morass? I could
easily drive home, eat breakfast, and rest for
the remainder of the morning until it was
time to leave for Charity's Memorial Meeting. If I didn't nap off my fatigue at being
awake all night, I was at risk of falling asleep
in Meeting, which was frowned upon, even
though it happened to certain members regularly.

On the other hand, I very much wished to
learn who had threatened me. I could drop

a note by to Emmaline if I learned the identity. I would then rest easy knowing the matter was in the capable hands of Kevin Donovan. I spied a boy standing near a hitching post and beckoned him over.

"Will thee watch Peaches for me? I'll only be a few minutes, and there's a coin in it for thee."

"Certainly, miss."

"I appreciate it." I climbed down, holding my skirts above the mud and muck of the street and handed him the reins. I made my way into the hotel, giving a rough-looking gang of young men a wide berth. I felt their gaze follow me.

"I swan, boys, it's the Quaker Detective," one proclaimed in a rowdy voice. Guffawing commenced all around.

I stood tall and kept moving toward the hotel's front door. I was accustomed to receiving curious looks, admonishing comments, questions about the language and dress of Friends. But I was rarely the object of such derision. The children's adage, "Sticks and stones may break my bones, but words will never harm me," was certainly true in this case.

Inside I paused to take my bearings. The lobby was a large room, but a dark, dingy, and noisy one. No gleaming ornate woodwork here, no fancy brocade draperies. Not a potted plant to be seen. Manure had clearly been tracked in, because the air was ripe with scents of both man and beast. I was relieved to see a wooden enclosure in the far corner. It had a glass window in the door and was clearly labeled TELEPHONE. Despite being well before noon, a bar that ran along one wall of the lobby was fully subscribed. Men hoisted pints of beer in glass tankards, and I spied more than one small glass of amber liquid being consumed, too.

I turned my back on the imbibers and headed to the front desk opposite the bar. A harried-looking man in an ill-fitting suit greeted me.

"Yes, miss?" His narrow face matched his high voice — pinched, not full. A big board of numbers and hooks hung behind the clerk. A few of the hooks held keys. Below the key board was a set of wooden slots, some of which held envelopes or slips of paper. "I hope you're not wanting a room, because we're full up."

"No, not at all. What I wish to see is the ledger where you record the names of people who use your telephone cabinet." I was careful not to touch the long counter, which was so grimy it couldn't have been cleaned in a year, perhaps a decade

"Why, I can't show that to you. Management policy and all like that."

I leaned a little closer over the counter. I glanced around before speaking and then peered at him over the tops of my spectacles. "It's secret police business, you see. I'm a private detective." I was hardly following Friends' principle of integrity, but if my tiny white lie got me answers and brought justice, perhaps it could be forgiven.

The clerk's eyebrows flew up. "One of them Pinkertons, are you? I read all those stories. What an exciting life you must lead."

"I can't divulge who employs me. Now, the ledger, please."

This book was thicker, plainer, and dirtier than the one at the Grand Hotel. I flipped back to yesterday's page and ran my gloved finger down the list of names. Far more calls had been made from this public telephone than from the previous one, and the hours after noon were crowded with names. I found two thirty, two fifty, three ten, three fifteen, and finally, three thirty. My heart fell when I tried to decipher the scribbled name. I peered at it, stood back and examined it with a cocked head, and lifted the book to get better light. But I couldn't make out the Christian name nor the surname.

The caller either had abysmal handwriting or had deliberately tried to obscure his name. It occurred to me that whoever called me might have scribbled a false moniker, rendering my entire search for the caller moot.

I opened my mouth to ask the clerk if he remembered who made the call but he was busy with a man built like a stone pillar, with a voice equally as heavy and rough. When the clerk became available, I gestured for him to help me.

"Can thee make out this name at three thirty yesterday? Does thee remember who made that call?"

"For your second question, I only work on the weekends. It's the boss's wife who works during the week, but she says she needs two days of rest." He also peered closely at the book. "No, I'm sorry, miss. I can't make it out, either." He looked up and shrugged. "Wish I could help you. Is there any other detecting you need done?" He rubbed his hands together.

I nearly laughed out loud despite my dejection at not discovering my caller's identity. "You can detect if there are any other hotels in town besides this one and the Grand Hotel. Or any other telephones available to the public."

"There aren't any other hotels, but doesn't the post office have a new telephone cabinet?"

Of course. How had I forgotten that? Bertie had told me a couple of months ago about the cabinet's installation. "I thank thee greatly for thy assistance."

"I am happy to serve. Perhaps I'll turn up in one of the Pinkerton novels sometime soon." His excitement was like a boy's.

"Perhaps." I bade him farewell and hied off to fetch my horse and buggy. And maybe discern the name of Charity's killer, too.

THIRTY-EIGHT

But I didn't get that far.

"If it isn't lovely Midwife Carroll," a voice called out before I was out the door of the Mechanics Hotel.

I turned my head in the direction of the voice, which was also the bar's location. As I'd thought, the speaker was Joey Swift, who now walked toward me with a big smile on his face. A number of men's heads also turned in my direction. I did my best to ignore them.

"I've been looking for you, Miss Carroll," he said when he neared. The fumes of alcohol on his breath were enough to intoxicate me and four other people. His words were not slurred, though, and his gait had looked normal. Perhaps he'd just now commenced to drink.

"Is that so, Joey?" I decided to play it innocent and not let on that I'd seen him banging on my door both times.

"Yes, ma'am. Oh, but you're a miss, aren't you? What are you doing consorting with the riff-raff down here?"

"I had an inquiry to make. Why was thee looking for me?"

"Will you sit for a moment?" With a formal gesture that didn't comport with everything else I'd seen of him, he indicated two empty upholstered chairs near the big coal stove that heated the lobby.

If sitting here and talking with him would forestall any future angry visits, I would do it. I examined the chair, which had seen better days, before perching gingerly on the edge. I folded my hands in my lap and waited. Joey sat at right angles to me.

"It's this way, Miss Carroll." He gave me an earnest look. "I have a friend, a lady friend. She's with child but she doesn't want the baby. I heard you might know of a way for her to get rid of it."

"Is thee the father, Joey?"

"Me? What?" His eyes shifted to a spot to the side and beyond me, and he rubbed his ear. "No, no, it's not like that."

If those weren't clues he was lying, I didn't know what were.

"She's a, uh, lady of the night, you see. She's got her business to think of. She can't be raising a baby and all that."

"I see." In my experience, prostitutes were some of the best at knowing how to avoid becoming pregnant and were aware of effective solutions in case they did. "Did she ask thee for assistance?"

"No, as a matter of fact. But I want to help her. She's a very nice lady." His gaze met mine again.

I sat for a moment discerning how to answer as I watched the busy foot traffic flow around us. I was the only woman in the place, so I received my fair share of odd looks. "I don't think I can help thy friend."

"Why ever not?" he asked, his rising ire evidenced by his reddening neck and face.

"My own business is that of helping women give birth, not preventing it. Like I helped thy cousin Charity, may God keep her soul. I can recommend two others who might be able to assist thy friend."

Joey lowered his voice to a conspiratorial tone. "Ransom said somebody tried to help Charity get rid of a baby and killed her instead."

"Thee is friendly with Ransom?" They hadn't seemed particularly so outside of Virtue's home the day Charity died.

"He's my cousin, isn't he?" He lifted his chin but averted his gaze again. "Listen, this is a bit urgent. My lady friend can't be working once she gets bigger." He made a gesture in front of his stomach, rounding his hands to indicate a pregnant belly.

"Then have her contact either Wallace Buckham on Moody Street or Savoire Restante on Clark." I watched him closely for signs of a reaction. If he had hired one of the two to kill Charity, he should be nervous at my knowledge of them.

"Thanks for that. I'll let her know." He rubbed his ear again but otherwise didn't appear anxious or on edge.

"Either of them might be able to help her." I stood. "I expect I'll see thee at Charity's Memorial Meeting for Worship this afternoon?"

He rose. "Oh, for corn—" He stopped himself. "Excuse me. I'd forgotten all about that. Yes, of course I'll be there. Have to honor my cuz, don't I?" He peered at me. "Since it's with the Quakers, I guess I'm going to have to get all silent and such."

I smiled. "We will keep worshipful silence when it's rightly ordered, but at a Memorial Meeting all are welcome to share memories of the deceased."

He swiped his forehead with the back of his hand. "That's a relief. Well, thanks for those names, Miss Carroll. I'll be seeing you." He sauntered back to the bar.

We would have one inebriated cousin in our midst while we remembered poor Charity. As I headed for the door, I wondered if his story about needing an abortionist for his lady friend was true. Would simply wanting help merit such ire as he'd exhibited at my house? Or perhaps it was merely frustration because he'd just learned of his lady friend's pregnancy and felt helpless in the face of it. Or was he also the likely father?

Thirty-Nine

I made my way to the post office, tying Peaches to a post when I arrived. The horse and buggy were a great convenience when I needed to travel to the other side of town. They greatly simplified my life when I needed to go out or come home late at night, even though I'd been assaulted this week as I drove. But for small trips within the downtown area, it was more of a bother. I sighed. I was here now, and I'd be home soon.

The post office was packed with people. Ladies holding boxes to mail, men jostling at the counter to buy a stamp or pick up a waiting parcel, a woman twirling the knob of her locked postal box. I spied Bertie and her young assistant, Eva, behind the counter. Eva looked frazzled and at her wits' ends, while Bertie took the rush in stride. There was, in fact, a small telephone cabinet in the back corner, but I wouldn't bother

Bertie at such a busy time for the call ledger. I waved at my friend and turned to go, then decided to give a peek inside the cabinet before I left.

I saw through the window in the door that nobody was within, so I pushed it open. I was surprised to spy a ledger hanging from a chain fixed to the wall next to the telephone box. A pencil hung from a string next to the ledger, so the system must be for users to enter their own names. The telephone itself was a wall model, not the type that sat on a desk like ours at home. I entered, pushed the door shut, and sat on the small seat protruding from the back wall of the cabinet.

Again I found yesterday's page and ran my finger down the list of times and scrawled names. I slowed when I came to the early afternoon. But luck was not with me. The ledger showed a call at two fifty, and then was blank until four thirty. I slammed the book shut. I stood too fast, bumping my elbow on the back wall. Tingles of pain shot up and down my arm. People called that sensation the result of bumping the funny bone. It didn't feel particularly funny to me.

I climbed slowly back into my buggy. Fatigue combined with frustration dragged me down. I should convey the news of the threatening call to Kevin by way of Emmaline, and also tell him what David had said about Wallace Buckham, but I was too tired to even consider one more outing. I closed my eyes for a moment, holding myself and the investigation in the Light of God, praying that Way would open for the truth to be revealed. But the bustling street was too noisy for my prayer to calm me.

I sighed, opening my eyes, then scanned up and down the busy street for an opening to join the flow of vehicles. I smiled when I saw Kevin hurrying in my direction.

"Kevin Donovan," I called to him. My problem looked like it had been solved by the grace of God. Or maybe of Kevin's errand.

When he looked around to see who had hailed him, I waved, and he strode up to the buggy.

"Thee is just the person I wanted to see," I said.

"Why am I not happy to hear that?" he said in a sardonic tone. "What nefarious deeds have you discovered now, Miss Rose?"

Two women in elegant wool coats passed by at that moment. Their hands in fur muffs, they glanced at Kevin with a look of alarm. One pursed her lips while the other took an extra step away from us before they hurried down the street.

"Does thee have time to sit for a moment?" I patted the seat next to me. "I don't want the world to hear what I have to say."

Kevin climbed in the other side. "What's happened now?"

"I was speaking with David Dodge about Charity's death. He was in Portsmouth all week at a physicians' meeting and returned only yesterday. I asked him about Wallace Buckham, and he said he thought the doctor had been involved in a case that besmirched his reputation as an orthopedist. He thought Wallace might even have been censured by the medical association."

"Interesting. I am planning to investigate this Buckham."

"David said he would, too. Being a doctor might open more doors to him."

"What else do you have?" Kevin asked.

I told him about the telephone threat, and about my search of public telephone cabinets. "I couldn't find a thing. I'm exceedingly disappointed."

"That was a good thought, to search the ledgers. But the call could very well have come from a device in someone's home, you know."

"Perhaps. After the call, I asked the operator if she knew where the call originated. She said she didn't, but mentioned the public cabinets."

"I'll see what I can find out, Miss Rose."

"I thank thee. Has thee made any progress at all? Has thee learned anything else about Savoire — that is, Sally Davies?" I heard a plaintive tone in my voice and hated it. It wasn't like me to whine, and it showed I truly needed some rest.

Kevin frowned. "We're checking alibis of all concerned, and following up all leads." The nearest church bell tolled once for the half hour. "Ten thirty already. I must go. Chief is waiting for a report, which will be woefully thin of fact and result. But I can use all your information and am grateful for it." He climbed out of the buggy, but leaned back in and frowned at me. "However, you must stop traveling about asking questions, Miss Rose. It will only lead to even more trouble for you."

"I know, and frankly, I agree. The next two days are full with Friends Meeting affairs and I won't have a moment to get into trouble."

"Good. The victim's service is this afternoon, I understand."

I nodded.

"I'll be in attendance," Kevin said, crossing himself with a quick small movement. "As a show of respect for the family."

"But also because the killer might well attend, too?"

"Precisely."

FORTY

I turned over again in my bed an hour later, but sleep eluded me. I'd experienced this before, when my body was so overtired it wouldn't let me rest. My nerves jangled like my arm had earlier when I'd bumped my elbow. Thoughts and images from the past two days flooded my brain. Joey's request of me to help his lady friend stop a pregnancy. The scribbled illegible name on the three thirty line in the Mechanics Hotel ledger. The hoarse voice of my caller. Wallace Buckham in his fancy house taking umbrage at my questions. How would I ever sort through it all?

At last I gave in to the inevitable. I would not sleep this morning. I sat up and tidied my hair and dress. The house was quiet at present, with the family out at school and work for the morning. I wandered into the front hall and collected the mail from the floor. My cheeks grew warm and my heart skipped a beat when I spied a letter in David's hand addressed to me. The stack also included a letter from Orpha. I sat at my desk and slit open Orpha's envelope first, saving David's for afterward like the special sweet it was.

Dear Rose,
     Would you do me the favor of taking me to Charity Skells's service this afternoon? I feel a need to convey my respects to her family. I shall be ready by one thirty.

                                        Orpha

Of course I would transport my elderly mentor. She must have seen a notice in the newspaper about the service. Or simply heard about the arrangements around town. Orpha knew many people and had ever been a source of much information. Now I turned to David's note.

My dear and cherished Rose,
     How splendid it was to dine and visit with you yesterday. I had missed you greatly during our days apart and I couldn't have asked for a better homecoming.

I stopped reading for a moment and held my cool hands to my warm face, smiling, then continued.

I want to tell you that I have investigated Wallace Buckham's history, and it is as I suspected. The AMA censured him last fall for ethical lapses and took away his license to practice medicine. The hospital withdrew his privileges in the operating theater.

Of course David could have telephoned me with this information, but a letter was private with no chance of a nosy operator listening in.

My memory served me well. The lapse in question involved Buckham performing a mechanical abortion on the mother of one of his pediatric patients. Your instincts were correct in this matter. Buckham was lucky the AMA didn't turn him in to the police for a violation of the Comstock laws, and the mother in question was lucky to survive the procedure.

I was right about Wallace. Kevin had probably already discovered the same, so I felt no need to convey this bit. And if he hadn't, I could tell him in person this afternoon. I read on to the end.

Buckham's crimes and indiscretions also resulted in his wife and children leaving him. I shall bid you farewell now, but very much look forward to spending the day tomorrow with you as we celebrate Faith and Zebulon's blessed union. Ours will be along soon enough, I promise.

With deep and everlasting affection,
I remain ever your humble servant,
David

I sat back, smoothing the fine paper with my hand. Silly David with his flowery ending salutation. I didn't sign my messages thusly, but I loved him for it.

I reread the results of his queries. So Buckham was a confirmed abortionist. I wished Kevin had been able to discern whether Savoire was, too. Based on what my client had told me, Madame Restante also offered mechanical terminations. Charity's death had to have been at the hands of one of the two. Didn't it? But neither of them needed motive to want Charity dead. Either could have been hired for the job. Or the killer could be someone else entirely.

Orpha's words of caution came to mind. She'd asked me to proceed carefully and with consideration. She'd said those who studied the best methods of mechanical abortion and offered them to women also provided contraceptive information, that this was a great service in spacing pregnancies to conserve women's health. Of course I was in favor of spacing children in a family. Orpha had ended by asking me not to prosecute too hastily.

Which was fine if, say, Charity had gone to Savoire of her own free will. Savoire might believe she was helping women gain health by spacing out their pregnancies. An incompetent abortionist wasn't much help, though. And what if the killer had persuaded Charity to go to the abortionist he — or she — had hired to commit murder? Even if Charity's death was the result of innocent incompetence, that person still should not be allowed to continue offering a dangerous solution.

FORTY-ONE

At ten before two o'clock, I handed the reins to the young man our Meeting had hired for the day and hurried around to help Orpha down from the buggy. The Bailey family hadn't accompanied me, with Betsy nursing a cold, Frederick out with the fast-growing twins to buy them new clothes for the wedding, and Faith hurriedly stitching the hem on her marital sheets. None in the family had known Charity well and I doubted their absence would be noted by the Swifts.

A light snow fell, making the world look like a giant had sprinkled confectioner's sugar over every surface. I handed Orpha her cane once she was down.

"Carefully now." I tucked Orpha's hand firmly through my elbow and held her close. "It's likely to be slippery." I worried about my mentor and her increasing frailty, but she was a strong-minded woman and didn't let much stop her.

"Yes, Mother," she said in a wry tone. "I have my cane, you know."

I laughed softly and squeezed her gloved hand.

We followed others up the broad granite steps into the Meetinghouse and into the door on the left. One could enter the main room from two interior doors, but when the central divider was raised it became a single space inside, with wooden pews in rows facing the far end. The building, which John Whittier had helped design, was now nearly forty years old, and the tall broad windows cast light within from three sides. The simplicity of the configuration and lack of ornate trappings freed the heart and mind to listen quietly in the company of Friends for God's guidance.

On a day like today, though, with a sad service to which all friends of the deceased were invited whether Quaker or not, the atmosphere was anything but quiet and calming. Skirts rustled. Townspeople whispered among themselves. A boy spoke in a loud voice and was quickly hushed. Benches creaked with restless bodies. Few rested with eyes closed to wait for the Light.

The family sat on the facing bench at the front, the seat usually reserved for Meeting elders. Virtue was in the middle with Elias to her left. Beyond him was a younger woman, likely Charity's sister who lived several towns distant, with her two young children. On Virtue's other side sat Ransom and the children except for the youngest, and then Joey Swift. Ransom must have left the baby in the care of a neighbor or perhaps Virtue's nursemaid. Virtue's eyes were reddened and she kneaded a handkerchief in her lap, but sat with her usual erect posture. Charity's sister also looked grief-stricken, and Elias sat with a hand shielding his forehead — and maybe his emotions, too. Ransom, on the other hand, looked harassed. He held Howie on his lap and was busy trying to keep him and two of the girls quiet. Charity's sister's older daughter, who looked about twelve, fetched her five-year-old cousin and brought her back to sit with her family.

Nine-year-old Priscilla surveyed the filling room with a solemn air, her chin held high. When her gaze passed over me, I raised my hand in a small wave and smiled at her. She lifted her hand in return and it looked like she was fighting to keep a smile from her face. *Good.* She knew I was an ally.

Everyone in the room kept their wraps on. The space would warm a bit once it was full, simply from the heat of all the bodies, but the furnace in the cellar wasn't making much of a dent in the temperature of the room today.

Kevin was perched near the back on one of the benches built into the side wall. I took a seat next to him, with Orpha on my other side. I knew he'd chosen that vantage point from which to observe the room. I couldn't help but want to do the same. We exchanged a brief glance.

Instead of observing, I folded my hands in my lap and closed my eyes. I held Charity's released soul in the Light and prayed for her children, that they might find peace in their newly motherless life. I held Ransom, too, although that brought up thoughts of homicide, on which I did not care to dwell this afternoon. I opened my eyes when someone began to speak. It was the Clerk of Meeting.

"We are gathered here today to remember the too-short life of our sister, Charity Swift Skells, whose soul was released to God this week. For those of you not familiar with the ways of Friends, we sit in silent expectant waiting for a message from God. We have no sermon, no hymns, and no single minister, as we believe we all minister to one another. Today we ask you to also remain quiet until you are so moved to share a message about Charity. Please stand and do so in a loud and clear voice so all may hear. It is our custom to then leave a period of silence before the next message. May Charity rest well in God's Light." He sat again.

I spied raised eyebrows and frowns as well as small nods and smiles of approval. For those used to the busy rituals of the Catholic or Episcopalian churches, or even the hymns and sermons of the Protestant faiths, our ways were unusual and could be unsettling. Many people were not comfortable with silence, with communicating directly with God.

I shut out the world again. I hoped a message would arise for me to share, and let my thoughts roam over what I knew of Charity before this week. She had most recently come to me for an antenatal visit in Eleventh Month, well along in her pregnancy, but too thin. She'd said Ransom had been out of work for some time and what monies they had went to food for the other children. I had encouraged her to accept aid from the women of the Meeting, saying starving herself was also starving the baby inside her. She'd responded that, despite her name, she much preferred giving charity than accepting it, but agreed reluctantly to let donations of food begin.

A woman cleared her throat and the room quieted. I opened my eyes to see a stalwart and kindly Friend, the one who had organized the food donations.

"I knew Charity for her entire life. She cared very much for others, and never hesitated to lend a helping hand. May she rest easy in her heavenly home, and may we all follow her example, giving charity where it is needed." The bench thumped when she sat again. After a minute, another woman stood. She looked familiar but I couldn't place her until she began to speak, and then I realized it was Jeanne Peele, the nurse from the hospital. I hadn't recognized her without her white hat and starched uniform.

"I had the privilege of sitting with Mrs. Skells as her soul passed from this earthly sphere," Jeanne said in a clear voice. "I didn't know her except in her last hours, but I want to express my appreciation for allowing me to help ease her final journey. May the good Lord bless her and keep her, and her family, too, in their hour of need." She sat.

I wiped away a tear. What a lovely thing to say. It was, indeed, a privilege to sit with someone who was dying. It was as much a privilege as that of watching life come into this world of ours, which of course I did much more frequently.

Several more messages followed, all from Quakers who had known Charity and her family.

A minute after the last one ended, Orpha stirred next to me and pushed herself to her feet, leaning on her cane. "I helped Charity birth her babies and I saw what a devoted mother she was. Children," she said directly to the girls and Howie, her voice wobbling with age but still strong, "your mama loved you deeply. You keep that in your hearts, and do your best to live as she did, as all these people are attesting." She lowered herself down again.

A lovely message, and an important one for the children. I squeezed Orpha's hand.

With a sidelong glance at Kevin I caught him frowning at the door to the far side. Two women paused in the doorway. My eyes widened. It was Delia and Savoire Davies. Savoire wore a black lace mantilla over her face and a long purple cloak. Delia, a stylish black hat pinned to her hair, brushed snow off her black coat.

My goodness, what motivated them to come? I watched as they slid into a back pew on the other side after a family scooted over to make room.

Orpha murmured a soft "Hmm," and nudged me. When I looked at her, she raised her eyebrows in a knowing glance.

I shot my gaze toward Ransom. Had he seen them? I couldn't tell. Delia, his lover from all appearances, as well as his fellow employee. Her mother, who dabbled in abortifacients. More than dabbled; she prescribed them. If she had inadvertently or willfully killed Charity, appearing here was a brazen act, indeed, as was Delia's.

As my gaze traveled over others of those gathered, I paused on the sight of Sophie in one of the pews, with Bertie perched next to her. I knew Bertie, as a public servant, attended every funeral she could. And Sophie was the Swift estate's lawyer, of which the Skells children were beneficiaries.

Movement on the facing bench brought my attention there. Virtue stood, regal in her grief.

"My daughter was a good woman." She looked over at her grandchildren. "As that lady said, children, thee each should follow in Mama's footsteps. Heed well that thee acts charitably and with love toward others." She gazed out at the assemblage again. "I am distraught beyond words, however, at the way Charity's life ended. Her time as a wife did not turn out the way she had hoped it would."

Ransom shot her a venomous glare.

"And the life of this gentle woman ended in violence," Virtue continued. The color was high in her face.

Young Priscilla turned her head to look at her grandmother with alarm on her face. The adults must have been successful in keeping the news from her and her siblings as to how their mother died. She whispered to her father, but he only shook his head, a finger to his lips. Why had Virtue said that in such a public gathering, and in front of the children?

"May God deliver a swift and just retribution." Virtue set her lips in a grim line as she sat. She closed her eyes, but tears leaked out. They tracked down her cheek as she faced the room, as if challenging anyone to say otherwise.

FORTY-TWO

An extended period of silence followed Virtue's shocking message, which had caused a thrum of whispers. A soft "Amen" popped up here and there. Who didn't want a swift and just retribution for Charity's death? The killer certainly didn't, but otherwise it seemed to be a shared sentiment. The words Virtue uttered were the shocking part. Didn't retribution mean punishment? We who frequented this room were more often heard to express a wish for love, for understanding, for grace. And yet we also stood on the side of justice.

The silence was punctuated by Priscilla's next-younger sister's kicks on the wooden bench support. My heart wrenched to see Priscilla reach out a hand to still her young sibling's fidgets. Even at her tender age, Priscilla was already standing in for her mother. Depending on how Ransom handled his family, Priscilla's childhood might be over if he relied on her to be a little mother. I'd seen it happen in other large families where the mother died too young.

In the quiet a soft snore droned. This was not unusual in First Day Meeting for Worship but was uncommon in a public meeting like this one. I surveyed the room, and frowned to see the snoozer was Joey Swift, right there on the facing bench for all to see. Head hung down and body slumped in the corner of the bench, he was sleeping off his liquid lunch, no doubt. I tried not to judge others for their weaknesses, as I had plenty of my own, and Orpha had cautioned me about leaping to condemn. But this was too blatant to ignore. He should be ashamed of himself.

The absence of voices was broken by a woman who had been childhood friends with Charity, and other messages followed in that vein. Outside the snow had gathered strength and was falling heavily. I watched through the far windows. At least it wasn't windy, too. Windblown storms tended to do more damage and be much harder to navigate.

Just when I thought the Clerk might signal the end of the Memorial Meeting, a man stood in the other room at the far back corner. I craned my neck but couldn't see him clearly. When he spoke, I realized it was Jonathan Sherwood.

"Ransom Skells works for me at Lowell's Boat Shop. I met his wife several times over the last months and very much admired her devotion to her husband and her family. May she rest in peace, knowing that many of us are working to ensure justice will be done." He lowered himself into his seat.

Many of us? A quick glance at Kevin showed not the same surprise I felt, but rather a quick nod toward Jonathan. Had Jonathan conveyed information to Kevin about Ransom and Delia? Had the benevolent manager turned against his employee? I longed to engage Kevin in conversation, except that couldn't happen here or now.

The Clerk stood and invited all gathered to greet their neighbors with the handshake of fellowship.

"We thank you all for coming today. The Swift family invites you to join them in a light refreshment at their home." He gave the address. "Please remain seated until the family enters the hall." He gestured to those seated on the facing bench, who stood and filed out.

I turned to Kevin. I opened my mouth to speak but he raised a palm.

"Not here, Miss Rose. Will you be going

to the Swift house?"

"I'm not sure," I replied. "I hadn't realized there was going to be a gathering."

"It's the proper thing to do," Orpha chimed in from my other side. "I'd like to go, if you'll take me."

"Of course I will." I smiled at her. "Then, yes, Kevin, I'll be there. You?"

He heaved a sigh. "My boy wanted me to get home and play snow fort with him. But duty calls. I'll be there."

The collected assemblage was already filing out of the room when raised male voices came through the open door to the entryway.

"You were never good enough for my girl."

Those angry words sounded like Elias Swift's voice.

"She loved me, Elias," Ransom's reedy voice shouted. "And I loved her."

All around me women's eyes widened, men's brows furrowed. Was Elias speaking out of guilt because he hadn't helped his daughter sufficiently, if at all?

"I know you mean I was never good enough for you," Ransom added. "But you took it out on your daughter, didn't you? Shunning her because she chose me over her daddy's advice. And now she's dead and you'll never be able to make it right with her."

"How dare you?" Elias's voice shook with ire.

The Friend in front of me shook her head, making a *tsking* sound.

"Gentlemen, gentlemen, gentlemen," Joey's voice slurred. "The Quakers aren't gonna like you fighting here in their sacred place."

Kevin pushed through the crowd, excusing himself, apologizing, but not stopping until he disappeared through the door. The shouts ceased.

"Tempers are high, Rose," Orpha murmured. "I'd watch my back, if I were you."

FORTY-THREE

Inside the front door of the Swift home a maid took the mourners' snowy outerwear. I kept a firm hold on Orpha's elbow, making sure she didn't get jostled in the crush of arrivals. The drive over had been slow going, as the snow on the roads had not yet been packed down by the town's big horse-drawn rollers. With any luck the return trip would be easier by the time we left.

Elias, Virtue, and Ransom stood in a line in the parlor. Despite the spacious nature of the lamplit room, it felt confining. Stuffy, full of grief. Elias sniffed frequently and wiped tears from the corners of his eyes as he greeted visitors expressing their condolences. Ransom shifted from one foot to another, ran his finger between his collar and his neck, and patted his brow with a handkerchief every chance he got. Virtue, in contrast to them both, never lost her straight bearing nor her apparent resolve not to plaster her emotions on her sleeve.

I clasped Charity's father's hand in both of mine after Orpha had spoken with him in a low voice and moved on to Virtue.

"Elias," I began, "I —"

He interrupted me. "Rose, tell me she wasn't in pain at the end." His low voice creaked. "Can thee tell me that?"

"In truth, I don't believe she was in pain. I am just so sorry none of us could save her. Modern medicine goes only so far." I squeezed his hand and released it. At least now he was showing grief rather than anger toward his son-in-law.

He stared at the floor for a moment before looking up. "I know." He shot a glance sideways, but I could tell it skipped Virtue and was directed toward Ransom. Elias leaned toward me. "I think he killed her," he whispered.

I inhaled sharply, then swallowed. "I'm sure the authorities are looking into every possibility. But right now thee has an obligation to thy guests." I peered over my spectacles with a small smile.

"Yes, of course. I apologize. This is all just so very difficult . . ." His voice broke as he patted away tears again.

The poor man. It seemed his sorrow moved him to grasp at answers to his daughter's death. It was one thing to dislike one's son-in-law and quite another to believe him a murderer. I didn't know if Ransom had been violent toward Charity during their marriage, but it was possible. Elias might have felt frustrated at not being able to stop it. Maybe Ransom had been a ne'er-do-well before he'd married Charity and her parents disliked him for not being a better supporter. Or Elias could have forbade Charity to marry Ransom and since she'd refused to comply, he'd held a grudge against the couple. A stubborn parent often experienced additional grief at not reconciling with an adult child before his or her death. The finality of that sorrow, that bitter pill, could easily be expressed as anger.

"It's difficult for all of us. Be well, Elias. I hold Charity's released soul in the Light of God, and thee and Virtue, as well."

I moved on to Virtue, who simply thanked me for coming. It must have been painful for her to stand next to Ransom, but etiquette demanded it, no matter her feelings about him as Charity's husband. Did Virtue share her husband's opinion of Ransom as the man responsible for Charity's death? Her behavior the day her daughter died had indicated she might. I moved on to Ransom.

"How does thee fare, Ransom?" I kept my

expression kindly and concerned, hoping to encourage an honest response.

"I just want all this to be over." He waved vaguely at the room and the many visitors. "I want to settle in with my children, return to my job, and not be reminded at every turn of my poor wife's death." His fingers rubbed his thumbs on both hands, over and over.

Over his shoulder I spied Kevin standing in a corner of the room. He was close enough to hear most of what the family said. He held a small plate of food in his hands but wasn't eating. To my eyes he was clearly on duty, but to others he probably appeared to be just one more mourner. I hoped I could grab him alone for a minute and report what Elias had said about Ransom. To whom I now returned my attention. "It will take some time."

Ransom's shoulders slumped. "I suppose so."

"Hello, Rose," a small voice piped up. "Thank thee for coming." Priscilla was next in line.

I patted Ransom's shoulder and stepped in front of the child. "Priscilla, thee is also greeting the guests?"

"Yes, of course. Granny said I should. It's the proper thing to do." Her face was pale but her erect carriage was a miniature version of her grandmother's. Her manners were, too.

I knelt and took her small hand in mine. "Thee is doing very nicely. But I'm sure thee can leave and run play with thy sisters and brother if thee wishes."

"I shan't be playing any longer." Her words were those of a much older girl, but her lips quavered as she spoke. "I'm the lady of the house now."

As I had feared. She shouldn't have to go through this ordeal. "I'll speak to thy grandmother. Go on upstairs and play now. It's fine."

"May I truly?" Her face lit up like the nine-year-old she was.

"Of course."

She glanced up at Ransom, who nodded.

I watched her slip out of the room and heard footsteps trotting upwards. Myself, I slipped into the dining room and filled a plate with small sandwiches, a portion of creamed oysters, and a slice of coffee cake.

Orpha sat in a chair at the periphery. My interest was piqued when I saw the person in the next seat was none other than Savoire, a plate of food balanced on her lap. She'd folded her lace mantilla back over her head, and wore yet another flowing gown, this one in black.

Had she and Orpha already known each other? Given my knowledge of Orpha, I wouldn't be surprised. Savoire might well have been one of the abortionists Orpha had referred to. I sidled in their direction, munching a sandwich as I went. But instead of talking about abortifacients as I'd expected, they were chatting about what they intended to plant in their herb gardens come spring. Most midwives, myself included, grew as many of our own herbs as we could. Talk of herbs could certainly double as talk of abortifacients, I realized.

"A sad occasion, Savoire," I said.

Orpha opened her eyes wide. "You two know each other, then."

"Miss Carroll paid me a visit recently," Savoire said. She gave me a perfunctory smile.

"Rose was my last apprentice," Orpha said. "And my best student."

"Savoire, I thought thee told me thee didn't know Charity Skells." Or had she?

The tall herbalist swallowed. "I came to pay my respects to a poor victim of malice."

"And very thoughtful of you, it was," Orpha told her.

"It was murder, wasn't it?" Savoire asked. "That's what everyone is saying."

"I can't speak to what everyone is saying." I popped the last bit of sandwich in my mouth as Orpha gave me the slightest wink of approval.

"Charity's death might have been the result of incompetence." I watched Savoire, but the only sign of a reaction was her nostrils flaring ever so slightly. "Did Delia come here with you?"

Savoire didn't hide her surprised reaction to this. "You know my daughter?"

"I've had the occasion to meet her, yes, at the boat shop."

Savoire nodded once. "Delia works with Mr. Skells and met his wife at the workplace. My daughter and Mr. Skells are friendly. Paying our respects to the family was the decent thing to do."

"Quite rightly so," Orpha said. She glanced up at me. "You're not in a hurry to leave, are you?"

"No, not if thee isn't."

"I'm quite enjoying myself, as improper as that sounds. I don't get out as much these days, you see." She directed her words at Savoire.

I smiled at Orpha. She thrived on being with a wide range of people, something her midwifery practice had afforded her but no longer did. "Then I'll be back in a little while to see if thee is ready. Good day, Savoire."

Savoire gave a little wave but didn't speak. She definitely didn't smile.

FORTY-FOUR

I wandered into the comfortable sitting room where I'd been received several days earlier and accepted a cup of tea from a uniformed maid. Clumps of people stood here and there talking, sipping sherry or tea, nibbling the proffered delicacies. Quite a crowd had turned out to pay their respects. I spied a few faces I was positive had not attended the memorial meeting. I wasn't surprised. Many who attend more conventional religious services were uncomfortable in the absence of familiar ritual. Virtue and Elias must have let their friends and business associates know it would be fine to skip the memorial meeting and instead come directly to this gathering.

I felt increasingly frustrated at not yet having discovered the identity of Charity's killer. Tomorrow would be completely taken up with Meeting for Worship followed by the happy Meeting for Marriage, with David by my side. I wouldn't have a moment free for sleuthing, and rightly so. But the more time that passed since Charity's death, the more difficult the crime would be to solve. Who else could I talk to here? What else could I discover now while I had the chance? Joey surely was here, although I hadn't seen him yet. For all I knew, he was somewhere sleeping off his morning inebriation.

I moved into the foyer, thinking I could peek into the parlor and maybe grab a minute with Kevin before he left. Instead, he stood with arms folded leaning against a wall, not even pretending he wasn't watching who came and went. In the corner nearest the door stood a uniformed officer, hands behind his back in the "at ease" position. Except he was at full attention and didn't look a bit at ease. Kevin beckoned me over when he caught sight of me.

"A heartfelt gathering, wouldn't you say, Miss Rose?"

I doubted anyone within earshot but me caught the sardonic note in his voice. I faced him. "Or not," I murmured. "Was thee able to uncover information on Wallace Buckham?"

"No, I haven't, more's the pity."

"David did. He said the American Medical Society censured Wallace for ethical lapses, and he can no longer operate at the hospital."

"What were the lapses?" he asked.

Sophie strode into the hall and Bertie followed at a saunter. "If it isn't the detective and the midwife." Bertie smiled at us.

"A mechanical abortion," I quickly whispered to Kevin.

He stared at me in alarm.

"Yes," I murmured.

Kevin whistled, then turned his attention to my friends. "Good afternoon, Miss Winslow, Miss Ribeiro," Kevin said.

"Are you off?" I asked them.

"Soon," Sophie answered. "I've been looking for you, Detective Donovan."

"Is that so, Miss Ribeiro? How can I help you?"

"I am the lawyer for an estate connected in complicated ways with this family. I was hoping for a definitive accusation of the guilty party in the recent death of Mrs. Skells. It's possible the outcome could affect our settlement."

Bertie grinned and rolled her eyes. "Once a lawyer, always a lawyer," she whispered to me.

I wondered if an arrest would, in fact, affect the conditions of Joseph's will, or if

Sophie was simply curious about the case.

Kevin cleared his throat. "I'm afraid we're not yet in a position to supply that, Counselor. With any luck, it'll be soon. Very soon."

"Please inform my office when you are." She drew a calling card from her reticule and handed it to him.

"Happy to oblige. Travel safely home."

Bertie bussed my cheek and slid into the coat Sophie held for her. When they opened the door I was startled to see night had nearly fallen. I had lamps on the buggy but should be getting Orpha home soon, regardless.

"Thee saw Madame Restante and her daughter appear at the Meetinghouse," I said in a soft voice to Kevin after the door closed behind Sophie and Bertie. "The former is in the dining room conversing with Orpha. I haven't yet seen the latter."

"I have." He also kept his tone low but used his eyebrows to gesture toward the parlor. "She appears to be lying in wait to catch a moment alone with the grieving widower." His expression looked like he'd tasted a bite of spoiled cabbage.

"Speaking of same," I said. "When I spoke with Elias Swift in the receiving line, he

316

confided in me he thinks Ransom killed his wife."

"Did he now? Those two have never reconciled their differences. To wit, the disturbance in your holy place just this afternoon."

"I know. That was most shocking, but truly not a surprise to hear." I was about to continue when the front door swung open.

"Jus' the two I been lookin' for," a hatless Joey Swift said in a jovial tone, bursting in from the outside in a rush of cold air and swirling snow. His breath reeked, as usual, of smoke and liquor.

"The door, Swift." Kevin's voice brokered no rebellion as he pointed toward the wide-open door.

So Kevin and Joey were acquainted. Because of past criminal behavior by Joey, I supposed.

"Right you are, Detective. Right you are." Joey turned to slam the door and then faced us again, hands in pockets, cheeks flushed, apparently not caring that melting snow trickled its way down his face.

"Why was thee looking for us, Joey?" I asked.

"It appears I'm in possession of an important piece of evidence in regards to my poor cousin's demise." He rocked back and forth on his heels with a satisfied expression.

"And what might that be?" Kevin frowned at him.

Joey leaned in toward Kevin, who inclined farther back toward the wall. I wouldn't want Joey's foul expirations in my face, either.

"What might it be worth to you, copper?" Joey asked, leering.

Kevin stepped neatly to the side. "Do you or do you not have evidence in the murder of your cousin?" His voice was stern, his face sterner, but I thought I detected a soft sigh after he spoke. I knew he was eager to get home to his family.

"I might, if it's worth a dollar or two."

Kevin laid a hand on Joey's arm. "Joseph Swift, I charge you with withholding evidence in a homicide case. You are coming to the station with me. Perhaps then we can convince you to share this valuable information you might have in your possession." The touch of his hand turned into a grip. "Officer?" Kevin glanced at the man next to the door, who hurried over to clasp Joey's other arm.

"You can't do this!" Joey protested. "I'm here mourning my poor dead cousin."

"Indeed we can." Kevin's expression was grim. "You have the rest of your life to mourn Mrs. Skells. She's not coming back."

FORTY-FIVE

I stared at the front door in the suddenly empty foyer. Kevin charging Joey with withholding evidence seemed an extreme measure. But Kevin had to be even more frustrated than I at the lack of progress in the case. Joey's asking for money in exchange for information might have been the last straw for the detective. Or maybe it was Joey's general disrespect for the law. Either way, the arrest meant Kevin would miss even more family time. I wouldn't want to be married to a homicide detective, but Emmaline must be used to it by now.

I roused myself to fetch Orpha and get ourselves home. As I turned to head into the sitting room, I caught a furtive movement farther down the hall under the stairs. I flattened myself against the wall and peered in that direction. All I saw was a black feather exactly like the one on Delia's fanciful hat. What was she doing under the stairs? A man's voice spoke from the same place. I quieted my breathing to listen.

"I just can't."

My eyes widened. It was Ransom's voice.

"But we had an understanding," Delia replied with a plaintive note. "You said you loved me."

"It's true. I adore you. But I can't do this anymore. Don't you see?"

The two were clearly having a dalliance, as Jonathan and the neighbor woman had suggested, and Ransom was trying to break it off. My lips pressed together. Why now? Why not end it when his poor wife was home with a half dozen children and another on the way? I did not like this man, nor Delia for consorting with him.

"No, I don't see." Delia's tone turned harsh. "Wasn't I the reason you —"

"Hush, now." Ransom spoke equally harshly. "Don't speak of that."

"I might just need to talk to that policeman who is here. Don't you think he'd want to know?"

"You can't do that!"

"Oh, can't I?" she taunted.

"You'll ruin me. Think of my children, Delia."

"Maybe you should have thought of them back when you first kissed me. Let go of my arm, now."

"Don't tell him, please."

A moment later Delia emerged into the hall proper and swept toward me. I didn't have time to even turn away before she saw me and stopped short.

Her nostrils flared and she set her fists on her hips. "What are you doing there? Were you spying on me?"

Caught in the act. Could I extricate myself? "Hello, Delia," I said. "I was just, ah, looking for my cloak. Are there hooks there under the stairs?"

She snorted. "Somehow I doubt that's what you were doing. I don't care." She tossed her head. "Tell me, where's that detective you're so chummy with? I have something juicy to tell him."

"Kevin Donovan?"

She nodded.

"He left a few minutes ago."

"Damnation." She must have seen my reaction, because she added, "Excuse my language." The apology did not sound sincere in the slightest.

"What does thee need to tell him?"

"Like I'd share that with you, Miss Proper Quaker." She tossed her head and flounced into the sitting room.

I was torn between wanting to follow her

and wishing to speak with Ransom. I chose the latter and continued down the hall. I found the space where the two had conversed, indeed a nook where coats and jackets hung from hooks and hats rested on a shelf above. But Ransom had vanished. I peered down the hallway, which likely led to the kitchen. I sighed. I wasn't going to chase him through the house. I went back into the foyer and was about to head off in search of Orpha when I heard rustling from the stairs. I looked up to see Priscilla perched about ten steps up, her chin resting on her knees. Had she heard everything?

"Rose, what does *damnation* mean?" she asked. "And why does my daddy not want that lady to talk to the police?"

My heart sank. The poor girl. I climbed up to sit beside her.

"*Damnation* is something grown-ups say when they're mad, but it's not a nice word. Thee should put it out of thy mind."

"All right. But why did that lady say she wanted to talk to the policeman? Is it about Mama?" She sniffed and swallowed back a sob, her eyes full.

"I'm not sure, Priscilla. Delia wouldn't tell me. But the detective is a friend of mine. I can ask him tomorrow if she spoke to him."

She gazed down the stairs for a moment. "Did my daddy really kiss that lady?" she whispered.

I had to be as honest as I could be with her. I owed her that. "He might have. They work together and maybe they are friendly. Do you kiss your friends?"

She nodded slowly. "But only my best friend. Does thee think that lady wants to be our new mother?" She pleated a bit of her skirt between her fingers and rubbed it.

I very much doubted that. "Nobody can take the place of thy mother, sweetheart." I stroked her hunched-over back. "And I don't think thy father will be kissing Delia again. Don't worry about what you heard."

Priscilla let out the sigh not of a nine-year-old but of someone much older, that of a person shouldering heavy cares. "Thee can't unhear things, Rose."

What else had she overheard?

"And I saw her," Priscilla went on. "The day Mama died."

I froze. "Who did thee see?"

"That lady that Daddy kissed. That one he called Delia."

"Did thee truly?"

She nodded solemnly.

"Where did thee see her?"

"It was right after Granny came for the

324

little ones, so it was half past seven. I remember hearing the clock chime the half hour. Daddy had already gone to work and we left for school. I was halfway there when I remembered I forgot my primer. I had to run back to fetch it. That lady was helping Mama get into the front of a dark wagon." She gazed at me with liquid eyes. "Did she do something bad to my mother?" she whispered. "Is that why Mama died?"

FORTY-SIX

I guided a plodding Peaches through the snowy streets after I helped Orpha into her house. The new electric streetlights provided a modicum of illumination, although they did not shine at all brightly. Still, I was certain they were safer than the old gaslights.

Stunned by Priscilla's revelation, I wasn't sure where to go. In prior days I would have simply driven to the police station to report this new piece of information about Delia helping Charity to her death. I couldn't appear there now, what with the police chief having put Kevin on notice about my assistance.

As I made my way toward the center of town, the facts of this new discovery kept rolling through my brain. Priscilla was a smart, observant girl, and I didn't doubt her story for a moment. But why had Charity and Delia come to know each other?

Maybe Charity had visited Ransom at the boat shop and Delia had befriended her. I'd gone looking for Delia at the Swifts after I convinced Priscilla to go back upstairs, but Delia had departed along with Savoire, Orpha told me.

The burning question remained: had Delia delivered Charity to Savoire for an abortion? Or to Wallace Buckham? Or perhaps she'd made use of her mother's office and done the deed herself. Delia had been neatly put together at her workplace the afternoon of the death, but I hadn't thought to ask her supervisor if she'd arrived late that day. I didn't think I'd seen him at the Swift's reception. If she was part of the abortion plan, what was she threatening to tell Kevin about? And what did Joey know? I resolved to drive by Kevin's house one more time. If he wasn't there, I'd leave a note with Emmaline.

I heaved a heavy sigh when I arrived at Kevin's home. The windows were dark. Emmaline and Sean must be out somewhere. He would have telephoned her that he had to deal with a witness in custody and wouldn't be home soon. I was simply going to have to pay the police station a visit. The chief couldn't find fault with a responsible citizen reporting a vital piece of information. Could he?

Off we went, my trusty steed and me, and soon I once again handed him off to the stablehand behind the station. I trudged up the steps and made my way to the front desk.

"I'd like to leave a message for Kevin Donovan."

"He's just in the back." The officer behind the desk stood. "I'll get him for you, miss. What name can I say?"

"No. Please don't disturb him." And more important, don't let the chief see me talking with him. "I can jot down the information if thee would be so kind as to provide me with paper and pencil."

"If you're sure, miss." The officer, a fresh-faced young man whose cheeks looked like he barely needed a razor, seemed deflated at not being asked to fetch the important detective. He slid the requested items across the desktop to me.

"I thank thee." I frowned at the paper. Where to begin?

Overheard Delia Davies speaking in what she thought was privacy with Ransom Skells. He wanted to end their dalliance. She threatened him with divulging something to thee.

I tapped the pencil on the table. What in the world would Delia have on Ransom? The matter of their affair? But she was the one with something to hide. How brazen of her to threaten him. I returned to my scribing.

After the two finished, the Skells's eldest child told me she had seen Delia helping Charity into a carriage the morning of Charity's death, at seven thirty. Thee must ascertain where Delia took her, and if Delia was late arriving to work that day. Also get alibis for Savoire and for Wallace Buckham that morn —

The door to the back offices flew open. I looked up from my missive to see Norman Talbot ushering Delia through the doorway. So she'd made good on her threat. What had she told the chief?

"Thank you very much for your information, Miss Davies," Norman told her in a smooth oily voice, speaking through a smile. "I assure you we'll take it under advisement."

Norman's gaze fell on me and the smile disappeared. Delia glanced over.

"I believe strongly in citizens performing their civic duty, Chief Talbot. I'll be going now. Evening, Miss Carroll." She swept through the door to the outside.

"Miss Carroll, what brings you in this evening?" Norman asked, and not through a smile.

"I came into possession of some interesting information pertinent to the case of Charity Skells's death. I was just outlining it for Kevin's benefit." I finished writing the word *morning,* and added *Call me at home when you can* and my signature before I looked up.

"But I trust you have not been playing the sleuth," the chief said sternly.

"Oh, not at all, Norman. Thee asked me not to." I mustered my best fake smile. "I'm only being a responsible citizen. Just like Delia."

"Very good. I'll take that note and make sure it reaches Detective Donovan." He extended his hand.

"I'd rather give it to him myself." I picked up the piece of paper and folded it in half.

The young officer looked bewildered and opened his mouth to remind me that he'd offered and I'd refused exactly that only minutes ago. Instead, Kevin himself hurried through the door to the back, which the chief had left ajar.

"Did I hear my name? Hello there, Miss

Rose. I dare say you've come here with news for me."

Norman pursed his lips and cleared his throat.

How I wished I could sit down in private with the detective and hash through all the particulars of the case, including if he'd managed to get information out of Joey, and what it was. Since that wasn't possible, I replied, "Yes, I do, and I've written the essentials on this note for thee." I handed the folded paper to Kevin. "Good night, gentlemen."

FORTY-SEVEN

It was dark out but not late at all. It only felt late because I'd been up for two days running. Tonight I would . . . I remembered with a start that my parents were arriving this evening. What had Faith said? Their train was due at seven, and she and Zeb would fetch them, likely borrowing Zeb's father's carriage. I needed to get home and make sure things were ready for them. Faith and I hadn't talked about sleeping arrangements. When my mother visited by herself, she slept in Betsy's bed and we made up a bed for Betsy on the floor of the room she shared with Faith. But that wouldn't do for both my parents. I shook my head, expecting that the ever resourceful Faith had likely thought of a solution.

My tired eyes felt full of sand by the time I arrived home from my too-long afternoon out. I was chilled through from all the driving around town and from taking time to properly care for Peaches once we reached the house. Zeb's family's horse and carriage were waiting inside the stable, so space was tight, but I managed.

Once I gained entrance to the house, though, it was warm and had never smelled so inviting, the air full of the delectable aromas of roasted chicken and vegetables, fried potatoes, and apple pie. The family had eaten, but plenty was left over for me and for my parents after they arrived.

"Did you do all this, Faith?" I asked after I'd washed up and served myself a plate of supper.

"Winnie and I cooked together." Faith sat across from me with a cup of tea. "I like her very much," she whispered.

The rest of the family, plus Winnie and Zeb, were gathered in the sitting room. I had greeted them all upon my arrival.

"I do, too," I murmured. I closed my eyes and held the blessing of this meal in God's Light before I ate, but it was a particularly short moment of prayer. I was hungry despite what I'd eaten at the Swifts. I took a bite of chicken, and it was so tender and juicy it melted in my mouth. The roasted carrots, parsnips, and celery from the root cellar were also cooked to perfection.

"This is heaven," I mumbled. "I thank

thee, and Winnie, too." I swallowed. "Is there any word about the trains? Are they running on time?"

"Zeb went down to the depot to check before he came for supper. They told him the train Granny and Grandfather are taking will arrive no more than half an hour late. How was thy day, Rose? The Memorial Meeting, was it well attended?"

"Yes, it was, and even more people came to the reception at the Swifts' home." On the sideboard I spied an envelope with David's handwriting on the front. "For me?"

Faith handed it me. "Yes, it came in the afternoon mail."

I opened it to read a short message from my beau, simply saying how much he looked forward to seeing me tomorrow and that he would be here by one o'clock with a large carriage to convey me and my family members to the Meetinghouse if we wished. I smiled and tucked it in my pocket, then told Faith what he'd written.

"How sweet of him. Rose, you landed a good man in David." She patted my hand.

"I know," I said softly, then savored another bite of meat. "This is a perfect chicken, by the way."

"Thanks." She sipped her tea. "Did thee

learn anything today about poor Charity's death?"

I didn't want to bother my niece's head with thoughts of murder. "Just a little. It's in Kevin's capable hands. I think he's getting close."

"Good." She tapped her teacup lightly with a spoon. "I obtained some supplies today." She spoke softly and her eyes gleamed. "For family spacing." Her smile was both broad and shy.

"Excellent. So thee is ready for thy big day."

"I am, dear Rose. I am."

Faith was calmer now than previously. Maybe worrying about not becoming pregnant had been her primary concern, and now that was assuaged.

Tall Zeb ambled into the kitchen. "I think we should be making our way to the station, Faith. I'll go out and bring the carriage around." He slid into his coat and topped his head with the flat-brimmed hat most Friends wore. The men, that is.

"I'll be right out, darling." She smiled up at her betrothed.

"We'll be back with them soon, Rose." Zeb went out.

Faith took her cup to the sink. Donning her cloak, she turned to me. "Rose, I still worry that thee feels left behind because I am marrying before thee. It was perhaps thoughtless of us to hurry into our wedding before thee and David are able to say your vows." She stood beside me as she tied on her bonnet.

I took her hand. "I don't feel bad, and thee must believe me. David and I shall marry as Way opens. In the meantime, I could not be happier for thee. Please don't worry about this matter. Thee and Zeb had no obstacles and thy marriage is rightly ordered. We shall all celebrate with thee tomorrow." I squeezed her hand.

She leaned down to brush my forehead with a kiss. "We'll be back shortly."

As the door closed, I returned to my meal. Of course deep inside I did feel a speck of envy, but I would never voice it. I truly believed my destiny lay with David and that we would find our path to a blessed union. I just wished his mother — and Amesbury Friends Meeting — felt the same.

I forked up a bit of fried potatoes, on which the cooks had sprinkled salt and curry powder, and savored it. The potatoes were as delicious as the chicken and vegetables. Despite the tasty and nourishing meal, my thoughts dwelt not here but on what I had witnessed at Virtue and Elias's reception. I longed for David to talk matters over with, but that would have to wait until tomorrow. He'd had to put in a command performance elsewhere tonight — or what amounted to one, since Clarinda had specially requested he accompany her to a musical soiree in Newburyport.

I was desperate to know what Delia had told the police chief, and could only hope Kevin would share that information with me when he was able. Under the stairs Delia had been on the verge of voicing what she and Ransom had done and he'd shushed her. Or, no, it was something he'd done for her. Had he convinced his wife to have an abortion? I doubted it, because he wouldn't even deign to use contraceptive devices, although that could be because they diminished his pleasure. Or had he arranged for Charity to be killed by a purposefully botched curettage of the uterus? It wasn't a particularly efficient way of killing someone, and the very thought made me shudder. Also, it hadn't been Ransom helping Charity into a carriage, according to Priscilla. It had been Delia herself. The one helping her obtain an abortion and thereby her death. I trusted the girl. Priscilla wouldn't have lied about such a weighty matter.

Priscilla. I sucked in air and clapped my

hand to my mouth. I prayed no one had heard Priscilla tell me what she'd seen. If the murderer had been listening nearby, the girl herself could be in danger. I needed to warn Virtue to keep her granddaughter safe. But the telephone was in the sitting room along with the rest of the family. As I recalled, however, the device was equipped with a very long cord.

A minute later I stood behind the closed door of my room asking Gertrude to put me through to Virtue. As I waited, I tried to compose my message in a way that Virtue would understand but without nosy Gertrude learning anything she shouldn't.

Virtue finally came on the line. "Rose? Is thee well?" She sounded alarmed.

"Yes. Nothing is wrong, Virtue. The service was lovely, didn't thee think?"

She paused before speaking, and her voice wobbled when she did. "Of course. But I cannot engage in niceties tonight. This has been the most difficult week of my entire life. Did you — ?"

"I apologize. My purpose in calling was to ask thee to keep Priscilla close to thy side until further notice."

"Prissy? Why ever?"

"I overheard a perhaps alarming conversation in the hallway before I left thy home.

Unbeknownst to me Priscilla heard it, too. When she and I spoke about it, she also told me something else she saw. Priscilla could be in danger, Virtue. Thee must protect her. If thee ventures out of the house, don't let the girl out of thy sight."

"What?" Her voice shot up. "In danger from someone who was in my house? Whoever could it be?"

"I can't reveal the details on the telephone. Please trust me."

FORTY-EIGHT

After my call to Virtue, I returned to sit musing at the kitchen table, nursing a cup of tea with my apple pie. Virtue had promised to protect Priscilla and to keep all the children nearby until I told her things were safe. That took one worry off my plate. And it was just as well I wasn't able to give her details. I didn't want my suspicions spread beyond Kevin's ears.

Mother and Daddy bustled in an hour later, followed closely by Faith and Zeb. I jumped up when I saw my parents. "They're here," I called into the other room. I hurried to hug my father, who brushed snow off his full white beard and beamed at me. I embraced my mother, too, after she'd hung her cloak on a hook.

Within moments the children were gathered around in the usual clamor for attention from their grandparents, whom none of us had seen since Christmas. Faith and

Zeb shed their own coats and busied themselves at the stove preparing supper plates for the newcomers. After Frederick and Winnie came into the kitchen, he introduced her to Dorothy and Allan.

My mother took Winnie's hand in both of hers. "I am pleased to make thy acquaintance, Winnie. We are a big and noisy brood, as I'm sure thee is aware, but the children are smart and as polite as we can convince them to be."

Winnie smiled. "We are becoming fast friends, and I am so happy to meet thee and Allan."

Daddy sat at the table, wiping his fogged-up glasses with a handkerchief. Within a minute of them being back on his nose, he had Betsy on his lap and the twins vying with each other to relay their latest adventures. My father glanced up at Luke, who hung back as if uncertain of his place. He was no longer a child at fourteen, but wasn't quite an adult, either. "We'll have a man-to-man a bit later, my Luke. Yes?"

Luke smiled. "Yes, Grandfather."

"One at a time now, boys," Daddy said in his usual jovial tone. "Tell you what, I'll flip a coin. Mark, thee is heads and Matthew is tails. All right? Whoever's side lands up gets to talk first." He dug a nickel out of a pocket and expertly flipped it in the air. It landed on the table and spun for a second before rolling on its edge, finally becoming still.

Betsy peered at it, then frowned at her grandfather. "I don't see any tails. Those are leaves, Grandfather."

My father threw his head back and laughed. "That's just a figure of speech, dear Betsy. Heads and tails are considered opposite parts of a body. It doesn't much matter what's on the back, we call it tails."

As Matthew commenced to talking, Mother pulled me to the side. "Is everything ready for tomorrow?"

"Yes, I think so. Faith has a lovely new dress, and the women of the Meeting are preparing refreshments. I'm so pleased thee and Daddy came."

"We wouldn't have missed this for the world."

"I'm doing my best to stand in, but Faith is missing Harriet a great deal right now."

"Of course she is." Mother gazed into my face, laying a hand on my cheek. "Land sakes, thee looks tired, my Rose. Up all night birthing a baby, was thee?"

I nodded, her care bringing sudden tears to my eyes. "Yes, and chasing down the facts of a very worrisome violent death, as well. One of my mothers was the victim, in fact."

I sniffed and swiped at my eye.

"Another murder?"

"I'm afraid so. I'll tell thee about it later."

Mother closed her eyes for a moment, sending up a prayer, no doubt. "Thee should retire for the night then," she said upon opening them.

"But I want to catch up with thy news."

"We'll have time, dear. We're staying the week, thee knows. The Weeds have offered us the use of their spare room." She dropped her warm hand but kissed my cheek where it had rested.

"Oh, good," I said. "I wasn't sure where we'd put everyone in this house, which is a bit cramped as it is." Three growing boys in one room, two girls in another, and Frederick in the third, plus me downstairs in the parlor made for a full house.

The telephone jangled insistently in the sitting room.

Frederick looked at me. "A call on Seventh Day night? I dare say it's for thee, Rose."

"I expect it is. Please excuse me." I hurried into the sitting room, once again stretching the cord so I could talk in my parlor with the door closed. The operator, someone other than Gertrude this time, connected me with Kevin.

"I hoped it was thee calling," I told him

after I greeted him.

"It's me, all right, and I'm finally at home where I can speak with you in peace."

"I did stop by thy house before I went to the station, but it was dark."

"Yes, my sainted wife gave up my getting free of this blasted case and took the boy to her parents for supper."

"I hope my visit didn't cause trouble for thee with the chief."

"No. Leaving a note was a good idea, Rose, even though I received it in person."

"What did thee think of my news?" I moved about the room, the telephone stand in one hand, the listening device at my ear in the other. "Doesn't thee think it is significant?"

"If this girl is telling the truth, it's an important piece of the puzzle."

"She is. I'm sure of it. Has thee or thy men questioned the doctor, Buckham, or Savoire Davies as to their whereabouts that morning?"

"Miss Rose, it's Saturday night. We can't be bursting into people's homes this late in the evening."

"I suppose not." But I wished they could, even though my grandmother's clock now gave its soft *bong* eight times. "Thee hadn't already investigated Wallace Buckham? I left thee a note about him on Sixth Day." I heard my scolding tone and breathed in a calming breath. It would do no good to nag the hardworking Kevin.

"That was yesterday. I got the note after I arrived home Friday evening. And this morning we couldn't find Buckham."

What? "What does thee mean, thee couldn't find him? Did he leave town?"

"I don't know. Could be he was simply out at the hospital or the market. Or skating on the pond. We couldn't find him."

"I hope he didn't become suspicious and go into hiding."

"I hope the same." Kevin cleared his throat. "We did ascertain that Madame Restante, that is, Mrs. Davies, was at her office on Tuesday morning."

"Truly?" This could be the break we needed. My heart beat faster in anticipation. "Then perhaps Delia took Charity there and Savoire performed the abortion."

"Perhaps. Except we have only Mrs. Davies's word on the matter, and she said she didn't arrive at her, uh, *bureau,* as she put it, until nine o'clock."

I thought fast. "I don't think there would be enough time to do the procedure and for Charity to have traveled home and summoned me, all before ten o'clock. Unless

Savoire was particularly brutal with the instrument." I shuddered to think of it. "She could be lying about the time, couldn't she? Surely some neighbor or tradesman would have seen her in the street. Did you ask people in the area?"

"Not yet. It was too bad Miss Davies left tonight before I got your note," Kevin continued. "I plan to question her at first light Monday morning."

"Not tomorrow?"

Kevin didn't speak for a moment. "Miss Rose, you know that tomorrow is the Lord's blessed day of rest, don't you?"

I sighed. "Of course I do. But the murderer might not respect that. What if there is another killing tomorrow? Will thee honor the day of rest then?" I heard the impatience in my voice but I was too exhausted to tame it.

"Now, now. No need to get testy with me," he said. "Of course in extreme case of need, I shall work on the morrow."

"What did Delia have to say to Norman Talbot?"

He made a frustrated *pshh* sound. "Some falderal about Joe Swift. Said he was blackmailing Mr. Skells."

"About what?"

"She claimed not to know."

And well she might. Otherwise she would be admitting to adultery — to the police.

"Maybe he is. Maybe Joey knew about Ransom and Delia's affair and threatened to go public with it. But wait, thee brought Joey in for questioning. What did he say?"

"The scoundrel called his late father's lawyer and then clamped his mouth shut. Didn't get a thing out of him. The lawyer told us unless we had evidence Swift committed a crime, we couldn't lawfully keep him. We're not getting any breaks in this case."

We certainly weren't.

FORTY-NINE

I clucked to Peaches at eight thirty the next morning on my way to visit Lucy and her baby son. The snow had stopped during the night and now, in the bright morning sunlight, the whitened world sparkled with tiny diamonds. But the clear air had also brought frigid temperatures. Even the heavy wool driving blanket wrapped around me and all the woolen layers I'd dressed in couldn't keep my feet warm.

I'd left a little early because I wanted to drive by Wallace's house to see if he was within. Surely it was the mark of a guilty person to flee. I turned onto Moody Street and walked Peaches until we were across from the doctor's big house. I pulled Peaches to a halt. Wallace did seem to be at home, after all. I spied a lit lamp through the window of his examination room. It didn't mean he was innocent of the crime, though.

As I sat there in the street, I considered the timing of that fateful morning again. I'd received Charity's note before ten o'clock because I'd noted the time in my parlor when a boy had arrived with the message. Priscilla had said Delia came with a hired conveyance to fetch her mother at seven thirty. So where had Charity been between seven thirty and nine? And if Savoire was telling the truth, could she have purposefully or accidentally perforated Charity's uterus between, say, nine and nine thirty?

I exclaimed out loud. When I conjured up the image of the room where I found Charity, I saw that red piece of paper I'd found in the drawer. Why hadn't I made this connection earlier? It could easily have been Wallace Buckham's brochure listing his services, the very one he'd let me take, that I'd left with Emmaline for Kevin. Was it coincidence that Charity had slipped the red brochure into her bureau? She might have been to see him for other family spacing advice. Or . . . he could be the man who killed her.

My heart pounded as I considered my options. I needed to pay Lucy a visit this morning. The afternoon would be taken up with Faith's wedding, David, and the family gathering. With this idea about Wallace, I ought to have Peaches gallop straight to Kevin's home. But I couldn't bother him so early on a First Day morning. What my duty, my calling, told me to do was rap the knocker on Wallace Buckham's front door and confront him with what I knew. But if I'd learned anything from the several murder investigations in which I'd been embroiled, it was to not insert myself in a potentially dangerous situation. My duty to the case didn't need to extend that far. I would let the police do their expert job and I'd do mine, that of midwifery. I resolved to continue on to Lucy and Henryk's farm.

Before I left, I glanced over at the house again and spied a carriage house to the right and toward the back of the main building. My eyes widened. A black enclosed wagon sat in front of the closed carriage house doors, its traces resting on a stump, its harness hanging slack. Except it was free of snow. It hadn't sat outside all night. It must have been driven here this morning and the horse put up inside the carriage house. Why would Wallace have taken such a wagon out so early in the morning? David had said Wallace's family had deserted him, so it could only be the doctor himself who would go for a drive. The police hadn't been able to locate him yesterday. Perhaps the doctor had been away overnight and had just returned. I pulled Peaches across the street, climbed down, and tied him to a hitching post so I could take a closer look first at the driveway and then at the wagon.

The driveway showed only the tracks leading toward the carriage house. My eyes widened. If Wallace had taken a wagon out this morning, there should be two sets of tracks in the fresh snow: one set for leaving, one for returning.

I checked the residence but didn't see anyone watching me, so I took a half dozen steps into the driveway. I couldn't help myself from moving closer, drawn like an iron filing to a magnet. I'd thought my heart was hammering a minute ago, but it doubled its rate now, and my throat thickened, making it hard to swallow. The vehicle looked very much like the one that had run me off the road on my way home from Bertie and Sophie's a few nights ago. I wished I'd had the chance to look for markings on the wagon that had attacked me but I hadn't. All I knew was that it was a dark closed wagon. And so was the one in front of me. The steed the other night had been black, too. When I examined the wide leather breeching where it would run under the horse's tail, I was not surprised to discover a long black horsehair stuck to it. Definitely not from Peaches. I stood rooted in place like a swamp oak, running the hair through my fingers. If I opened the carriage house, I had no doubt I would find that black horse.

But . . . I frowned as I curled the hair into a coil and pocketed it, thinking back over the events of the week. I hadn't spoken to Wallace until the morning after being attacked on the road. Why would he have accosted me, trying to hurt or even kill me? I could understand him wanting me to disappear after I came to see him, asking about his services and alluding to abortion. But before? And if the wagon wasn't his, whose was it?

A sudden wind set branches to rattling. It blew snow off the tree above, plopping clumps onto my bonnet and cloak. I shivered. What was I doing out here on a suspect's private property staring at a horsehair? I had a newly delivered mother to attend to, a worship service to participate in, and after that a family event to celebrate, the happiest one in a long time. It was high time for me to get moving. A church bell in the distance began to toll as I turned to leave, and a crow high in a bare tree croaked a warning.

"Where do you think you're going, Rose Carroll?" Delia's voice sounded behind me even as her hand grasped my left arm and something very sharp poked a spot of bare skin just below my right ear.

Where had she come from? "Delia?" I tried to twist to see her but the sharpness threatened to pierce my skin.

Her low laugh was the scariest sound I'd ever heard.

FIFTY

"You couldn't leave other people's business alone, could you?" Delia's voice was low and as cold as the frigid ground. "Telling stories to your detective pal."

The sharp object pricked harder. An ice pick? A hat pin? Whatever it was, it hurt. I winced. "What does thee mean?" I asked, even though telling stories was exactly what I'd been doing. True stories, too.

"I've been watching you, and I've had enough of it. Following me here today was a bad idea."

"I wasn't following thee." With any luck Wallace would look out a window and notice us. He would come to my rescue. Except . . . no. My heart sank. Delia being here must mean the two of them were working together. I cast my mind about for a response, thinking as fast as my galloping heart. "I have something of Wallace's I wanted to return."

"On a Sunday morning? Hardly," she scoffed.

"It's true. Thee can ask him."

She barked a harsh laugh. "No, I can't."

"Why not?"

"He's dead." She pressed the object into my neck until it stung. "Just like you will be soon."

A chill of dread rippled through me. "Wallace is dead? What happened to him?"

"I'm not at liberty to divulge that right now. Let's just say it wasn't from natural causes. He was threatening to go to the police. I couldn't let that happen."

She'd killed him because he was going to turn her in. She planned to kill me, too. If I could keep her talking, surely someone would drive by and take notice. We were out here in plain sight, after all. "Did he kill Charity?"

"No, the idiot refused. I had to do it myself."

May God rest his soul. Wallace had had some morals in the end. She must have done away with him yesterday morning, which is why Kevin's men couldn't find him. My thoughts raced on to the obvious conclusion. "Thee used thy mother's office to murder Charity."

She barked out a laugh. "The woman was

a simpleton. I'd befriended her when Ransom and I fell in with each other. After I intercepted Charity's letter to my mother, I told the woman I had trained with my mother, and that I would give her a lower price for her abortion than the famous Madame Restante. She believed every word of it."

Poor, poor Charity. She wasn't a simpleton, but she had indeed been a desperate and trusting soul. She hadn't divulged Delia's name to me because she'd thought they were friends. "What did thee see in Ransom? Doesn't thee know he has six young ones?"

"Of course." She scoffed at my questions. "The grandmother will take the children. And the money Charity was inheriting changed everything." As I had suspected. She clearly didn't know Ransom would not have control over the funds.

"I know thee took Charity to thy mother's office in this very wagon." Why didn't someone drive by? Where was the milk wagon, an early churchgoer, anyone?

"How do you know that?" she demanded.

"Thee was seen with Charity that morning." The crow in the tree scratched out more warnings, as if it was telling me, "Go-go, go!"

"Who saw us?" she demanded. "Who told you? I'll attend to him when I'm finished with you. Unless you're lying."

"I am not." However, I would die before I would give her sweet Priscilla's name. "Does thee own this wagon?"

"You ask too many questions. But I'll tell you what, you get to have the special tour." Her icy words cut the air worse than the freezing wind. She pushed my shoulder and poked my neck until I stood facing the back of the wagon. "Open the door," she snarled.

I pulled on the handle with some effort until the door creaked open. All I wished to hear was a clanging police bell growing ever nearer, but that was not to be. Not yet.

A reek of blood stained the crisp winter air. The vehicle was, or had been, a meat wagon. A length of rope lay coiled in one corner near the door.

"Where did thee obtain this vehicle?" I asked.

"It's my uncle's. Now shut up and get in before somebody sees us."

No. I was not going to be locked in a windowless wagon and left to freeze to death. I had to get away from her, and quickly. My brain raced, seeking a plan.

"Move!" she commanded.

"Very well." I'd move, if that was what she

wanted. Fast and furious, I ducked down and away, freeing my neck from the sharp object. I twisted my left arm free of her grasp and jabbed my right elbow hard into her solar plexus.

Delia cried out and crumpled to the ground. She curled up, wrapping her arms around herself, gasping.

I grabbed the rope from the wagon and knelt behind her feet. I began to loop the cord around her ankles but she kicked back at me. I cried out as her heel hit my knee. My ire rose. She was not going to win this battle. I quickly twisted to sit on her knees, which immobilized her legs.

"That hurts!" She scrabbled at me with her hand.

I turned my back. "I don't care." I tied her feet together as fast as I could. I pulled the knot tight and tied a second, for good measure, then rolled off her and stood. Near her head I spied her sharp object sticking up out of the snow. I gave her a wide berth as she began thrashing about.

"You untie me this minute," she screamed, her breath still weak from my blow. Her fanciful velvet bonnet now hung down her back, and a long strand of light hair had come loose from its pins, lying limp on her cheek.

"I will not free thee."

She grabbed for my ankle but I was too fast for her. I sidestepped and quickly scooped up the object, then stepped back again as I examined it. It was a curette, used for scraping the uterus, except the curved end had been honed to a point as acute as a needle. *The murder weapon.* Had she used this on Wallace, too? The police would learn that soon enough. Again I skirted her at a safe distance and picked up the end of the long rope.

"Two can play at this game, Delia." I brandished the tool in one hand. "Put thy hands behind thy back or thee will feel the point of this weapon thee so carefully sharpened. Thee won't like it, I promise." I prayed I would not have to carry out my threat and harm her. But if I had to hurt her to prevent her from attacking me or anyone else in the future, I would. This killer was not going free.

She cursed but complied, wrestling herself into a seated position with her hands to the rear. I didn't help her. I didn't trust her not to try to grab me again. The rope was long enough to secure her gloved hands. I had to put down the tool, so I worked quickly, pulling these knots snug, too.

"That's too tight," she complained. "And

it's cold here on the ground."

This from someone who was going to lock me in an unheated wagon? Her whining would have been funny if it hadn't been so pathetic, so desperate. It was a vivid contrast to what this disturbed person had done to Charity and Wallace, and had been about to do to me.

"Don't worry, you won't be there long. Just until the police arrive." I gave her one last glance, then hurried toward the house. My visit to Lucy was going to have to wait.

FIFTY-ONE

I slid into Wallace Buckham's home, grateful the door was unlocked. I gaped, halting in my tracks. He lay dead in the foyer. I slid off a glove to touch his cheek, but his skin was cold to the touch in the chilly air. Wallace wore a silk dressing gown over a long night shirt, except the collar of the pale blue gown was now stained by the congealed blood which had poured from his neck. The portraits of happy families with well-spaced children watched silently from the walls.

I closed my eyes and sent up a prayer for his released soul, then made my way around his body and into his office to ring the police.

"This is Rose Carroll," I said once we were connected. "I have a murder suspect by the name of Delia Davies tied up at a private residence on Moody Street." I gave the address.

"What's that you say?" The young officer

sounded skeptical.

I sighed inwardly. "Would Kevin Donovan happen to be there?"

"No, miss. He'll be going to mass with his family, I'm sure."

I started anew. "I was attacked by a person of interest in Charity Skells's murder. Delia Davies confessed to killing Charity. She also took the life of a physician named Wallace Buckham. I was able to overcome Delia."

"You were?" His voice screeched.

I held the listening device away from my ear for a moment. "Yes." I made every attempt to keep my tone from becoming impatient. "She is outside and her hands and feet are tied. I'd appreciate it if thee would please notify Detective Donovan and send transport to come pick her up as soon as possible."

"I'm impressed, Miss Carroll. We'll get on it right away."

"I thank thee. I shall wait here until someone arrives." I hung up the receiver and sank into the office chair, my knees wobbly from what I'd just been through. My gaze traveled over the jars of herbs, the red pamphlets, the binaural stethoscope, the tidy desk. A sheet of paper sat near the phone. I took a closer look and shook my head slowly. On it was written *Call Detective*

Donovan. What a pity Wallace hadn't telephoned earlier. He might have hesitated for fear the authorities would detain him, too.

I pushed up to standing. It wouldn't do to leave Delia alone much longer. Who knew what she could get up to, even bound like she was. Before I left the house, I took a moment to kneel next to Wallace's body. I tried to slide his eyelids shut. Unfortunately they had already stiffened in place. He might have been a censured doctor, but he had done the right thing in the end. He didn't deserve to die for his crimes.

I slid my glove back on and opened the door only to hear an alarmed whinny. *Peaches.* I'd left him tied to the hitching post in front. Sure enough, Delia had somehow risen and was hopping through the snow with both feet toward my horse and buggy. She still had a good ten feet to go and wasn't moving fast. I lifted my skirts and raced toward her, positioning myself between her and my horse.

"Thee isn't going anywhere, Delia." Behind me Peaches *whuffed* and stomped his feet.

Delia glared at me with rage on her face. Her ire combined with her forward momentum to unbalance her. With a cry she tipped face front into the snow. She turned her head to the side and cursed me with words that should have embarrassed anyone in earshot. I stepped behind her and grabbed the length of rope connecting her hands and feet. I pulled it until it was taut, ignoring her tirade.

Dressed for church, Kevin arrived with the wagon before ten minutes had passed. The music of the ever louder police bells that preceded him had never sounded so sweet.

FIFTY-TWO

I sat in Kevin's office at the police station as the town's church bells rang eleven. He and I had agreed I would meet him back here after I paid my visit to Lucy and her baby. Blessedly, both mother and child were in the bloom of good health, as were their equine counterparts. The newborn boy was already nursing like a champ, just like his colt brother. And my heart rate was finally back to normal.

"I guess we both missed church this morning," Kevin now said with a wry smile.

"Sometimes God's work takes us elsewhere. Did Delia go easily?"

"You must be joshing. She snarled and scratched and loudly proclaimed her innocence. She's still making a nuisance of herself in the lockup downstairs. Nice knots you tied, by the way."

"My father taught me well."

"Now fill me in on what Miss Davies told

you, if you will."

I relayed everything I could remember. Finding the wagon. Discovering the black horse hair. Delia seizing me and saying she'd killed Charity after Wallace refused to. "Good for Wallace, refusing to kill Charity. I'm sorry I ever suspected him."

"It's what a good detective does, Miss Rose. He was on my suspect list, too. Did Miss Davies confess to killing him, as well?"

"No, she stopped short of that. She did say he hadn't died of natural causes. She told me he'd been about to turn her in to the authorities. And I saw your name written on a piece of paper next to the telephone in his office."

"What a shame he waited so long."

"Yes." I thought for a moment. "So Savoire was telling the truth about her own morning."

"She was. A neighbor came forward and said she'd seen Mrs. Davies at home until eight thirty that morning."

Likely the same neighbor with whom I had conversed. I frowned. "But Savoire knew of Charity's death. I wonder if she suspected her daughter was to blame."

"It's possible. We'll have her in for another round of questioning." He tapped a pencil on the desk. "It's the motive that puzzles me. Was Miss Davies so enamored of Mr. Skells that she had to do away with his wife? Was she really going to take on all those children?"

"I believe she thought Ransom was going to have control over the funds from Charity's uncle Joseph, not realizing that Sophie was going to administer them. And she said Virtue would take in the children, which I imagine she would have."

"Yes, the money might have been the real draw. It's often the motive for homicide once we weed out spurious causes for killing." Kevin nodded. "We'll get her to talk sooner or later. I should tell you Joe Swift's lawyer convinced him to divulge what he was hiding. It was nothing more than the affair between Mr. Skells and Miss Davies."

I nodded. "Good."

"Is there anything else Miss Davies told you this morning?"

"Delia convinced Charity she knew how to perform a safe abortion. She said she told Charity she'd apprenticed with her mother." I shook my head. "Poor Charity, thinking she was going to improve her situation by not having yet one more child. Instead she lost her life entirely."

Kevin *tsk-tsked.* "It's a good thing Mr. Skells is guilty of nothing more than adul-

367

tery or those children would have been left orphans."

"Like the ones last fall."

"Like them, indeed. Why people think they can get away with committing murder is a question to which I'll never have a satisfactory answer."

"Does thee know if he will keep the children with him or give them over to Virtue's care?"

"I spoke to him a few minutes ago. He's hanging his head in shame, and rightly so, but he is resolved to keep the children. The funds Miss Ribeiro will disburse will help him greatly, I'm sure."

"And I imagine Virtue will continue to offer her support." I hoped she would, anyway.

A small knock on the door preceded Norman Talbot sticking his head in. "Ah, Miss Carroll. I heard you were here."

I stood hastily. "I'm just going." I glanced at Kevin. I truly didn't wish to cause him problems with his chief.

"Let me shake your hand first, young lady." Norman's tone was gruff, begrudging. "You did good work this morning."

"She most surely did," Kevin said proudly, also standing.

Norman extended his hand to me. Feeling a bit like my world had stood on end, I shook it.

"I thank thee," I said after I managed to extricate my hand from his overly firm grasp. "It was an act of self-preservation, truly. Delia Davies was about to lock me into an unheated windowless wagon. I couldn't have that, now, could I?"

The chief smiled as if he was obliged to. "Henceforth you are welcome to act in self-preservation with any criminal you encounter. That said, my caution about staying away from police work stands. Following it will obviate the need to defend yourself. Good day, Miss Carroll." He slipped out the way he came in.

"Both a commendation and a chastisement," Kevin murmured, staring at the door.

"I perceived as much." As if I ever *tried* to get into dangerous predicaments. "I do have to be going. I have a wedding to prepare for."

"Miss Faith and Mr. Weed, isn't it?" Kevin raised his eyebrows. "That's a happy occasion. Please convey my congratulations to the couple."

"It will be my pleasure to do that. I hope thee finally gets some time to build that snow fort with thy boy." I pointed to the pencil likeness of Sean.

"I'm on my way, Miss Rose. I'm on my way."

FIFTY-THREE

David and I sat next to my parents in the second pew of the Meetinghouse a few minutes before two o'clock, with Betsy perched beyond my parents. We had left a seat empty to remember our dear Harriet. Annie and Bertie sat behind us, and Matthew, Mark, and Luke were in front of us with Frederick and Winnie. The front pews on the other side of the aisle were filled with Zeb's parents, his aged grandmother, his younger siblings, and other close relatives. They'd also left a vacant place, in their case to honor Isaiah, the brother who had died in the Great Fire last year.

When David had arrived, a stern-faced older Friend had pressed her lips together in disapproval and then looked away. She was one of the women who had cautioned me about the consequences of marrying out. I merely squeezed my beau's hand and smiled at him. She couldn't turn David away from a happy Meeting like this one, where plentiful non-Friends were in attendance.

Between the front pews and the facing bench, empty of elders this afternoon, stood a small table on which rested the large parchment marriage certificate, with two fountain pens at the ready.

Annie leaned forward from the pew behind me. "When will it begin, Rose?" she murmured.

"When the couple enters," I whispered in return. The winter sun, low in the sky, created the shadows of dark branches dancing on the wide pine floorboards. The air smelled familiarly of wool, antimacassar, and expectation. Benches creaked and a buzz of whispers and quiet words from the non-Quakers in attendance filled the air, as it had during Charity's much less happy service yesterday.

Mother and Daddy sat with eyes closed, as did other Friends in the room. Betsy and I had greeted guests until only a couple of minutes ago, handing visitors who were not members of the congregation a small printed sheet outlining the customs for the Meeting for Worship for Marriage. We'd given an especially warm welcome to Orpha and Alma. Orpha had whispered, "Nice work this morning," to me and squeezed my hand. Once again I was amazed but not surprised at how fast news traveled. I'd whispered back, "All's well that ends well."

John Whittier had written to express his regret that his health did not allow him to leave Danvers at this time, but he'd wished Faith and Zeb many happy years together. He'd also enclosed a copy of a poem he'd written a decade and a half earlier, "The Golden Wedding of Longwood," which he'd written for friends celebrating their fiftieth anniversary of marriage. His inscription to Faith and Zeb on the poem read, *May your joyful union also last fifty years and more.*

Now even the murmur of conversation ceased. I twisted in my seat to see Faith and Zeb poised in the doorway at the back of the room, she in her lovely blue gown, he in a freshly starched collar above a new dark suit. He glanced down at her. She nodded and took his hand, and they walked slowly to the front. They lifted their joined hands over the table and then dropped them to sit, hands folded and eyes closed, on the facing bench.

How I wished Harriet could have lived to see this joyous union. To help Faith prepare to leave her childhood home and become a wife. To see her eldest join in matrimony with a fine young man. To rejoice in the continuation of life. My eyes filled, but I blinked away the tears. This was not a moment for grief, and I knew Harriet's fine spirit lived on in her daughter.

I sank into worship, clearing myself of worldly thoughts, leaving room for God's Light to enter. I held the loving couple in prayer. I held also Savoire Davies, and the family of Wallace Buckham, wherever they were. I held the released souls of Charity and Wallace. I held Ransom and his children, and Virtue and Elias Swift. I held the disturbed criminal, Delia. And I held David and myself in prayer, too, that we also might arrive at a moment like this one right here.

After some minutes I opened my eyes at a rustling in front. Zeb rose and extended his right hand to Faith, who took it with her right hand as she stood. My eyes filled again to see my beautiful niece, her back straight in that simple dress, her face open and filled with joy, about to marry. How I wished Harriet were here to see this.

Zeb cleared his throat. "In the presence of God and before these friends, I take thee, Faith Harriet Bailey, to be my wife, promising, with Divine assistance, to be unto thee a loving and faithful husband as long as we both shall live." He gazed at Faith with his head slightly tilted, love writ large on his face.

David took my hand into his and squeezed as I sniffed.

Faith smiled at Zeb. "In the presence of God and before these friends, I take thee, Zebulon Harris Weed, to be my husband, promising, with Divine assistance, to be unto thee a loving and faithful wife as long as we both shall live." She bent to sign the top line of the certificate. She handed him the pen and he did the same. They sat.

I stood and made my way to the table. They had asked me to do the honor of reading the certificate to the assembly. I hoped I wouldn't burst into happy tears halfway through. I took a deep breath and began to read.

"Whereas Zebulon Harris Weed of Amesbury, County of Essex, and state of Massachusetts, son of Ezekiel Weed and Patience, his wife, of Amesbury, and Faith Harriet Bailey of Amesbury, County of Essex, and state of Massachusetts, daughter of Frederick Bailey and his late wife, Harriet, of Amesbury, having declared their intentions of marriage with each other to Amesbury Monthly Meeting of the Religious Society of Friends held at Amesbury, Massachusetts, according to the good order used among them, their proposed marriage was allowed by that Meeting."

I read on, detailing today's date, that the couple had appeared in a duly appointed meeting under the oversight of this Meeting, and repeating the vows they had uttered. The certificate ended thusly:

"And in further confirmation thereof, they, the said Zebulon Harris Weed and Faith Harriet Bailey, she, according to the custom of marriage, adopting surname of her husband, did then and there to these presents set their hands. And we, having been present at the solemnization of the said marriage, have as witnesses thereto, set our hands." Under Faith's and Zeb's signatures were drawn dozens of lines ready for the signatures of everyone present old enough to know how to use a pen.

I set down the certificate with a deep breath. I smiled at Faith's brand-new name — Faith Harriet Bailey Weed — and at the newlyweds. I signed my full name under hers before returning to my seat.

"We're next, my darling," David whispered.

I turned my head and stared at him.

"Mother has given us her blessing. Just this morning."

My mouth dropped open. He nodded

once. I'd never seen him look so happy and so proud. I covered my mouth, about to cry from joy once more.

"Truly?" I whispered to him.

"Yes," he murmured, taking my hand again.

A loud clearing of throat came from several rows back. I held a finger to my smiling lips. This was a time to hold the married couple in silent prayer and await messages about their union, not to talk among ourselves. But all I wanted to do was throw my arms around my betrothed, my beloved David.

ACKNOWLEDGMENTS

Thanks as always to editors Amy Glaser and Nicole Nugent and the Midnight Ink team for publishing this series. With every book, Amy and Nicole point out crucial improvements and catch small but important errors of detail. Greg Newbold once again created the art for the beautiful original cover and captured the sense of the story.

I was grateful to join Tiger Wiseman again for a high word-count week at her Mystery Acres in Vermont and for her Scrivener consulting. I also was able to spend a productive week with Ramona DeFelice Long and others in another Clare House writing retreat. Ramona gave a fourth brilliant performance with her developmental edit of the manuscript, too. Thank you, my friend.

As always, my Wicked Cozy Authors gang has my back, both on the blog and behind the scenes: Barbara Ross, Liz

Mugavero, Julie Hennrikus, Sherry Harris, and Jessie Crockett. Please come visit us at wickedauthors.com, check out all their other names, and read these ladies' books. You won't regret it.

Rose's father Allan is modeled on my late father, Allan Maxwell, Jr. I'd rather have him still here to read the manuscripts, but I know he's beaming at my literary successes from wherever his soul rests.

Catriona McPherson helped me with Scottish flavor for one scene, and KB Inglee again read a draft and fixed a few historical faux pas. Thanks, author pals! Midwife Risa Rispoli checked the birthing details, for which I am ever grateful.

I was privileged to attend, in a labor support role, the birth of my goddaughter Anna Yanco Papa's first baby over the course of a weekend while this book was in progress. (I was in the room when Anna was born to my best friend thirty-three years ago, so this was a special completion of a cycle.) We all rejoiced in a healthy baby girl born to Anna and her darling husband, Kevin Braxton, and the experience was a mini-refresher course in labor and delivery for me. I thank them both for allowing me to be there.

Last year was Amesbury's 350th birthday and the year was filled with events celebrating the town's long and rich history. At the kickoff party live auction, I donated naming rights to a character in this book. Jonathan Sherwood, I hope you like being a supervisor at Lowell's Boat Shop!

I'm blessed and grateful for the love and support of Amesbury Friends, Sisters in Crime, my good friends, my sons and sisters, and my beau — I love you all back.

ABOUT THE AUTHOR

Agatha- and Macavity-nominated **Edith Maxwell** (Amesbury, MA) is a member of Sisters in Crime and Mystery Writers of America, cochair of the New England Crime Bake, and a longtime member of the Society of Friends. She also writes the Local Foods Mysteries, the Country Store Mysteries, and the Cozy Capers Book Group Mysteries (the last two penned as Maddie Day), as well as award-winning short crime fiction. You can find her at edithmaxwell.com and blogging at wickedauthors.com and killercharacters .com.

The employees of Thorndike Press hope you have enjoyed this Large Print book. All our Thorndike, Wheeler, and Kennebec Large Print titles are designed for easy reading, and all our books are made to last. Other Thorndike Press Large Print books are available at your library, through selected bookstores, or directly from us.

For information about titles, please call:
  (800) 223-1244

or visit our website at:
  gale.com/thorndike

To share your comments, please write:
  Publisher
  Thorndike Press
  10 Water St., Suite 310
  Waterville, ME 04901